THE
WILDWATER
WOMEN

THE WILDWATER WOMEN

ELLIE WOOD

Harper
North

HarperNorth
Windmill Green,
Mount Street,
Manchester, M2 3NX

A division of
HarperCollins*Publishers*
1 London Bridge Street
London SE1 9GF

www.harpercollins.co.uk

HarperCollinsPublishers
1st Floor, Watermarque Building, Ringsend Road
Dublin 4, Ireland

First published by HarperNorth in 2022

1 3 5 7 9 10 8 6 4 2

A catalogue record for this book
is available from the British Library

ISBN: 978-0-00-847117-0

Printed and bound in the UK using 100%
renewable electricity at CPI Group (UK) Ltd

MIX
Paper from
responsible sources
FSC™ C007454

This book is produced from independently certified FSC™ paper
to ensure responsible forest management.

For more information visit: www.harpercollins.co.uk/green

*For everyone who has fallen in love with the
Lake District, and those who are yet to discover it*

Prologue

The roar inside her head was louder than the noise of the traffic as she stepped out of the sliding glass doors and into the busy street beyond, her heart pounding a frenzied beat. She'd had her suspicions, but nothing could have prepared her for the shock of hearing the news outright. Beneath the rain-soaked sky, she searched the snake of cars for shiny smudges of yellow, and was about to fling a hand in the air to hail a vacant cab, when she noticed her fingers were shaking. Her tears mingled with the rain, blurring her vision. *Breathe,* she told herself. *Breathe.* But suddenly the idea of being stuck in a taxi felt suffocating. She started to put one foot in front of the other instead, trying to force herself to focus on the here and now, not the future with all its unknowns.

She took a circuitous route home, detouring through the park as though instinctively craving respite from the relentless hustle of the city. A plane caught her eye, glinting in the early evening light as it took off in the distance, soaring towards the blush-coloured clouds. But the idea didn't come to her at that point. It was only when she got back to the apartment, caught sight of the little painting hanging there on the wall of the spare room as it always had, now cast in the pink glow of dusk, that she knew exactly what she was going to do.

1

A glimmer of rose-gold light was visible over the fells, so it had to be after six, thought Abby. Maybe she should get up. She had barely managed to sleep so far; there was little to be gained from lying there any longer. So this was it. The day was here: September the third. Abby turned her head away from the window, where her still-open curtains framed the dawn, to Ben's side of the bed. She closed her eyes, awake but dreaming.

She saw Rowan, wriggling in her arms as a baby; then as a toddler, wobbling as she learned to walk. Now another milestone was here: her first day of school.

'She'll be fine,' she thought she heard Ben say, his voice a muffled whisper.

He'd never been one to stress. Always said Abby worried enough for two.

She wished he'd kiss her now, like he used to. Say he loved her again.

She reached an arm out beneath the duvet, in the hope he'd pull her in for a cuddle, but of course the sheets were cold. She opened her eyes, and reality bore down on her. Ben was gone and he wasn't coming back. She was on her own. Just like she had been since before their daughter was even born.

She pushed back the covers, and pressed her palms to her cheeks, as though physically plastering on a brave face for Rowan's sake. She walked into the bathroom and looked at her reflection in the mirror. Five years older since she'd last seen Ben. Longer since they'd spoken. He'd disappeared in the same way the last streaks of sunset slunk from the sky, suddenly leaving night-time in their wake; one moment Abby had a husband and a beautiful life, the next minute she'd been plunged into darkness. How time slipped away. Rowan was growing up. And he'd never even met her.

Today felt like such a big step. An unexpected burst of anger surged through her body and she braced her arms against the sink, waiting for it to subside into sadness and exhaustion. She summoned all her strength. She was going to need it to get through today. She didn't relish the thought of dropping Rowan off at the school gates alongside all the other pairs of parents.

'Mummy?'

Rowan pulled her back to the present, from the brink of her helter-skelter of despair. She stood in the doorway, her pyjama top on inside out, and rubbed her eyes. Her blonde hair, the same hay-bale shade as Ben's, was sleep-ruffled. 'I don't want to go today.'

Abby knew how she felt. She crouched down, and gazed into her daughter's moss-green eyes. 'You were excited yesterday, sweetheart.'

Rowan's forehead rumpled. 'Can we stay here and make a cake instead?'

Abby wished more than anything that they could.

'You'll like it when you get there. Make lots of new friends.' She smoothed straw-coloured strands away from Rowan's face.

Her daughter shook her head. Which one of them had she inherited her stubbornness from? Abby wondered. *Please don't make this harder than it already is*, she pleaded with her child in silence. 'Come on, darling, let's get you dressed.'

She was still battling to get breakfast cereal from Rowan's spoon into her stomach, when the doorbell rang.

Rowan glanced up, intrigued by the interruption.

Abby sighed.

'You carry on, please, poppet,' instructed Abby, walking out of the kitchen and into the hallway. A shiver shot across her skin like an ice cube sliding down her spine. Was it going to be the landlord? But Ben had told her he'd taken care of their rent. He'd said she didn't have to fret about that, at least.

Abby swallowed as she opened the door – and came face to face with a complete stranger.

'Hi there. Good morning,' the woman said with a transatlantic twang, greeting her twice as though in compensation for the disturbance.

Great, a cold-caller was exactly what she needed; the missing ingredient from her morning, thought Abby, scratching her neck as though sarcasm was worn like a scarf.

'I apologise for interrupting . . .' began the woman, beaming back at her, buttermilk locks bouncing on her shoulders.

She didn't look sorry, thought Abby, squinting in the stark September light. The woman appeared to be around her mother's age, and certainly had the same knack for an ill-timed visit.

3

'I wonder if you could help me, if you had a spare second?'

Abby bit her lip, stopping a quip about all the surplus minutes she had at her disposal from slipping out of her mouth.

The woman's shoulders sagged in the ensuing silence. 'No worries . . .' She swatted the crisp air and turned to leave, pulling her cashmere cardigan closer around her.

Abby felt Rowan's warm body press itself to her hip, her daughter clearly overcome by curiosity.

'Will you go to school so I don't have to?' Rowan called out into the still, chill morning.

The woman spun round. 'Hey!' she said to Rowan, with a wide smile and such warmth Abby felt her core thaw a little. 'I've already been to school, honey,' she said in answer to Rowan's question. 'A long time ago,' she added with a laugh. 'But it's a lot of fun, I promise, and I can't imagine a more beautiful part of the world to go to kindergarten in. You're a very lucky girl, sweetie.'

Abby was struck by that last sentence: she wondered how many other people would say the same about Rowan. She squeezed her daughter's shoulder.

'Thanks,' she said to the woman, her breath visible in the cold fresh air. 'What was it you wanted to ask?' she added, tilting her head to one side.

'Oh, it's just I can't switch on the darn heater, and my cell phone is dead – I forgot one of those, er, what do you call them? The gadgets for power overseas.'

'Adapter.'

'That's it.' The woman blew out a breath. 'So I can't call the rental company.'

Ah, she was from the holiday cottage next door.

'But I'll figure it all out. You both have a great day.'

4

Abby watched as she struggled with the latch on the adjacent cottage's wrought-iron gate. 'Wait a second. I can take a quick look if you like?'

The gratitude on the woman's face caused guilt to course through her. Had she become less giving now she was used to doing everything herself? She must have.

'Are you sure?'

Abby nodded. She'd need to be fast, but she felt for the woman: seemingly alone in an unfamiliar place.

'I'm Lori, by the way. Your neighbour for the time being.'

'Hello. I'm Abby, and this is Rowan.'

'You sound like Elsa!' declared her daughter. 'From *Frozen*.'

Lori laughed as she led them both into Silver Ghyll Cottage. 'It's just over here,' she said, pointing at the hearth. 'I can't seem to find any way of turning it on. There must be an ignitor somewhere . . .'

Abby frowned at the fireplace, flanked by two neat stacks of wood either side. 'Er, it's a log burner.'

A beetroot bloom crept into Lori's cheeks. 'I'm from New York City,' she said by way of explanation.

'I can show you how to light it, don't worry.' Abby crouched down.

Lori marvelled as though she was watching a magic trick, and when amber flames began to flicker behind the glass, she clapped. 'Thank you so much!'

Abby grinned as she got to her feet. 'You're welcome. Right, I better get this little rascal to school,' she said, glancing round for her daughter.

Rowan was delving about in the top drawer of an oak sideboard on the far wall.

'Darling, stop that!' Abby strode over to her. If they didn't get a move on they were going to be late. But there beside a

5

stack of leaflets on local attractions and a leatherbound visitors' book, was a converter plug. She plucked it out.

Lori squealed with glee. 'Jeez, aren't you an *angel*.'

'All sorted!' Abby grinned despite herself. She glanced around Silver Ghyll's living room with its old, exposed beams and gleaming flag floors. The place had a welcoming charm like her house had once had.

'What's the best way to get to lake Rydal?' asked Lori with a foreigner's turn of phrase as Abby corralled Rowan out of the door.

She didn't really have time for any more questions. There was a tourist information centre in town, for that sort of thing.

'Can I walk there?' Lori added.

Abby resisted the urge to reply that you could walk anywhere if you kept going long enough. 'Um.' She took in Lori's expensive-looking, biscuits-and-cream-coloured clothing. She didn't strike her as being a long-distance hiker. But appearances could conceal hidden depths. 'It's about half an hour on foot,' she said.

Lori's eyes widened expectantly and Abby stifled a sigh. 'Go through the park and follow the river Rothay to the packhorse bridge.'

Lori's gaze didn't leave hers, as though she was listening to a fairy tale, not a set of directions.

'Cross over the beck, then follow the track to the lake shore. You can't miss it.'

'Let me write this down . . .' Lori patted her cardigan's pockets as though a Biro could have stowed away in its cashmere folds.

Abby pursed her lips. Rowan's fingers wriggled for freedom in her clasp, desperate to explore the undiscovered corners of the house.

'One second,' said Lori.

Abby grasped her last grain of patience with the same tenacity as she gripped her daughter's hand.

'Here we are,' said Lori, now poised with a pen and a gold-edged notebook.

The instructions for how to get to the lake were as imprinted on Abby's mind as her daughter's name and date of birth, but when was the last time she herself had been down to the water's edge? she wondered as she ran through the way there once more. How long had it been since she'd wandered along one of the winding pebbly paths, watched the sun's rays dance on Rydal's rippled surface, or seen the rosy shimmer of twilight on the river?

Then Rowan tugged on her arm, and yanked her back to the present.

Abby looked down at her wrist and caught sight of the time on her watch: Oh Jesus, they should have set off ten minutes ago.

Rowan skipped alongside her, clutching her *Frozen* lunchbox, as they hurried down the lane that led to the primary school, and Abby couldn't help thinking that Lori's kind words of encouragement must have lifted her daughter's spirits and made the day seem less daunting. She was thankful – but the same couldn't be said for herself. Her insides were churning like the river Rothay in a winter storm, and a swell of sadness was bubbling to the surface that she was struggling to suppress.

At the school gates, she hugged Rowan twice, wanting her to feel just as much love as any of the other children. As the teachers beckoned in the new starters, she waved her daughter off, watching until her corn-coloured curls disappeared from view. Then she took a deep breath, and began to walk to work through the park, cutting up towards the top end of Ambleside.

Time was passing – Rowan was no longer a baby; she was a lively little girl – but she herself seemed to be snagged in a thorny thicket of memories from before. A brisk walk on a bright morning like this one ought to make her feel better, she thought, as loneliness needled her skin like stinging nettles. Lori was here on her own, had travelled all the way from America for that luxury. She would be seeing all this – every sight she took for granted each day – for the first time.

Abby glanced up from the gravel path she was plodding along, wishing there was always a clearly marked path to take in life. The grass glittered with dew, as though diamonds had dropped from the sky during the night – perhaps a goddess up there had been crying, too, she thought to herself with a wry smile. She realised she'd had her head down the whole way to school in her haste that morning – and perhaps she'd had her gaze turned away from the rest of the world for a very long while. She looked around: at the auburn-tinged trees and the birds flitting in between, and Wansfell in the distance, watching over the town. Nature was wrapping her up in a 360-degree show of its splendour. A small seed of solace started to stir inside her somewhere.

Abby pushed open the door to the Plum Pie Bakery at twenty-five to nine.

'*Afternoon,*' said Joy, the inappropriately named owner. Abby knew her employer to be a dragon for many reasons, but mainly because her grumpiness seemed to correlate directly with the weather, proving that she was a cold-blooded creature who certainly shouldn't have settled in Cumbria, one of the wettest counties in the country. Abby was surprised her boss had needed to install ovens in the kitchen: surely she could've baked the goods with her fire breath alone, instead.

'Sorry,' Abby said, her forehead furrowed. 'It's Rowan's first day at school—'

'But it's not *your* first day *here*: you should know you're meant to start at eight-thirty – *sharp*.'

Shame spiked the back of her neck as she tied on her apron, a protective purple carapace that shielded her from the onslaught of tourists and locals who would soon start to pour in once the clock struck nine – but wasn't armour enough against Joy's meanness.

Abby ducked into the kitchens at the rear of the shop, already in need of some respite.

'Hey, Abs!'

She smiled as she watched Tom take a tray of raisin-speckled scones out of the oven.

'These'll be ready to go out in a second.' He glanced over his shoulder as he began to lay the golden-glazed treats out on wire racks to cool.

Abby's stomach rumbled like a grumble of thunder at the aroma of warm, freshly baked cake. She'd been so busy trying to get Rowan sorted for school, then rushing to work, she hadn't had chance for breakfast.

'Want one?' he asked, nodding at the scones.

She felt a flash of embarrassment flush her cheeks.

'Yes, please,' she said with a sheepish smile.

Tom grinned. 'Help yourself.'

Abby searched for one that was wonky, or looked lacking in fruit, intending to select one not fit for front of house, but of course Tom's creations looked faultless.

'The proof's in the pudding,' he said, as though reading her mind.

She picked up a scone and bit into it. 'Mmm,' she said through a mouthful of buttery crumbs. '*Delicious.*'

'Good,' Tom said, brushing flour from his front. 'How'd it go, then?'

Abby finished chewing, unsure what he was referring to.

'Rowan's first day,' Tom clarified, eyebrows raised.

Abby was surprised to find the tension in her tummy had eased slightly, whether it was because of Tom's thoughtfulness or the sublime taste of the still-warm scone, she didn't know. Perhaps it was a mixture of both.

'Our Freddie settled in straightaway – I'm sure Row'll be just the same.'

'I hope so,' replied Abby, about to take another bite of her breakfast just as Joy appeared in the doorway, wearing a scowl. She made a point of glancing at her watch, and dispensing a tut, before spinning on her heel.

Tom jerked his head at an enormous bag of sugar sitting on the worktop. 'D'you think if Joy ate all that, she'd *still* be so sour?' he whispered, making Abby snort with laughter. She stuffed the rest of the scone in a paper bag, saving it as a snack for later, and signalled a 'thank you' to Tom with her eyes as she picked up a stack of straight-from-the-kitchen cakes, then scurried out to the shop floor just as Joy turned the sign on the door to 'open'.

The morning had been quiet for the time of year but at midday, a steady stream of the Plum Pie's regulars started to trickle in, including the glossiest woman Abby had ever seen. '*Rebecca Braithwaite*' she'd once overheard her say into her mobile while she stood at the counter, too busy to pause her conversation while she paid at the till. With her flawless makeup, sleek hair and spa-fresh nails, Rebecca was the image of everything she was not. Abby had often pondered what her story was. *What does she do?* she wondered. She was always on the phone, as though her life was bursting with both chatter and possibility. *What must it be like to be so put-together?* She appeared to be in her mid-twenties, with her glowing, wrinkle-free complexion and an impeccable wardrobe of pencil skirts and silky shirts.

Today, Rebecca was gesturing at the selection of sandwich fillings through the glass cabinet with a fire-engine-red fingernail, her iPhone clamped to her ear.

Was she wanting roast ham? Abby jabbed the air above it, awaiting a nod of approval from Rebecca. A backlog of customers was beginning to block the pavement outside, and it was only a matter of moments before Joy would bark at her to hurry up.

But no confirmation came, and Rebecca's expression remained as glazed as the ham. Abby reached for the platter of honey-coated slices and hoped for the best.

Did she want a baguette or a bap, though? White or wholemeal? Any salad? She searched Rebecca's features for any available clues but she wasn't even looking now. This was impossible, she thought. She'd just have to do the same order as yesterday.

She started to cut open a roll – and Rebecca glanced up and shook her head. 'Sorry, one second,' she said into her mobile, and her eyes met Abby's. Tears pooled there like two puddles, and Abby felt a pang of compassion as Rebecca ran through her request. Clearly her polished surface belied a troubled undercurrent. Abby slipped a piece of Borrowdale tea bread into her paper carrier bag for her to find as a surprise, while Joy was busy glaring at someone who'd dared to ask her whether any of the cakes were gluten-free.

In the post-lunchtime lull, Abby plucked up the courage to speak to her boss. 'Is it still okay to finish at three, from today? Like we discussed?'

Joy sighed like a sagging balloon. 'Well, it makes things *very* difficult for me,' she said with a glower.

'I need to collect Rowan.'

'And I need my staff to work a whole shift, Abigail.'

Abby texted her mother to see if she could do the pick-up instead, wincing at the thought of Rowan looking out for her amongst all the other unfamiliar figures in the fading autumn light.

Got bridge club today xx came the reply.

Abby swallowed. She'd spent so long insisting she could manage; she couldn't blame her mother for simply getting on with her own life. She'd have to ask Rowan's other grandma. Ben's mum.

At four-thirty, a full hour and fifteen minutes after Rowan had finished school, Abby finally left work.

'I'm so sorry it was such short notice,' she said, standing on the doorstep of Fairfield View.

'It's okay.' Marie attempted a smile, the crinkles in her skin illuminated by the soft glow of the hall lamp, like crags silhouetted by sunlight. 'I'm the one who ought to apologise. I should do more . . . I love spending time with Rowan . . . but it's just I see Ben—'

'I know. I understand.' Abby felt a waterfall of sorrow wash over her.

'Mummy!' Rowan bounded along the corridor and leaped into her arms. 'I did you a picture!'

Abby looked at the red and green blobs of paint before her. 'It's beautiful, darling!' Her gaze met Marie's. *What is it?* she asked with a crease of her brow.

Marie gave a shrug. 'A masterpiece!' she cooed to her granddaughter.

Rowan beamed in between them; chest puffed out like a robin.

'So, you've had a good day, then, sweetheart?' asked Abby, her shoulders taut, once they'd waved goodbye to Marie.

When her daughter's head bobbed back and forth in an enthusiastic nod, she slowly blew out the breath she realised she'd been holding. As they walked back home, weaving through the wiggling lanes, Rowan launched into a list of all the activities she'd done, scattering in a steady stream of new friends' names, and Abby allowed the stiffness in her frame to subside.

'Hey, girls!' came a familiar-sounding American voice, just as they reached their gate.

Abby turned to see Lori coming down the street behind them, carrying shopping bags bulging with groceries. 'Hi,' she said, ushering her artwork-clutching daughter inside off the pavement. *What food do we have in the house?* she wondered, jolted into thinking about dinner by the sight of Lori's provisions.

'Look what I did at school!' Rowan held up her picture for Lori to see, tracing a finger over the dried globules of paint to showcase her work.

Lori stopped as she reached the entrance to Silver Ghyll. 'Wow!' She grinned.

Abby smiled as she watched her take the time to regard the brush strokes of a four-year-old.

'A mountain ash, huh?' Lori jerked her head towards their cottage garden, and Abby followed her line of vision to the red-berry-laden tree standing in the far corner. *Goodness me, so it is*. Abby blinked, startled.

She stared at her daughter's namesake: the rowan. She'd almost forgotten it was there, despite once partly choosing the house because of it: a symbol of protection, according to folklore. Seeing it standing guard outside the cottage had seemed like a sign: she and Ben and their unborn baby would be safe here. Now that notion felt so stupid.

'I sure know talent when I see it!' said Lori, breaking Abby out of her thoughts.

Her daughter giggled with glee.

Abby glanced at Rowan's picture, saw for the first time the emerald fronds and ruby beads of the tree. Perhaps there were a lot of things, right in front of her, that she wasn't able to see.

'Oh, I have something for you,' said Lori, setting her bags down on the doorstep of her cottage. 'Just give me one second.'

Abby squashed a sigh: she had supper to be making and – she peered at the front of Rowan's new blue sweatshirt – yoghurt stains to be sponging off her daughter's jumper – wait a minute, where was her lunchbox? Had she left it at Marie's? She didn't have time to stand about . . . She rubbed her forehead, reminding herself that Lori had been kind, and deserved to be shown the same generosity of spirit in return.

'I got a little lost on the way home, couldn't seem to remember where this place was,' Lori explained, shaking out her arms. 'Good workout, though,' she added with a laugh, flexing her fingers to get the feeling back in them after lugging the heavy bags round the Ambleside streets.

Abby smiled sympathetically. 'You'll get your bearings, don't worry.'

'I sure hope so!' Lori replied, searching around for her key in her handbag.

'How long are you here for?' asked Abby, forcing herself to be chatty.

'Oh, er, I've got two weeks in this place, but I can always extend – explore some more . . . I'm just, you know, keeping things open . . .'

'Playing it by ear,' said Abby, stroking the top of Rowan's hair whilst mentally running through all the things she had to do.

'Exactly . . . Oh, I don't know where I've put my – aha!' Lori held a glint of brass aloft in her hand triumphantly.

The trees shivered in the breeze and Abby clutched her coat closer as a cluster of clouds covered the sun. She needed to light the fire, give Rowan a bath . . . exhaustion ached in her bones.

'I'll just put these things in the kitchen.' Lori bent to pick up her shopping. 'Back in one moment – or you're welcome to come in . . .?'

Abby opened her mouth to say no, but Lori had a motherliness she was missing with a physical intensity – and before she could help it she found herself saying 'Yes, please.'

'Make yourself at home,' Lori said, as Abby and Rowan followed her into the cottage.

'Shall I fix us some coffee?' she called from over by the fridge, rooting around in a carrier bag before pulling out a pint of fresh milk.

'Er, that would be lovely,' replied Abby, not sure what to do with herself when someone else was the one waiting on.

'And I'm pretty sure I have some OJ here somewhere, for you, sweetie,' she said to Rowan, but the little girl wasn't listening; she was straining to be released from Abby's grasp.

'Please, sit down – relax!' said Lori, flapping her hands at the two of them.

Rowan launched herself onto Silver Ghyll's plump sofa with a squeal of delight, and Abby sank down beside her, resting her head against the back cushion. She shut her eyes, momentarily succumbing to tiredness, but she was conscious of Rowan squirming about next to her, so she opened them again.

'Did you find the lake? Rydal?' she called through to Lori, scanning the inside of the cottage as she waited for her response. Silver Ghyll could be the set of a film: a cosy rom-com where the characters would live happily ever after.

'Not today. I put that slip of paper down somewhere and . . .' Lori shook her head as she stirred milk into mugs. 'I couldn't find it anywhere.'

'I'll write the directions down for you again, don't worry,' said Abby, rummaging around in her handbag debris for a scrap of paper and a pen.

'Now, this is for you, honey,' Lori said to Rowan as she set a tumbler of juice down on the coffee table in front of her. Abby's stomach lurched as a premonitory vision – a cascade of kicked-over orange being spilled onto the plush carpet – assailed her. She sat upright to supervise her daughter, just as Lori handed her a hot cup of coffee. 'There you go,' she said, and Abby swallowed down the swell of emotion such a small gesture unexpectedly kindled inside her. She wrapped her hands round the mug as though she could conduct the warmth straight to her worn-out heart. 'Thank you,' she said.

'No problem.' Lori took a seat in the armchair opposite. 'It's nice to have some company.'

'So, where did you get to, then?' Abby asked.

'Ah, let me see,' said Lori. 'I've been all over!' She circled a cashmere-swathed arm in the air to illustrate her point. 'It's been a-mazing. Oh, let me show you – it's easier.' She put her coffee down and got to her feet.

'*Six lakes in a day*,' Abby read aloud from the front of the flyer Lori gave her. 'Windermere, Brotherswater, Ullswater, Thirlmere—'

'It's even more gorgeous here than I imagined.' Lori had a dreamy expression on her face, and for a fleeting moment Abby wondered if there was more to her trip here than just simply a holiday.

'So you feel you've got a bit more of an idea of the area now?' she asked, when Lori stayed lost in her thoughts.

'Absolutely!' she said, coming to her senses, a smile spreading across her lips. 'There's so much to see! I can totally see why artists from all over the world fell in love with this place.'

Abby nodded. She supposed it was true. Writers and poets throughout history, too.

'I got a whole lot of leaflets from the visitors' centre in town,' continued Lori, babbling like a brook. 'There's all sorts of things I want to do. Hey, I'm going to try this if you're interested.'

Abby looked up. Lori was proffering a pamphlet for some sort of local attraction. *But I live here, why would I want to go on trips for tourists?* Abby took the piece of paper she was holding out to be polite.

17

'It could turn out to be a real blast!'

'What's that, Mummy?' asked Rowan, peering over her arm.

Abby stared at the shiny sheet of paper in silence for a few seconds. The photograph on the front was of five figures standing on a jetty which jutted out into a lake – Coniston, perhaps. They were facing towards the water, as though focusing on the new journey they were embarking on together.

'Wild swimming,' she breathed. She'd heard of it, of course, in the same way she knew about the myths and legends that abounded the Cumbrian mountains, but it was something others did – those who were braver, fitter, stronger.

'I saw a whole bunch of people doing it today,' said Lori.

'In *September*?' Abby had splashed around in the shallows of the lakes in summer, as a youngster, but this was something else.

'Uh-huh. Meant to do wonders for your wellness, you know.'

Abby gazed at the rippled reflections in the image; the water almost looked to be moving, the sunlight playing on its surface, casting the lake in a spectrum of blue.

'Of course, you've gotta do it properly – can't just go jumping straight in at the deep end.' Lori took a mouthful of coffee. 'That's why I'm gonna join this group.' She nodded at the flyer.

'You are?' said Abby, full of admiration for her dynamic attitude. This woman was here in a completely foreign place, seizing every opportunity that came her way.

'Why not?' Lori shrugged her shawl-shrouded shoulders. 'When in Rome . . .'

But we aren't, thought Abby. *It's probably still scorching over there at this time of year.*

'I thought you might wanna try it out too,' continued Lori. 'We could go together.'

Abby slid the leaflet onto the coffee table. 'Oh no, that's not for me.'

'How can you be so sure?' said Lori.

'I don't have time . . . I've got work and Rowan and . . .'

'The classes are flexible – I spoke to the lady who runs them. Beginners welcome, apparently. Said she takes groups out at all hours of the day.'

'Thanks for the offer, but—'

'Think about it,' said Lori, sitting forward in her chair. Her conker-brown eyes shone. 'I'm going to give it a whirl tomorrow. You never know, it might be exactly what you need.'

Abby shifted on the sofa. How could an ice-cold dip in a freezing lake with total strangers possibly solve her problems? 'I'm fine.'

Lori cocked her head on one side as though she was studying a curious portrait in a gallery. 'All right. Well, let me know if you change your mind. It's not as if I'm exactly far from you,' she said.

'Okay,' said Abby, displaying a placatory smile. 'Right,' she said, standing up. 'We'd better be getting back.' She scooped up a droopy Rowan, who seemed to have suddenly flopped after all the excitement of a full day at school. 'Thank you for the coffee.'

'Any time,' said Lori, pushing herself out of the armchair. 'Goodbye, sweetie,' she added, waving at Rowan. 'Keep on painting!' She jerked her head at the cardboard-mounted artwork in the little girl's hands.

'Oh, what was it you wanted to give me?' asked Abby, remembering the reason they'd come in in the first place as she stepped over the threshold into the blustery night.

'Jeez, of course!' Lori leaped off the doorstep and disappeared back inside the house. She returned with a distinctive little blue-and-white branded paper bag. 'A little thank-you, for your help this morning.'

Abby felt a shudder of shame as she remembered her reluctance: she could certainly have been more welcoming.

'It's only a little something . . .' said Lori.

'Grasmere gingerbread,' murmured Abby. The sight of the packet itself stirred a swirl of memories within her. She hadn't tasted any for *years*. Rowan had probably never experienced it. A flashback unfurled inside her mind: she and Ben breaking off chunks with frozen fingers on a frosty walk.

'Present!' proclaimed Rowan, perking up.

Lori gave the package to her instead, leaving Abby to her reverie. The little girl giggled, giddy at the sight of the gift, dragging her mother back to the moment.

'Thank you,' Abby said, finally finding her voice.

Rowan's little hands were fumbling with the folds of wrapping, eager to investigate the contents.

Abby reached out, about to stop her eating it before her dinner. 'Shall we save it for later, sweetheart . . .?' she started to say, but all of a sudden she herself was hankering for a chunk of the spicy-sweet biscuit-cake. The confection had a unique magic; tourists travelled from far and wide to get their hands on it, and sampling the secret recipe for the first time was something truly special.

Rowan peered inside the paper bag and a waft of fragrant ginger drifted towards Abby. If she closed her eyes she could almost be back there, outside the tiny shop in Grasmere town, enveloped in one of Ben's hugs as they cuddled to keep warm as they waited in the queue. She bit her lip and concentrated on soaking in her daughter's thrilled expression.

Rowan snapped off a square piece and popped it into her mouth. 'Mmmmm.'

'Good, right?' said Lori.

Abby offered her the bag, before breaking off a bit too.

'I bet you guys have it all the time, but I can't get enough of the stuff! I practically bought out the shop getting souvenirs for the folks back home . . .'

But Abby didn't hear any of what she said, her surroundings fading away as the chewy concoction melted on her tongue. The instantly recognisable, inimitable flavour transported her to Before more effectively than any time machine ever could. She marvelled at how taste could evoke such strong feelings. Grasmere gingerbread tasted like home.

Her daughter started to skip down the flagstone path back next door to Little Garth, singing a song she hadn't heard before, that she must have learned at school.

'Goodbye,' she said to Lori, with a last look inside the interior of Silver Ghyll: a cocoon of comfort that she was loath to leave.

2

Abby was stacking syrupy squares of flapjack in the glass display cabinet beside the counter when she spotted Rebecca Braithwaite coming into the Plum Pie Bakery just after noon the following day. The little bell above the door tinkled, as though with delight at the sight of her lustrous tumble of hair and the shiny slash of letter-box red on her lips.

How on earth is she so perfect? Abby wondered, sweeping a bloom of flour she'd only just noticed was there from the front of her apron. She straightened up, catching the scent of Rebecca's fresh, floral perfume as she did so: like a breath of summer air. *She even smells beautiful.* Abby couldn't remember the last time she'd spritzed fragrance on her skin – probably before Rowan was born. It used to be a ritual she relished, but now it belonged to a bygone era; the bottle Ben had bought her, the last Christmas they'd spent together, stood on top of the dressing table in her bedroom, like a relic from when he was still around. She couldn't bear to wear it, but neither could she bring herself to throw it away.

'What can I get for you?' Abby asked, pulling herself together.

As soon as Rebecca had given her answer, she was instantly tapping away on her phone.

Typical, thought Abby, turning round to reach for a roll. Rebecca was absolutely stunning, but it did strike her as just the slightest bit rude that she always stood at the till on her phone, sometimes not even looking up. *So much for saying thank you for the—*

'I think I got given some Borrowdale tea bread by mistake yesterday.'

Abby spun back round to the counter.

Rebecca was holding out a collection of coins to pay for the cake in the palm of her hand; her iPhone clasped in the other, its screen now black and lifeless.

Abby blinked.

'It was *delicious*, by the way.' Rebecca's lipstick shimmered as she spoke.

Abby waggled her hand, shooing the change out of sight before Joy could twig what was going on. 'It was a freebie, don't worry about it,' she whispered, after glancing around to check her boss was out of earshot. 'You looked like you needed a pick-me-up.' Abby recalled the sheen of sadness she'd seen in Rebecca's eyes the day before.

'Oh, thank you.' Rebecca's shoulders slanted suddenly with surprise. 'That's very kind.' She smiled, but then her phone began to ring. 'Sorry . . . I've got to take this,' she said, before clicking to silence the insistent electronic sound.

'It's okay,' Abby mouthed as she sprinkled shredded lettuce on buttered bread. She finished making the sandwich, doing her best not to listen in while Rebecca carried out her conversation. But there seemed to be a momentary pause in Plum Pie customers coming into the shop and she couldn't help hearing the gist.

'I'm just grabbing lunch. I'll be back at my desk in five minutes . . .' Rebecca said into the receiver.

Abby wondered what her job was. The most glamorous place around was the Loveland. But that wasn't a place she wanted to think about. Hadn't stepped inside the hotel since—

'Work,' Rebecca explained with a sigh as she ended her call and picked up the paper bag Abby had prepared for her.

'Tell me about it,' said Abby under her breath as Joy patrolled past the counter, purely to check her employee wasn't having anything that could possibly be perceived as a pleasant time whilst on *her* payroll.

Abby jumped as Rebecca's mobile rang yet again.

'Hi, Mum . . .' she said into it, simultaneously extracting her card from her purse. 'I know, I haven't had chance to speak before now . . .'

Abby gave her a thumbs-up to signal the transaction had gone through.

'Yes, in a group . . . Yes, tonight . . .' she heard Rebecca say. 'It's my last hope . . . I've tried everything else . . . No, I'm sure I'll be in good hands . . . I don't know how long the session lasts . . .' Rebecca tucked her lunch under her arm as she zipped her handbag back up. 'Yes, I'll ring you straight after, I promise . . .' She was so absorbed in her discussion that she didn't so much as glance back in Abby's direction, before slipping out of the door and hurrying off down the street.

As Abby watched her disappear from view beyond the panes of the bakery's bay window, head bowed and back

24

hunched, she could almost see the stress pressing down on Rebecca's slight shoulders, and she wondered for the second time in the space of two days what was causing her suffering.

She was wiping down the counter, deciding whether she should get some shopping on the way to collecting Rowan from Maria's or she'd better do it afterwards, but with her daughter in tow, when a last-minute customer caused the bell to chime above the door.

'We're closed!' barked Joy, hands on hips, blockading entrance to the bakery with her body.

Abby glanced up.

It was Rebecca Braithwaite.

'Oh, no problem,' she said. 'I thought I might've made it in time, but it doesn't matter . . .'

Abby glimpsed the clock on the wall above the way into the kitchen. Strictly speaking, there were twelve more seconds till the minute hand struck four-thirty, and as Joy was a stickler for precision, she didn't see any reason why they shouldn't still be open.

'I haven't cashed up yet,' said Abby, and Joy flashed her a look that said she certainly wouldn't be compensating her if she chose not to stick to the exact hours of her schedule.

'Well, if you're sure it's all right . . . Please can I just buy another piece of that Borrowdale tea bread?' asked Rebecca. 'I'm about to go wild swimming,' she added, the words gushing out of her like water from a mountain spring.

Abby looked up. '*Are* you?' First Lori, now Rebecca.

Rebecca gulped, as if she might not really be so sure she wanted to. 'Yes.'

Abby could've sworn Rebecca would be more of a luxury-swimming-pool sort of girl. 'Gosh, you're adventurous.'

Rebecca gave a high-pitched laugh. 'Oh, no, I'm not *at all* . . .' She swallowed, as though she'd been about to say more but then stopped herself.

'Well, I think you are!' Abby selected the biggest slice of tea bread with the serving tongs. 'I wish *I* was like you.'

'Oh, you really don't.' Rebecca raised her eyebrows. 'And – trust me – if I can do it, *anyone* can.'

Abby took the money she handed her. 'I don't know how you cope with the water being so cold.' She gave a shiver.

'The temperature's the least of my worries . . .' Rebecca muttered as she slotted her container of cake in her bag. 'They teach you how to deal with it – the group leader does. God, I certainly couldn't do it alone . . .' She shook her head as though to extinguish the thought.

'So, there's a whole load of you who go?' Abby asked, curiosity unexpectedly uncurling in her chest.

'I'm told so.' Rebecca blew out a lungful of air, as though already practising her breathing technique. 'This'll be my first time.'

'Very impressive,' said Abby. An image of Lori, also bravely signing up for the session without knowing anyone, swam into her mind. Maybe she'd be in the same group as Rebecca. She opened her mouth to say so, but then stumbled over how to explain her connection: *an American tourist, who I've only just met and really know nothing about, might – or might not – be joining you, too?* She'd sound insane. Lori was barely an acquaintance—

'You should come.'

Abby's eyes met Rebecca's, with their soft taupe shadow and feline flicks of liner.

'I'm not brave enough for that.'

'I thought the same, but the instructor talked me through everything.' Rebecca prodded a scarlet-varnished finger towards the outside world. 'At that shop in town.'

Abby knew the one, had walked straight past it a thousand times. Swim Wild. She'd never been in because, surely, it was for sporty types.

'We'll all be beginners tonight . . .' Again Rebecca looked like she was battling not to blurt out something more. 'Anyway, it doesn't start till six. Just in case you change your mind. We're meeting at the White Crag car park by Rydal.'

Rebecca smiled goodbye and started to make her way towards the door.

Maybe she *should* give it a go? thought Abby. The fact she was even *considering* it came as a shock to her. No, she couldn't – what on earth had come over her? She should be picking up Rowan right about now—

A thudding sound made her head whip round.

Joy had dropped a carboard box at the foot of the counter with a thump. 'Didn't I ask you to put these in the stand over there, earlier?'

'Yes, I—'

'Don't tell me you haven't had time, when you seem to have *plenty* of it to waste.'

Abby felt a hot flush of humiliation.

'People don't pour money into marketing material for *fun*, Abigail.'

I'm surprised you know what the word means, thought Abby.

Then a clattering commotion in the kitchen caused Joy to march off in that direction instead, no doubt to torment Tom for a change.

Abby picked up the box and carried it over to the tourist information rack positioned beside the window. Then she crouched down next to it and bent back one of the top flaps to peer at the literature inside: neat piles of pamphlets placed face-down to showcase an advert for the Plum Pie Bakery that covered the back page – complete with a generous promotional discount voucher of five per cent off any purchases. *Classic Joy*, thought Abby. She turned over the top leaflet – and dropped it back into the box like she'd been burned.

Wild swimming.

The same flyer that Lori had shown her.

She stared at the tranquil-looking lake with its turquoise and indigo tones.

Then she heard footsteps and scrambled up – but, to her relief, it was Tom. At this rate, she was half-expecting *him* to declare he too was off for a dip in the lake.

'Don't you be staying any later than this, Abs,' he said as he shrugged on his coat. 'Joy doesn't deserve it, okay?' he added after glancing over his shoulder to check their boss hadn't appeared like a ghoul from a Lake District legend while his back was turned. 'This is *your* evening.'

His words seemed to echo around the empty shop floor once he'd gone.

Her evening.

Nights normally comprised of a repetitive pattern of Rowan-related routines. That was how it should be, surely. Her daughter came first. Her evenings weren't her own anymore and she wouldn't have it any other way.

But maybe I could have an hour that belonged to me.

A sudden surge of guilt gnawed at her gut, and she rubbed her eyes as though that would erase the heinous thought she'd just had.

She had to get going, she told herself. Rowan would be waiting.

She pushed the remaining pamphlets into the information stand and crushed the cardboard box they'd come in, standing on it to break it down for recycling, and simultaneously trying to stamp out any wild ideas of open-water swimming in the process.

Then she reached into her pocket for her phone, intending to send a quick text to Maria to tell her she'd be leaving any second and would be there to collect Rowan at five at the latest – but her thumbs began to battle with her brain: she couldn't seem to suppress the strange urge to be in on the action for once, part of the party. What was the harm in seeing what all the fuss was about, just as a one-off? On impulse, she sent a message to Maria asking if she could possibly pick her daughter up at seven instead.

Her reply came back almost instantly.

No problem. I'll make her something for supper x

Maybe this would be a good thing for Rowan too, Abby realised. It was healthy for her to spend time with people other than her, bond with her grandmother, and connect with more members of her not-so-large family.

She grabbed her jacket from the row of hooks in the back, and said goodbye to Joy, before stepping outside beneath the billowing grey sky. She took a big breath of cool night air and felt a frisson of excitement as she did so – for the first time in approximately five years.

3

As she turned the corner into Church Street, Abby found
herself being drawn towards the soft amber light that spilled
out from Silver Ghyll's sitting-room window as though she
were a moth. She rang the bell and stood on the flagstone
front step, waiting for Lori to answer the door. But each
second that passed by seemed to foster the feeling of foolishness that had begun to flicker inside her, and by the
time Lori finally appeared, it was in full flourish. *What am
I doing?*

'Hey there!' Lori said, her wide smile full of warmth.

'Hi!' Abby gave an awkward wave, like she belonged in
Rowan's Reception class.

'How're you?'

'Great!' The lie squeezed Abby's throat, making her voice
a squirrel-like squeak.

'You sure, doll?' Lori's forehead creased. 'You seem a little
on edge.'

'Yep . . . I just . . .' *Just what?*

'You wanna come in?' Lori stepped aside, and Abby spotted a stripy stuffed-full canvas tote sitting squat against the hallway wall.

Oh god, what gear would everyone be taking on this excursion? She really hadn't thought it all through. Suddenly her stomach was a knot of new-born eels. 'Oh, no, it's okay . . .' she replied. She could back out now and no one would know. *Except me: I will. When was the last time I did something different? Had a change?*

'Okay, well, how can I help, hon?'

'Er . . .' Abby bit her lip. The bushes whispered encouragement in the breeze.

'Look, I'm heading out for my swim session soon,' said Lori. 'But I've got time for a quick coffee first.' And with a waft of soft cream fabric, she shepherded Abby inside.

Abby glanced at Lori's already-packed bag as she walked past. She wasn't even one hundred per cent sure where her old swimming costume was. Was that even suitable? *What on earth was I thinking?*

'Where's the little one? She okay?' asked Lori, as she set about making the drinks.

'Rowan. Yes – at her grandma's.' Abby leaned against one of the kitchen chairs.

'Good, I'm glad to hear it,' Lori said as she opened and closed cupboards.

Abby slid into a seat; it was good to take the weight off her feet.

Lori handed her a steaming mug. 'Alrighty. So, are you going to tell me what's up?' she said, sitting down opposite her.

Abby took a sip of coffee, as though it were liquid courage. 'Sorry, I'm being *silly*—'

'Honey, you need to quit being so hard on yourself. When you get to my age, you learn to care a lot less about what other people think.' Lori smiled reassuringly.

Abby felt her self-consciousness dissolve, like a spoon of sugar in a hot drink. 'Okay . . . well . . . I thought I might give it a go, too – come wild swimming with you.'

'Is that *it*?!' Lori raised her eyebrows. 'Sweetie, you had me worried there for a second.' She clasped a hand to her chest.

'Sorry,' said Abby, fiddling with the handle on her cup.

'What is it with you Brits, always apologising.' Lori gave a laugh. 'This is *great*!' She reached over and touched Abby's arm. 'We're going to have *fun*.'

Lori said it with such conviction, Abby couldn't help but grin. Enthusiasm began to bubble up inside her once again.

Lori scraped her chair back. 'We need to get going, doll! We've got a wild swim to be swum!'

Abby stood up too. 'I'll go and grab my things.'

'I'll see you out front – I've got a cab coming at quarter to, if you want to jump in.'

'Are you sure?' Abby glanced at her watch; it was almost half five.

'Yeah, no problem. It's already fixed.'

'Okay. I'll give you a lift next time, then.'

'*Next time!*' echoed Lori delightedly. 'Yes, girl! That's the spirit!'

A minute or so later, Abby let herself into Little Garth, then raced upstairs to start sifting through her clothes for her swimsuit. *Where could it be?* She hadn't even seen it recently. She must have last worn it before she was pregnant. *Was it really that long ago?* She yanked out each of the drawers in her antique chest; searched amongst her socks, just in case, but to no avail. She rooted around in the walk-in wardrobe –

but still nothing. She let out a sigh of frustration. It was no use. *I shouldn't have left it so last minute anyway*, she scolded herself. She was just about to go back downstairs to tell Lori she wasn't able to come after all, when she caught sight of a woven beach bag Ben had bought her, slung on the hook on the back of the closet door. She pressed her lips together and blinked back the memories of that last holiday. *Honeymoon*, murmured the shadows. But Lori would be waiting; she didn't have time to be maudlin. She unzipped it and looked inside: the vision of her polka-dot bikini instantly whisked her back there to the hot white sand, and if she closed her eyes she could almost feel the touch of Ben's hand.

A horn sounded from the street outside.

She stuffed the two-piece souvenir of the woman she'd once been back into the raffia shoulder bag, then shoved a rolled-up towel in with it too. On the way out, she grabbed a woolly bobble hat, practical and purposeful, as though that might make up for the madcap kit she'd managed to scrape together.

White Crag car park was nestled at the foot of the lake, a short walk from the shore and only a few minutes' drive from the centre of town. Almost obscured by a screen of bronze-tinged beech trees, the clearing had an air of secrecy, as though only those in the know would ever realise it was there.

'Oh my *god*!' said Lori as the taxi pulled in off the road.

Abby turned to look at her: they hadn't even reached the water's edge yet.

'I can't believe we're actually doing this!'

Abby's insides squirmed; now wasn't the time for Lori's keenness to waver.

The taxi slowed to a halt, and Lori's doubt was illuminated by the orange interior light as she handed over a note to the driver.

'We're in this together, don't worry,' Abby said, as they picked up their bags from the centre of the black leather seat.

Lori smiled. 'You bet!' She bent forward, to speak to the driver. 'See you at seven,' she said before they both clambered out of the cab.

They stood side by side on the gravel ground in silence for a second or so, soaking in the scenery before them. The river Rothay frothed beyond the flittering leaves of the screen of beech trees, while birds frolicked between branches.

As the taxi swept round in a circle before disappearing off in the direction of Ambleside again, Abby felt a pulse of adrenaline. There was no going back now.

'Are we nuts?' asked Lori, as though telepathy was her hidden talent.

'I think so, yes,' said Abby.

Lori gave a companionable chuckle.

The sound of her laughter dispelled some of the dread pooling in Abby's abdomen.

A handful of other cars lined the grassy verges, but there was no sign of any other swimmers as yet.

Abby hitched her incongruous beach bag onto her shoulder.

'Cute,' Lori said with a nod.

Abby rolled her eyes. 'I look ridiculous!'

'Not at all! I like it.' Lori patted her tote. 'My bathing suit is bananas, you just wait.'

'I bet mine'll beat yours,' replied Abby, feeling a shudder of embarrassment at the idea of changing into her blue-and-white spotted bikini in front of a bunch of absolute strangers.

'*You came!*' said a voice, as a car door slammed.

Oh no, thought Abby, spinning round. Wearing a completely inappropriate tiny two-piece swimming costume in front of people she'd never met before in her life would be *far* more preferable to being seen in it by *Rebecca Braithwaite.*

'Hi!' Abby replied. 'Yes, I'm here!' she said, spreading her arms out wide as though to illustrate the point.

Rebecca was standing beside a shiny red car that'd been sitting there all along: of course, thought Abby, she probably always went everywhere in plenty of time.

Lori was already striding over to introduce herself.

Abby followed in her wake.

'Hey there, I'm Lori.' She grinned. 'So, you guys know each other, huh?'

Abby gazed at Rebecca: now wearing a berry-coloured quilted jacket and pristine green wellies, she looked like she should be on the cover of *Cumbria Life.* 'Yes. Sort of. I mean, we've met before . . .'

'At the Plum Pie Bakery,' added Rebecca. 'If you haven't been before, it's the *best.*'

Rebecca said it so sincerely, Abby couldn't help but smile. 'I work there,' she explained.

'Aha!' said Lori, her hands on her hips. 'Sounds like it's a place I need to check out!'

'Get the Borrowdale tea bread – it's *so* good!' Rebecca said, shielding her mouth with her hand as though dispensing a top-grade tip-off.

Abby giggled. 'I'm glad you liked it.'

'It's the only thing giving me the strength to stand here now.' Rebecca laughed, but it was laced with fear.

Abby noticed her cheeks bleach despite her expertly applied blusher. Her own anxiety seemed to fade into insignificance next to Rebecca's nerves. 'We're going to be *fine*,' she said, attempting to bolster her.

'Sure we are!' said Lori.

Rebecca rubbed her forehead, as though it were possible to massage away unpleasant thoughts.

Why is she here, if she hates the very idea? wondered Abby.

'Look, I think this might be the instructor!' Lori declared.

The three of them watched as a mud-spattered Land Rover swerved off the main road and then trundled to a standstill in the space opposite where they stood.

A sturdy, short-haired woman of about seventy stepped out of the driver's side and then surveyed the group. '*Wildwater Women!*' she shouted into the fresh night air, summoning her swimmers in the manner of a farmer rounding up their flock.

Abby shuffled forward, flanked by Lori and Rebecca.

'Clarissa Dimplethorpe,' the woman announced. 'Your guide.' Clarissa squinted as she studied her motley stock. 'Yan, tan, tethera.'

Rebecca and Lori looked baffled.

'*One, two, three,*' Abby translated. 'It's an old Cumbrian counting system,' she explained. 'Must just be us, then,' she added, when no further numbers came.

'You should all have filled in the questionnaire on the website,' Clarissa continued.

Lori and Rebecca nodded on either side of Abby, who felt her heart begin to pound. *What?*

'Oh, yeah . . . I did that at the shop in town . . .' Lori gave her a sideways glance and an apologetic grimace.

'I can send you the link,' said Rebecca.

'It's real quick,' Lori added with a sheepish smile. 'I should have said, but I totally forgot.'

Clarissa held a clipboard aloft. 'But for those of you *haven't*,' she said, pausing while she scanned their faces, as though this was a test she used in order to determine the instruction-averse from those who heeded the rules. 'I'll need you to fill out this form in block capital letters.'

So far, the outing had a similar level of fun to that of a school field trip, thought Abby, stepping forward. She stared at the list of questions on the sheet of paper. *Medical history. Emergency contact.* Oh god.

She swallowed as she started to scribble down her answers.

Clarissa was already speaking again. 'So, you're all first-timers here today.'

The general edginess of the group definitely gave that away, thought Abby, stealing a glance at the others – who were both listening intently.

'We're lucky today, the lake's fairly warm.'

Really? thought Abby, noticing Rebecca pull the zip of her quilted coat up right up to her chin, as though it were a crimson-coloured chrysalis she could crawl back into.

'There's a lingering bit of summer heat.' Clarissa flung open the rear door of the Land Rover. 'But we're still looking at around twelve – maybe thirteen – degrees, tops.'

Lori looked blank. 'Can I get that in Fahrenheit?'

Rebecca gave her a probably-best-if-you-don't shake of the head.

But Clarissa was busy rooting around in the back of the Defender.

Abby darted forward to return the clipboard and her completed form, and just as she was about to turn and scoot back to the safety of the others, Clarissa thrust something black and blubbery into her grasp. 'For you.'

Abby looked down at the object in her hands. *A wetsuit.* Relief flooded her system: the world wouldn't see her bikini after all. She clasped it tight; the fabric felt slick and smooth like seal skin.

'I've actually got my own,' said Rebecca.

Abby raised her eyebrows; *she'd* never even worn one before.

Clarissa nodded wordlessly, as though she could recall the details of everyone's questionnaires without the need for reminders.

'And this is yours,' she said as she passed a wetsuit to Lori, further demonstrating that all relevant information was efficiently filed away in her mind. Then she slung a rucksack onto her shoulder and slammed the back door of the Land Rover, signalling the introductory stage of the session was over.

'The lake's this way,' she shouted, striding off at a not inconsiderable pace. 'If you need me to slow down, just say,' she called, already on the other side of the car park.

'Alrighty,' said Lori, setting off at speed. 'Let's get this show on the road.'

Rebecca looked as though she was about to be sick.

'Are you okay?' asked Abby as they both followed suit.

'Mm,' she replied, keeping her eyes on the path ahead as the three of them scuttled to catch up with Clarissa.

Abby felt a shiver of anticipation: soon, they'd have their very first taste of wild swimming.

'So, you live in Ambleside too, huh?' Lori asked Rebecca, as though sensing she needed distracting from their imminent immersion.

'Yes,' said Rebecca, her voice barely audible above the breeze-rustled trees.

'I'm here on vacation,' offered Lori with a smile. 'Must be *amazing* to live in such a *gorgeous* place.'

'Yes.' Rebecca's gaze stayed on the winding track.

Abby marvelled at the mosaic carpet of leaves beneath her feet.

They came to a bridge, stopped to watch the Rothay burbling beneath its wooden slats for a second.

'Let's get a photo, girls!' said Lori, holding her phone at arm's length to take a selfie of their trio. 'Something to remember today by!' She motioned for Rebecca and Abby to squeeze in the shot. 'Wildwater Women!' she whooped as she snapped the picture. The others echoed her, and even Rebecca was persuaded to smile.

But Clarissa was now a speck in the distance.

'Hey, ma'am!' called Lori. 'Slow down!'

They scurried to close the space between them as Clarissa's shoulders visibly sagged with exasperation at the sight of them so far behind.

Lori puffed as the path started to incline slightly. Large, curved stones formed a set of gently sloping steps, through burnished bronze-and-brown woodland.

Abby tipped her head back to take in the gilded filigree canopy above them. '*Wow*,' she breathed. Even this short walk to the lake shore was stunning.

She forged on in front, eager to prove they were taking the open-water swim seriously.

Rebecca soldiered on in silence.

Clarissa, certainly not one to dilly-dally, so it seemed, stood waiting beside a small swing gate.

The sight of it caused a swell of nostalgia for Abby: Ben pulling her in for a kiss as he refastened the latch. But as she pushed the gate open and passed through to the other side, to the soundtrack of the squeaking hinge and the soft laughter of her fellow swimmers, for the first time, she felt as though she was physically beginning a new chapter.

4

'This is *awesome*!' cried Lori, cheeks pink with exertion, as she shut the wooden gate and clapped eyes on the sweeping vista laid out before them: Rydal in all its golden-hour glory. The lake shimmered below, a mirrored sheet of polished precious metal, framed with every shade of autumn splendour: the fields and foliage that fringed the shore were a range of rich jewel-like greens from emerald to jade. The surface of the water itself gleamed like it was made of molten platinum.

Abby stood stock-still and speechless, absorbing the view as though she could somehow steep her soul in it. The sight of such a panorama was enough to make even a doubter like her believe in the nurturing force of nature: she could feel the countryside seeping into her soul, restoring her, resuscitating her. She stayed there for several seconds, and was surprised when Clarissa did the same, allowing them a few moments to fall under the landscape's spell.

'The Lake District is an extremely special place,' she said solemnly, once they'd had plenty of chance to bask in the beauty of the lush scenery stretching out as far as they could see to a honey-hued horizon. 'And it must be treated with respect.'

'Absolutely,' murmured Lori at an uncharacteristically muted volume, and Abby turned her head to look at her face: she blinked as though her eyelids were camera shutters, and she was trying to imprint the image in front of her on her brain indelibly.

She twisted the other way and glimpsed Rebecca, who was intermittently glancing at the wide expanse of Rydal water before returning her gaze to the solid stony ground she stood on, seemingly steeling herself in preparation for getting any closer to the lake.

'We're custodians of the countryside,' continued Clarissa, commanding their attention once again. 'And we must always conduct ourselves to that effect.'

The wind appeared to have moved on to worry branches and leaves elsewhere, and Abby took a large gulp of chill still air.

'Onwards!' instructed Clarissa, setting off down the foot-path which descended to the lakeshore between grassy banks scattered with burnt-umber bracken.

Moments later, the women were lining the water's edge, merely a few metres away from Rydal's ice-cold embrace.

'We're lucky enough to have the perfect conditions tonight,' said Clarissa, tilting her head back towards the sky for a second as she spoke, as though in gratitude to the heavens for such good fortune. 'A nice calm surface,' – she nodded at the lake as though she was greeting a familiar friend – 'and very little breeze, which is much better for when you get out.'

They had to go *in*, yet – never mind the ideal environment for getting *out*, thought Abby.

Rebecca's stance was rigid.

Lori plonked down her tote bag on the pebbles while she took a photo of the snakeskin-like reflections in the shallows.

'So we'll get changed first, and then I'll take you through some breathing exercises.' Clarissa took off her rucksack at the same time as she talked, as if everything she did was an example of efficiency. 'The techniques I show you will help you to deal with the temperature.'

Lori scrunched across the stones and bent to dip a hand in the lake. 'Jeez, that's cold enough to freeze the balls off a brass monkey!' she declared, shaking water droplets from her fingers with an exaggerated shiver and retreating to the rest of the group.

Abby stifled a laugh and even Rebecca cracked a small smile at her dramatic reaction.

Clarissa's countenance remained constant. 'You're all required to wear wetsuits at this stage, because your bodies aren't yet acclimatised,' she continued. 'This is a gradual process and comes with time. As you swim more and more, you'll begin to notice the difference.'

More and more? thought Abby. She was doing well to be attempting it now, as a one-off.

Then Clarissa looked at each of them in turn, commanding their undivided attention as well as conveying the seriousness of the situation. 'This is wild swimming, after all. I wasn't keen on the phrase at first but if it reminds people how unpredictable the water can be, I'm all for it. Reckless behaviour when you're out here amongst nature can have dangerous – even fatal – consequences,' she said, evidently intending to shock the group into paying close attention to her safety instructions, but for Rebecca, such a stark statement seemed to spark pure panic. She sank down suddenly.

'But if you take due care, you'll be completely fine,' concluded Clarissa.

'I think I'll just sit here for today, watch how you all get on, if that's okay,' Rebecca muttered, her skin pale as sheep's wool.

'Carry on getting changed,' Clarissa called out to the others as she made her way over to where Rebecca was hunched over with her head in her hands. She crouched down next to her. 'One little step at a time. Just do what you're comfortable with,' Abby heard her say.

Rebecca stayed where she was, peeping out from the pulled-up hood of her coat like a reluctant caterpillar while the rest of the group struggled into their swimwear.

Thank god for the wetsuit, thought Abby as she shielded herself with a towel whilst wrestling on her bikini bottoms. She couldn't believe she'd actually contemplated only wearing a couple of scraps of spotted fabric to be submerged in a freezing lake.

'I'd highly recommend bringing water shoes in future,' said Clarissa, her voice reverberating out into the night.

Abby looked up to see Lori in an obviously designer bathing costume, in a spun-sugar shade of pink, complete with a ruffled neckline that flattered her decolletage and a wired bodice that made her figure curve in all the right places. She was quite possibly the most glamorous wild swimmer Abby could ever envisage.

Lori must have sensed her staring. 'Told you it was crazy,' she said with a chuckle.

Abby diverted her attention, concentrated once again on wrangling her limbs into her polka-dot top.

'I Googled spas before I got on the plane over here. I'd planned to visit one with a *dreamy* infinity pool, it was really near here – I can't remember the name of it now . . .'

'Not the Loveland?' Rebecca piped up.

'Yes!' said Lori, now trying to stuff the stiff frills of her swimming costume into the top of her wetsuit. 'But now look where I am instead!' she said.

'I actually work there,' said Rebecca.

I knew it, thought Abby. The hotel was the most stylish, elegant place imaginable. Of course she did.

Rebecca pointed to the other side of Rydal. 'You can see it from here.'

Abby's gaze swivelled to look across at the low butterscotch-coloured building that lay at the far edge of the water; an oblong ingot, its golden lights glittering out onto the lake. She'd tried to focus on everything apart from the Loveland; it was a small sliver of her surroundings, after all. The image blurred as she felt tears begin to puddle in her eyes. She turned away, shoved her legs into her wetsuit and yanked it up her body.

'So let's start breathing, nice and deeply,' instructed Clarissa, slipping off her slate-grey fleece to reveal the limestone-white flesh of her bare arms: beneath, she was wearing a black bathing costume.

Gosh, she's brave, thought Abby, fists clenched against the cold despite her full-length neoprene suit.

'Keep taking big, regular breaths,' continued Clarissa. 'Come on, Rebecca, you can join in with this bit at least.'

Abby pushed back her shoulders and did as Clarissa said, steadily blowing the air out of her lungs. The exercise seemed to be having an almost meditative effect, she felt her muscles start to relax.

'Keep this going as you enter the water,' said Clarissa, walking a few steps forward so she was standing ankle-deep in the lake. She gave a flick of her wrists to signal Abby and Lori should follow.

Lori shot Abby a smile. 'Here we go!' she sang.

Abby grinned back at her despite herself. It was exhilarating to be standing on the brink of an experience that was so close to home and yet so totally outside of her usual everyday life. She sucked in another cool breath.

Clarissa had already waded out to waist level and was now splashing water on her forearms as though she were washing in a warm bath.

Abby reached up to twist her tawny hair into a topknot, as she dipped a toe in the shallows.

'It's freezing!' Lori exclaimed with a wince.

Crikey, it is cold. Abby waggled her feet in the water. The rounded rocks were smooth beneath her soles. Ripples rumpled the surface of the spot where she stood, as though reminding her she was present, part of the picture now: every movement she made was mimicked by the lake, she was at one with the landscape. She watched as sunshine and shadow danced a pas de deux over the pebbles. The chill of the water was awakening her somehow, and she found herself being drawn towards it, walking another few paces closer to where Clarissa was waiting.

'That's it, keep going, very gradually – and carry on breathing,' said their instructor.

The water was up to Abby's midriff now. She drew infinity symbols in it with her fingers, watched the lake swirl as she moved her arms by her sides.

'Holy moly, my hands and feet!' said Lori. 'It's *brick*!' she declared, the cold causing a stream of what Abby assumed must be New Yorker terms to tumble out of her mouth.

'Gloves and booties,' called Clarissa in reply, like Jeremy Paxman announcing the correct answer on *University Challenge*.

Abby's exposed skin stung too, as though the sensation was intended to remind her she was *here* – she could touch and feel and experience the world around her.

She poured palmfuls of icy water on her wetsuit-clad arms, mirroring Clarissa's earlier movements. She saw Lori was doing the same, cupping sparkling scoops from Rydal's surface with bright-red hands.

She turned to look at Rebecca, who was peeking out through the gap in her raspberry hood to watch them, and on impulse she waved – a gesture to try and make her feel included, even if she wasn't in the water with them. She herself had needed a little encouragement from the other women, after all.

Rebecca raised a hand in response, her frown giving way to a hint of a smile; like sunshine breaking through clouds after a storm.

Abby glanced back over at their leader, who was now bobbing about in the water with all the ease of someone bathing in the balmy Caribbean. 'When you're ready, ease yourself in – and keep that breathing nice and regular!' Clarissa shouted.

Abby filled her lungs with fresh autumn air.

'Oh boy,' said Lori. 'We're really doing this.'

Abby nodded, a rush of excitement coursing through her. 'Yes, we are.'

They exchanged a look, an unspoken recognition they were sharing this incredible experience together.

'Ready?' said Abby, taking strength from the fact they were standing side by side at the same stage as one another.

'You betcha!' replied Lori.

Abby slowly lowered her shoulders into the lake – and it welcomed her with nothing but sharp pinpricks of pain. She

47

let out an animalistic shriek that surprised her – perhaps she'd been suppressing it for quite some time.

Lori squealed.

Abby winced as the water enfolded her. Wavelets nipped at her neck. *You're alive*, Rydal whispered in her ear with each biting stab.

'Take a moment to make sure your body has acclimatised to the temperature properly,' Clarissa called, drifting on the spot to demonstrate, like she was floating off the coast of Barbados.

Abby blew out a deep breath.

'Oh my goodness,' said Lori beside her. 'We're in!'

Abby shot her a grin. She couldn't really believe it. Then she began to move instinctively, as though her limbs were working of their own accord, trying to keep her warm. A bubble of laughter spontaneously erupted from her lips. *I'm doing it! I'm wild swimming!* She twisted her head to take in the spectacular views surrounding her. The low sun cast everything in an enchanting glow and beauty abounded in all directions: a little black bird with a white beak glided on the glassy water; lambs-fleece clouds whirled above her. She flipped onto her back and marvelled at the two magical-looking mounds of leaf-covered land that loomed out of the middle of the lake like the setting for a children's adventure story.

'Heron Island and Little Isle,' announced Clarissa.

How had she not appreciated all these things before? wondered Abby. These sights were minutes from her front door. Lori had traversed the globe for the privilege of being here, whereas she had spent her whole life with them in easy reach. She might have physically laid eyes on this scenery in the past, but it was as though she was truly seeing it all for the very first time.

'Stay in line with the shore,' shouted Clarissa, 'that way you can get out swiftly at any moment.'

Abby switched back to breaststroke and began to swim parallel with the pebbled bank. She felt her muscles tense and release as her arms and legs forced their way through the water, propelling her forward. She took a gulp of oxygen, chilled and sweet with the scent of imminent twilight, then felt her lungs push the air from her chest again, as though purging herself of the stresses and strains that she squashed deep down inside on a daily basis.

'God, it's all so *gorgeous!*' cried Lori.

Abby glanced over her shoulder at her; she looked utterly entranced by their environment. Then she turned back to see a swan, snowy and serene, skimming the shallows in the distance, and the peach-and-apricot sunshine kissing the fells goodnight on the skyline.

'Let's head back in now,' instructed Clarissa.

Abby started to head for solid ground.

'It's very important not to overdo it on your first time,' explained Clarissa. 'If you stay in for too long, you risk hypothermia.'

Even with her layer of neoprene, the cold seemed to have permeated Abby's skin and bored into her bones. Her extremities were beginning to feel numb already.

'Most of the benefits of freshwater swimming are gained in the first two minutes anyway,' Clarissa added. 'But you'll be able to build up your tolerance as you become accustomed to the temperature over time.'

Abby suddenly felt stones scrape her knees, so she scrabbled to her feet, struggling to stand on the slippery rocks and silty sediment of the lakebed. *I must get some swimming shoes*, she thought, before smiling to herself in surprise. She was

49

considering coming again before she'd even left the water! The lure of the lake was certainly strong; she felt the pull to return already.

'Oh my god, how amazing was that?' said Lori, spraying droplets of water that sparkled like sequins as she splashed her way to shore.

'It was incredible,' Abby agreed. 'I can't believe we did it.'

'Neither can I!' said Lori with a shiver.

'You need to get dry and dressed as quickly as possible now,' boomed Clarissa, who – somehow, by sheer wizardry – was already wearing the clothes she'd arrived in. 'Put lots of layers on as fast as you can.'

Abby began to wriggle out of her wetsuit, and when she next looked up – with her bobble hat pulled over her ears and her coat zipped up to her chin – Clarissa had set out a large flask and four mugs amongst the smooth stones.

'How was it?' asked Rebecca, once everyone was wrapped up again.

'Awesome!' declared Lori, beaming with euphoria.

'Really good!' said Abby, toning down her enthusiasm seeing as Rebecca hadn't felt able to join them. She flexed her fingers and made a mental note to add gloves to the list of gear she needed to bring in future.

'You can really feel the endorphins, huh?' said Lori, shaking out her arms with delight.

An aroma of rich cocoa hit Abby's nostrils and she turned to see Clarissa holding out a steaming mug topped with mini marshmallows for her. 'Oo, thank you!' she said. She couldn't remember when anyone had last made her a hot chocolate. She inhaled the indulgent fragrance, feeling like a child again. She wouldn't have had their instructor marked as the marshmallow type, she thought, as she took the drink grate-fully. But Clarissa certainly wasn't as fearsome as she'd first thought. With her grey fleece, stocky body and slightly upturned mouth, she reminded Abby of a Herdwick sheep.

'So, do you think you'll try and go in with us another time, Rebecca?' Clarissa said, once they all had a warm beverage cradled in their hands.

Rebecca clasped her cup of hot chocolate for courage as she contemplated the question. 'Yes,' she said, her voice so timid the word was almost whisked away by the barely-there breeze.

Clarissa gave a perfunctory nod. 'You come as many times as it takes before you feel confident enough to get in the water.' She was rummaging in her rucksack again. Abby heard a rustle of wax paper and saw the flash of a Swiss Army knife, and then Clarissa was dishing out wedges of fruit loaf.

'Westmorland pepper cake,' she said as she proffered it to the group.

Abby's stomach growled as soon as she glimpsed the dense, fruit-packed slices – she could almost taste the treacle on her tongue as she reached for a piece. The woman was a wonder, she thought, regarding Clarissa with wide eyes as she bit into a slab of the gently spiced cake. The heat of the pepper combined with the fire of fresh ginger began to warm her inside.

Rebecca shook her head and took a sip of her drink instead.

'You can have some, even though you didn't swim,' Clarissa said, as though she could sense Rebecca's reasoning without her having to speak. Perhaps she'd encountered so many different kinds of people over the years that she had an inbuilt talent for knowing how humans think.

'So British!' said Lori with a laugh as she picked up a chunk and sighed with happiness. 'You make this?' she said through a mouthful of crumbs. 'It's *yummy*.'

Clarissa briefly bowed her head in acknowledgement of the compliment, but then she bent down to put the wax wrapper back in her bag, as though she was born to be busy.

'How is everyone feeling?' she asked when she stood up again, swinging her rucksack onto her back as she spoke. She scanned the group, seemingly searching for any tell-tale signs of undesirable after-effects.

'*Unreal*,' replied Lori. Her hair had formed damp ringlets that framed the look of wonder on her face.

'Great!' said Abby, feeling flushed with a sense of achievement. She would never have dreamed she'd be capable of overcoming such a mental and physical challenge before today. But here she was, on the other side. Right at that moment, she felt as though she could conquer any obstacle that came her way. She couldn't recall having inner confidence like that since Ben had been by her side—

'Excellent,' said Clarissa. Then she sought out each pair of eyes that were gathered around her, to signal what she was about to say next was serious. 'Always keep a look out for your fellow swimmers,' she said soberly.

Abby noticed Rebecca swallow.

'Someone who appears to be okay, can be in trouble only minutes later,' Clarissa carried on. 'As soon as you leave the water, cold blood returns to your core and causes your deep body temperature to drop,' – she lowered her hand like she was plunging a cafetière of coffee to demonstrate her point – 'even if you're warmly dressed.' She surveyed the swimmers in her midst. 'This is why you often only start shivering about quarter of an hour later. You must get out of the lake before you become too cold, as you will continue to get colder after swimming.'

'Alrighty,' said Lori, giving a navy-style salute to acknowledge the message had been safely received.

Abby saw Rebecca's lips were trembling even though she'd clamped them together in a bid to make them obey. 'You okay?' she asked, spontaneously putting an arm around her shoulders.

Rebecca swept gloved fingers across her eyes. 'Yep.'

Clarissa gave a nod of approval, as though pleased to see they were taking care of each other already. 'Okay, shall we make a move?' she suggested, clearly not one to stand about aimlessly. Of course she was already packed and ready to go, so she waited for the others to collect up their soggy swimwear and towels. 'Our bodies are now recovering their core temperature,' she announced as they gathered their belongings, as though by continuing to impart useful information while she lingered, she wasn't wasting time.

Abby rolled up her bikini inside her towel and stuffed it into her beach bag, then picked up her dripping wetsuit. Her skin tingled beneath her clothes and her blood seemed to be buzzing round her body. She'd never experienced a sensation like it; she was so *refreshed*.

A dusk mist was now descending as the temperature dropped and night began to draw in, giving Rydal an ethereal appearance.

'You've all done well for your first foray,' Clarissa declared, including Rebecca in her comment with a quick nod. Then she spun round and started to stride back up the hill, leading the way for the other women in the fading light.

5

Abby looped her wringing wetsuit over her anoraked arm. 'After you,' she said to Rebecca, sandwiching her securely between herself and Lori for the return journey. 'I don't blame you for staying dry by the way,' she said empathetically as she brought up the rear. 'It's madness really,' she added, more quietly, to make sure Clarissa couldn't hear.

Rebecca gave her a small smile. 'Thanks for being understanding. I know swimming in the lake doesn't seem like that big a deal—'

'But it does! I never *ever* thought I'd be bold enough to be here . . .' Abby trailed off, as from the blanched look on Rebecca's face, she wasn't helping by stating how hard it had been to break out of her usual habits and throw herself out of her comfort zone. She sank into silence.

Lori stepped in to fill it. 'So, you work at the Loveland, huh?' she said, changing the subject.

Abby's stomach lurched at the mention of the hotel. A memory ambushed her: Ben standing at the top of the aisle, against a backdrop of blush-pink peonies, turning to look at her for the first time—

'Yep,' Rebecca replied. 'I'm head receptionist.' She let out a sigh, and Abby got the impression that the topic of her job was perhaps as unpleasant to talk about as wild swimming for Rebecca.

'You don't enjoy it, hey?' asked Lori, straight to the point.

'It's just busy . . . you know.' Rebecca exhaled deeply as though she was releasing a pressure valve, trying to rid her body of pent-up tension.

'Wanna talk about it?' said Lori.

Rebecca brushed stray strands of hair from her face. 'I don't mean to moan . . . just the owners think we *staff* belong to them, not just the hotel.'

As much as she didn't want to dwell on the Loveland a minute longer than she had to, Abby could appreciate exactly where Rebecca was coming from in terms of having a tyrant boss, and she felt a sudden affinity with her. She'd assumed Rebecca's life was perfect, judged her on the shiny shell she usually showed to the world, but underneath, she was just as vulnerable as she or anyone else. *Why do we do that?* She wondered. *Compare our anxious, muddled insides with other people's polished exteriors?*

'It's just so all-consuming and full-on. Sometimes I feel like work is taking over my whole life. Sorry,' she added suddenly, as though she really hadn't intended to spill her heart to the two of them.

'Don't apologise,' said Lori. 'Let it out, honey.'

'I know it doesn't help, but I know what it's like,' said Abby.

'And I have my own business now, but I've had *awful* employers in the past,' said Lori.

They reached the top of the track, where Clarissa was waiting by the wooden gate like a weary shepherd. But before they passed through, the three of them turned automatically, to take in the view, as though the sight of lake and its verdant surroundings was a salve.

'This landscape has remained largely unchanged for hundreds of years,' she said, sharing the moment with them. 'And we *must* preserve it for the future.'

'Absolutely,' breathed Lori.

Abby looked down at the silvery water and the darkening hills stretching beyond. Another day was drawing to a close. But she'd done something different. Changed the pattern she'd been stuck in for so long. For once, she felt at peace with her place in the world at that precise point in time.

'If you could put your wetsuits in the back of my car when we reach White Crag, that would be great,' said Clarissa, once again taking the opportunity to dispense instructions while her herd was gathered together in one spot.

'Sure thing,' said Lori.

Clarissa pushed open the gate and headed into the woodland beyond, the trio in her charge snaking along the path behind her.

'Um, did you both pay for the session when you signed up at the shop?' asked Abby in a hushed tone when Clarissa was far enough in front of them to be out of earshot.

Rebecca and Lori both shook their heads.

'Or do we do that when we get back to the car park?' So far, money hadn't been mentioned, and there was no fee stated on the safety form Abby had had to sign. She wondered how much cash she was carrying in her purse; she really ought to have checked the cost with Clarissa first. She tried to tot up what the figure might be in her mind: they'd had an hour of her time, and she really couldn't have been a better guide, plus the hire of a wetsuit—

'It's free,' said Lori. 'That's what she said to me, anyways.'

'Really? It can't be,' replied Abby, her voice high-pitched with surprise.

Rebecca was nodding to indicate she'd been told the same.

'What, as a taster, you mean?' asked Abby. She glanced up from the stone-slab staircase they were now descending, could see Clarissa already at the bottom, one boot on the first slat of the footbridge as she paused for them to catch up. 'For the first time, like a trial go?'

'No,' said Rebecca, before taking a breath as though she was about to say something more, but stopped herself.

'I don't understand,' said Abby. 'Why doesn't she charge people?'

Lori turned to look back at her, opened her mouth, then hesitated.

Abby frowned. They both seemed to be holding something back. But then, perhaps she had a tendency to do that sometimes too . . .

'Well, she has the Swim Wild shop in town,' said Rebecca. 'So, I reckon if we support that, maybe buy some bits of kit—'

'Oh, for *sure*,' said Lori. 'I need some mitts, man,' – she held up her hands for emphasis – 'and a whole lotta stuff before I *lake swim* again.'

Rebecca and Abby giggled at her turn of phrase. They'd reached the wooden bridge, but Clarissa was now standing beside her Land Rover, on the other side of the river, encircled by the intricate mesh of copper-coloured beech trees where their adventure had begun.

'Hey, so what made you wanna go all *wild* when you have that awesome pool at the Loveland?' Lori said, turning to Rebecca. 'Must get a discount if you're staff, huh?'

Rebecca kept her eyes fixed on the planks beneath her feet.

Abby watched the Rothay foam and froth as they crossed; she was intrigued too. If Rebecca was so scared of the water, then surely the Loveland's luxurious spa would seem like an easier starting point?

When they reached the gravelly ground beyond, still Rebecca's gaze stayed stuck on her wellington boots. 'I . . . I couldn't do it at the hotel.'

'I get it,' said Lori sympathetically. 'You don't wanna hang around work a minute longer than you have to, right?' She nodded to herself, as though she'd cracked a cryptic clue.

Rebecca's forehead creased, as though Lori hadn't entirely got the right answer, but correcting her would be too complex to articulate at that current moment – they were back at the car park now.

Abby saw a sudden flare of headlights through fine fog as a taxi swung off the main road then crunched across the stones towards them. She hurried over to Clarissa, who was opening up the rear doors of her Defender. 'Thank you so much,' she said, her breath clouding as she spoke.

Clarissa twisted round. 'You're welcome,' she replied crisply, before carrying on unfastening forms from clipboards.

'It's been a *wonderful* experience,' Abby continued, clutching her sodden wetsuit awkwardly. She meant it. Now she was back in the clearing, with the rumbling sound of the cab's running engine ringing in her ears, as it waited to whisk her back home, she found she was reluctant to return to real life. Crushing guilt seared through her as soon as the thought took shape in her mind. She had Rowan to think about – responsibilities. She shouldn't be spending her time swimming in lakes with strangers. It had been interesting – exhilarating – as a one-off, that was all. Then, to her horror, she felt tears threaten to tumble from her eyes. She choked back a swell of emotion. 'It's really made a difference to me,' she mumbled, and Clarissa turned back to meet her gaze.

'I'm glad.' Her dark eyes shone beneath the bright light of the Land Rover's interior. 'It's why I do it.' She took the wetsuit, and gave Abby a smile so brief she wondered whether she'd really seen it, like catching a rainbow in a spray of water, or a shooting star in a clear night sky.

'I must owe you something . . .' said Abby.

Clarissa tilted her head slightly. 'Just pass it on,' she replied. 'Kindness is the best currency, and certainly the only one I require.'

'Hey, Abby!' called Lori, across the sheltered glade. 'Our cab's here!' She strode over to deposit her wetsuit in the back of Clarissa's four-by-four. 'It's been *uh-mazing*,' she said to their instructor, clasping a hand to her chest. 'Honestly, thank you *so much*. I'll be back – one hundred per cent.'

'I'm glad you've enjoyed it,' Clarissa said, before seeking out Rebecca over Lori's shoulder. 'And are you okay?' she asked, clearly looking for comprehensive feedback from the group. 'The Lakes are always here. They'll be ready whenever you are.'

Rebecca nodded. 'Thank you.'

'Excellent,' said Clarissa, and with a slam of her Defender's doors and a roaring rev of her engine, she drove off in the opposite direction to Ambleside and disappeared like a creature from a Cumbrian myth.

6

Abby waved as she watched Rebecca walk back to her little red car alone.

'See you again, I hope!' Lori yelled, before leaping into the warmth of the waiting taxi, eager to tell anyone who'd listen about their exploits. 'We surviiiived!' she whooped to the driver.

But Abby stayed put for a second, wanting to make sure Rebecca didn't feel abandoned, before she got into the taxi beside Lori. It was strange; they all led completely different lives, and up until an hour or so ago had been steering their own separate courses through the world, but now Abby felt the beginnings of a bond forming between them, invisible and delicate, like a spun-silk spider's web.

Rebecca beeped her horn in farewell as she swung out of her parking space, and Lori and Abby grinned back as the taxi indicated onto the road.

But as she and Lori wound their way towards town, Abby couldn't escape the intense squeeze of anxiety that was scrunching her stomach and restricting her lungs. The weight of all the things she had to do once she was back seemed to be squashing her into the black leather seat.

'Oh my god, I feel sooo good, don't you?' said Lori.

Abby bit her lip and nodded. She'd felt invigorated at first; it had been refreshing to be so fully immersed in nature – a brief but brilliant sixty minutes of respite from her usual rut. But now she'd left the lake behind, and was crawling ever closer to her cottage, her initial feeling of elation was dwindling. *I can't make a habit of this*, she thought to herself. It was getting late and she hadn't collected Rowan, checked she'd got clean school uniform or made her packed lunch for the following day. Soon, she'd be by herself again, doing her best to bring up her daughter and battling against a never-ending list of chores, just like normal.

'You want dropping off at your place or in the centre?' asked Lori.

Maria's house was at the other end of Ambleside, but Abby didn't want to put Lori out by asking her to make an extra stop – she'd already been kind enough to let her hop in the taxi with her. 'Home is great, thank you,' she said with a smile.

'Alrighty,' said Lori, already chattering away to the driver again, giving him a blow-by-blow account of their excursion.

Little Garth looked gloomy and soulless when they pulled up beside the pavement outside, like a body with no light behind its eyes, thought Abby, lugging her leaden limbs from the comfortable leather seat. A long day at the bakery, followed by the adrenaline-filled escapades of the evening, had left her feeling exhausted. Stepping out of her everyday routine really only made it harder to force herself back into it again; like trying to stuff a sleeping bag back into its carrier or cramming a suitcase closed, post break.

'So, when can you next make it?' asked Lori, once she'd pressed a ten-pound note into the taxi driver's hand and extracted a promise from him to give open-water swimming a go.

Abby's tired brain struggled to compute the question.

'Which day works for you?' said Lori, leaning on the little metal gate that led to Silver Ghyll.

Abby felt the air leave her chest as though she were a deflated lilo at the end of a holiday. There just wasn't time for her to be off gallivanting; she had a little girl to raise. Swimming with the Wildwater Women was not something she should be wasting time doing. 'Er, I don't know . . .'

Lori's shoulders sank slightly, silhouetted by the milky moon. 'No worries,' she replied, batting a hand through the chilly night sky before bidding her goodnight. 'See you around, anyways!'

Abby felt a twist of remorse as she walked up the street – why hadn't she tried to explain? She hadn't meant to offend her. Now Lori probably thought she didn't see the point of hanging out with her: someone who'd soon be gone as quickly as they'd arrived. But it wasn't that. Abby wished she'd taken the time to make it clear – she'd enjoyed her night off from the norm, but she couldn't justify stepping out of reality regularly. She had too much to be concentrating on as it was. But what did it really matter whether Lori understood or not? Abby asked herself. Her neighbour would be back in America in a couple of weeks. Abby couldn't keep going to the swim sessions for her sake. Even so, she still hoped Lori didn't think less of her. She'd gone back on her word, in a way, and it bothered her. She glanced back at Silver Ghyll, but the door was already closed.

Abby looked at her watch: it would almost be seven-thirty by the time she reached Maria's. Nearly half an hour later than she'd originally said. She semi-jogged there, the physical exertion thawing her out.

'I'm so sorry,' she puffed when Maria opened the door to Fairfield View.

'Whatever for?' replied her mother-in-law.

Abby pressed the palms of her hands to her hot cheeks: no doubt they were ruddy from her half-run. 'I said I'd be here by seven . . .'

'Don't be silly,' Maria said as she ushered her inside. 'It's freezing out there – come in.'

'Oh, I won't stop, we'll get back,' said Abby, hovering in the hall. Rowan rushed out of the front room and flung her arms around her. Abby bent down to breathe in the scent of her daughter's soft skin and stroke the golden strands of hair from her face, wishing – not for the first time – there was a way to store moments like this so you could return to them in the future if you wanted to: a magical memory library. One day, Rowan's eagerness to see her would wane, but right now Abby savoured the sensation of having her sticky fingers wrapped round her neck and her chocolate-smeared face pressed close to hers.

'I had ice cream, Mummy!' she squealed, her hot breath in Abby's ear.

'That's nice, sweetheart.'

'She's had broccoli too,' said Maria.

'Not at the same time!' Rowan giggled loudly.

'Thank you for looking after her,' Abby said to Maria, standing up.

'It's been a pleasure,' she replied. 'Look,' she added, fiddling with her wedding ring. 'If you need me to babysit ever—'

'Oh, tonight was just . . . I . . . er . . .' Abby's cheeks burned. She hadn't picked up her daughter because she'd decided to go for a dusk dip in Rydal with people she didn't know. Her excuse sounded insane, even to herself. She didn't want Maria to think she wasn't managing. 'It's not going to happen again,' she mumbled.

Maria nodded slowly. 'All right. Well, the offer's there.'

She gave a small smile but Abby could see the shine of sadness in her gaze. She reached out and squeezed Maria's arm. *Maybe she does want to spend more time with Rowan after all?* she wondered. 'Whenever you want to see her,' – she jerked her head at Rowan, who was hopscotching on the spot – 'just say, okay?'

Maria's eyes roved Abby's face. 'And if you . . .' she began, her voice slightly hoarse. 'If there's . . . something you want to do, she's welcome here anytime.'

Did she know where she'd been? wondered Abby, abashed. Her sapped mind started to spiral. Did she think she wasn't doing a good enough job of raising Rowan by herself? She clutched her daughter's shoulder, as though demonstrating she was *everything* to her. 'Thank you,' she muttered, not sure what else to say, and at a loss as to how to get across she was doing her best, despite the circumstances.

'See you soon, sweetie pie,' said Maria, unhooking Rowan's coat from a peg in the hall and helping her into it.

Abby took the rucksack that was hanging next to it on the wall.

'Byeeeee, Grandmaaaa!' called Rowan as they began to walk down the road.

Back home, once Rowan was bathed and in bed, Abby set about making cheese sandwiches, stifling a yawn as she pulled an almost-stale loaf from the bread bin in the kitchen. She took far too long to find the block of cheddar in the fridge, failing to see it right in front of her at first, fatigue taking its toll. Her fingers fumbled with the tin foil as she wrapped up Rowan's for the following day, then she sat down on the sofa to eat hers, her stomach rumbling despite the dismally uninspired supper. She stared at the wall that separated Little Garth from Silver Ghyll as she did so. Her cottage was that quiet she could hear the faint sound of Lori speaking on the phone, her laughter intermittently permeating the wall, as though her infectious optimism refused to be contained. She'd been so generous-spirited when Rowan hadn't wanted to go to school at the start of the week, thought Abby.

When she'd finished her sandwich, she stood up, swept the crumbs off her plate into the bin, then started to empty out her daughter's bag. The sight of Elsa on Rowan's *Frozen* lunchbox made her think of Lori too, and Abby resolved that when she next saw her again, she'd do her best to explain: she'd enjoyed their wild swimming session, but she just didn't have space in her life for hobbies at present.

She ran a sink-full of hot soapy water, and then opened the Disney-character-covered container and upturned the remnants into the rubbish – the mulch of a half-eaten banana and some discarded crusts – the picnic she'd made the previous day now diminished to unappetising scraps. Representative of her existence really, she mused as she washed out the box: her life had been reduced to a shadow of what it had once been.

She finished making Rowan's lunch, wrote herself a note so she didn't forget to take it out of the fridge when she woke up, and then looped her daughter's rucksack over the back of a kitchen chair, ready to be packed in the morning. But as she did so, she caught sight of a sheet of paper inside,

65

covered in the pencil marks of a four-year-old. She pulled it out, intrigued to see what Rowan had been busy with – but felt a sharp stab in her abdomen as she recognised the people in front of her. She traced the shapes Rowan had scribbled above the words 'Mummy' and 'Me' and below the title 'My Family'. But it wasn't just the fact there were only two stark grey stick figures with disproportionately huge hands and exaggerated features on the page instead of three, like there should be, that made her heart sting and her stomach clench – it was the unmistakeable form of an enormous teardrop Rowan had drawn falling from her mother's face.

7

'You all right, Abs?' asked Tom.

Abby squinted back at him beneath the harsh lights of the bakery. Her eyes felt like shrivelled sultanas. 'Yeah, fine thanks,' she replied, swiftly diverting her gaze to the tray of just-made plum pies she'd now picked up, so he couldn't detect she hadn't slept. 'How about you?' she said, already inching towards the shop floor.

'You *sure*?' he said, cocking his head on one side, as though ducking the question she'd batted back. 'Is Rowan not settling in so well, is that it?'

Abby's mouth felt dry, like she'd tried to swallow a spoonful of flour. She couldn't ignore Tom's kindly meant enquiry, but neither was she able to find the words to answer him. She gripped the baking sheet with both hands. *Do not cry*, she instructed herself sternly. But the stick figures her daughter had drawn seemed to be etched behind her eyelids; she saw the image each time she blinked. The idea that her child knew she was struggling made her feel terrible. As a parent, she ought to be able to put her own emotions out of the picture, and focus on what was best for Rowan. She couldn't let her misery affect her.

'Kids are smart, Abs,' said Tom, his voice gentle. 'They're not easily fooled.' He stopped kneading his dough and took a step towards her. 'And neither am I, for that matter.' His brown eyes were wide and round like two melting Maltesers. If you ever want to talk, I'm here, okay?'

She nodded, half grateful for his concern, but equally as upset that he could see through her pretence that everything was all right too. Was everyone convinced she couldn't cope? The kitchen suddenly seemed suffocatingly stuffy, the walls and ceiling far too close.

'I know how hard it is,' Tom said as he returned to making his bread.

No you don't! Abby wanted to scream. He hadn't a clue how claustrophobic it was to be trapped in an endless cycle of single-handed responsibility for a precious little person – he wasn't bringing Freddie up by himself! Her shoulders were rigid with rage. But it wasn't Tom's fault, she was aware of that, and he didn't deserve her anger; he was doing his best to help. Yet no one could. They weren't able to get her husband back, were they?

'I think Rowan knows I miss her dad,' Abby said in an almost whisper, the words spilling out from inside her like she was an egg whose brittle shell Tom had cracked. She set the tray of pies on the work surface and sighed.

Tom turned towards her.

'I found a sketch she'd done at school . . . She can tell I'm sad . . .'

'See, she's a bright girl,' said Tom softly. 'Just like her mum,' he added.

Abby smiled at his compliment despite herself.

'I think you're missing *yourself*, as well as him,' he said.

She bristled. She was bound not to be the woman she was before! She'd been betrayed by life, had her happiness snatched away. How did everyone expect her to react, for god's sake?

'We need to get Abby back,' he said, nudging her arm. 'That's the most effective way to make sure Rowan's okay.'

Abby raised her eyebrows. 'What do you mean?'

'If you don't look after yourself right, you can't take care of her.'

Abby frowned. 'Everything I do is for Rowan—'

'I know,' Tom cut in. 'And that's my point, Abs. You can't pour from an empty cup, that's all I'm saying.'

But then they both heard the distinctive sound of Joy's footsteps approaching and sprang back to what they were each supposed to be doing. Abby hurried out of the kitchen with the freshly baked pies, catching Tom's eye as she did so and smiling a thank-you. Sometimes the hardest advice to hear was the kind you needed the most.

She was still mulling over Tom's words at midday, when the little bell above the door announced Rebecca's entrance.

Abby handed another customer their change, then raised a hand to wave.

Rebecca mouthed 'hello'; she was on the phone, of course. She stood next to the display cabinet of cakes, searching for her purse at the same time as talking into her mobile.

Abby served someone else, but she couldn't help over-hearing some of what Rebecca said.

'This Saturday? But . . . I've worked the last three weekends in a row . . .' Rebecca was glaring at the squares of chocolate brownie beyond the glass as though they were to blame for her rota.

Abby busied herself with checking how many bread rolls were left in the hanging bins behind her head.

'Okay,' she heard Rebecca say. 'Yes . . . I know. I'll be back on reception in a second anyway so— Yes . . . I understand. Bye.'

Abby turned back round. 'Hi!'

Rebecca rubbed her right temple, as though her phone conversation had caused the side of her head to pulse with pain. 'Hey,' she said, blowing air into her cheeks like an exasperated puffer fish. Then she pulled her red lips into a polished grin. 'Defrosted yet after yesterday?'

'Just about,' replied Abby, reaching for her serving tongs. 'How are you?'

'Ah, I'm okay,' Rebecca said. 'Didn't do quite so well as you, did I?' she added with a self-deprecating smile.

Abby remembered how scared Rebecca had seemed, before they'd even set off from the car park, and how she'd appeared panicked by the mere sight of the water. Maybe she was wrestling with an issue much larger than just enduring the cold conditions. But she'd still been brave enough to begin – to even contemplate the wild swim – when Abby suspected that it was something that felt almost insurmountable for her. It had clearly been a bigger deal for Rebecca than it had been for the rest of them. 'Perhaps you set off from a different starting point,' Abby said sagely, wondering whether some of Tom's wisdom had rubbed off on her.

A ruby bloom flamed in Rebecca's cheeks. 'You were very impressive, considering it was your first go,' she said, deflecting the focus away from herself.

'Oh, I don't think I'll be doing it again any time soon, though,' Abby replied, fiddling with one of the cuffs on her plastic gloves.

'Really?' asked Rebecca with a frown. 'You looked like you enjoyed it! Once you were in – or *out*, for that matter,' she quipped.

Abby laughed.

Rebecca gave her lunch order and then in walked Lori, the doorbell chiming as though in celebration of their reunion.

'Hello!' Abby and Rebecca both said simultaneously, turning to smile at her.

Lori looked momentarily taken aback, her face remaining blank for a few seconds before it broke into a grin, like a time lag on a video link. 'Oh, hey there!'

Abby wondered whether she hadn't recognised them for a minute; she supposed they did look pretty different, she in her purple apron and health-and-safety hair net, and Rebecca, now the epitome of glamour, all russet locks, red-lipstick and nipped-in workwear.

'How are you?' Lori greeted them with arms spread wide, her blow-dried hair bouncing on her bobbing shoulders, as though in compensation for the delay.

'Good,' replied Rebecca. 'How about you? Finally warmed up after yesterday?'

A flicker of a shadow passed over Lori's face, like a cloud obscuring the sun, then her full-beam smile was back. 'Oh, yeah! Took a hot shower and had takeout Thai . . . sooo good. What's up with you girls, huh?' She looked between the two of them.

'Ah, not much,' said Abby, with a shrug. 'Back to the grind-stone.'

'Yep,' added Rebecca. 'Me too.'

'Oh, *wow*,' exclaimed Lori, elongating the vowel, as her attention was lured by the array of sumptuous-looking cakes on display in the shop.

71

'You can see why I recommended this place, right?' said Rebecca, stepping aside slightly so she could see the full selection.

'Huh?' said Lori, glancing back at her, her smile slipping slightly, before she recovered herself. 'Oh, *sure*. It's *amazing*.'

Abby made up Rebecca's roll while the other women marvelled at the traybakes and pastries stacked on the glass shelves before them. Now wasn't the time to explain to Lori that she wasn't going swimming again because she lacked opportunity for any leisure activities full stop, not because she didn't want to spend time with her short-term neighbour. She'd wait till she bumped into her outside the cottage, or call round at some point. Perhaps make sure she was all right; she seemed a little flustered.

'Have you come to get some of the tea bread?' Rebecca asked Lori, jabbing a finger to indicate where it was amongst the spread of treats.

But Lori wasn't looking. 'I just want one of *everything*,' she replied with a chuckle.

'Are you going to sign up for another session with Clarissa?' Abby said to Rebecca, thinking that the other two could pair up and continue with the sessions, that way they'd each have someone to go with.

'I wanted to try again on Saturday, actually,' Rebecca replied, tightening the belt on her trench coat as though strapping herself into a stylish, state-of-the-art set of armour. 'But I have to work now; we've got a wedding at the Loveland this weekend.'

Abby concentrated on the little slivers of cucumber she was cramming into the ham sandwich she was making, but Rebecca's words whirled around her mind, stirring up memories like silt disturbed from the lakebed. *A wedding at the Loveland.* She hoped the tub of onion slices in the salad bar beside her would excuse her watery eyes.

'You wanna go swimming Sunday instead?' asked Lori, her eyebrows raised at Rebecca. Then she turned towards Abby. 'You're welcome too, of course, er . . . um . . .' she added, trailing off.

She's forgotten my name, thought Abby, *and I've been stressing that she's offended I wasn't being friendlier and spending more time with her!* She felt a rush of relief: as usual she was worrying about nothing. They'd only met a handful of times, after all.

'I can do Sunday,' said Rebecca, as she paid for her lunch. 'Shall I give you my number?'

'Oh, good idea,' said Lori, digging around in her tote bag for her mobile. 'It's in here *somewhere.*'

'Or I can take yours if that's easier,' said Rebecca, when the search started to look potentially fruitless. But then her own phone began to ring again, its screen blazing and the accompanying buzzing noise seeming to become increasingly insistent, demanding her attention. 'I have to get back to work . . .' she muttered. She leaned on the counter and scribbled her digits on her receipt, handed it to Lori and waved goodbye to them both before she rushed out of the door.

'Busy bee,' said Lori, giving up looking in her shoulder bag with a sigh, and meeting Abby's gaze.

Abby nodded; Rebecca certainly was. 'What can I get you?' she asked.

'I'll take a slice of Plum Pie, please,' said Lori. 'Seeing as it's the house specialty.'

Abby wrapped up a piece for her. 'Anything else?'

'That's all, thank you.'

Abby moved to the till.

'Actually,' began Lori. 'Do you mind if I ask you something?'

Abby looked up. There was an urgency in her eyes. 'Go ahead.'

'Just a second . . .' Lori was rummaging in her bag again. 'I hope you don't mind . . .'

'Not at all,' said Abby. She was just glad there was no awkwardness after she'd bowed out of going to any more of the wild swim sessions. And she owed Lori, anyway, for the taxi ride the previous day. The least she could do was help her with whatever question she had. Besides, no one else had entered the shop and Joy was nowhere to be seen.

Abby glanced back at Lori. 'Gosh!'

'You look like I just pulled a rabbit out of a hat!' declared Lori. She was holding her iPad, showing her a framed picture of a landscape painting on the screen.

'I wasn't expecting that!' said Abby, mesmerised by the translucent watercolours of the idyllic scene. 'Is it the Lake District?'

'Uh-huh. It was my grandpa's,' explained Lori.

'It's beautiful.'

'I think so too.'

Abby couldn't tear her gaze from the image: the iridescent lake with the majestic blue-green mountains behind. The light in the scene seemed mysterious and otherworldly; the picture seemed to have both a magic and a melancholy. And it was magnetic to look at.

'It's the reason I came all the way here from New York – I had to see this place with my own eyes,' said Lori. 'You're a local, right?'

Abby nodded.

'You know this spot?' Lori asked, holding the painting up hopefully.

Abby had lived in Cumbria for her entire life, but had no idea where that view was. She peered at it more closely, looking for distinguishing details. But there were no distinctive buildings to use as landmarks. The names and shapes of the hills were unfamiliar to her. She shook her head. 'Sorry.'

Lori looked crestfallen.

Abby bit her lip. 'I'm sure we could find it.' *We?* Where had that come from? What on earth was she saying?

'Really?' Lori's eyes widened. 'Do you think so?'

'I mean . . . someone's got to know,' Abby said.

Lori's shoulders sank. 'Oh.' She flipped the case of her iPad closed and slipped it back into her bag.

'Why don't you ask Clarissa?' suggested Abby.

'Who?'

'The leader of the swimming group.'

'Oh, yeah!'

Abby looked at Lori. 'She said the landscape's remained pretty much unchanged for centuries, remember?'

There was that cloud again.

'Right,' Lori said, fixing her smile back in place.

'I'm sure she'd know, she seems so well-acquainted with everywhere round here,' Abby carried on. 'I don't see why it wouldn't be possible to locate it somehow,' she concluded.

'Okay!' said Lori, seemingly appeased.

Tom appeared in the doorway that led to the kitchen, carrying a tray of delicious-smelling scones.

'Oh, sorry, Tom,' said Abby. 'Thank you.'

'No worries,' he said, sliding the metal baking sheet onto the counter behind her, before flashing Lori an inclusive smile. 'Heads up, by the way,' he whispered to Abby on his way out. 'Dragon ahoy!' Then he disappeared off in the direction of the kitchen again.

Abby's shoulders tensed in anticipation of her boss's arrival.

Lori glanced around, as though Cumbria was such an unearthly place it might actually be possible to encounter a flame-breathed monster. She yanked her bag further up her arm. 'I'll let you get back to work, anyways,' she said.

'Don't forget this!' Abby handed her the paper bag of plum pie.

'Oh, yeah. Thanks. Have a great day!'

'You too,' replied Abby.

Then Joy emerged from the back, bringing a firestorm of displeasure with her into the shop; Tom must have spied her coming in through the rear door.

'Are these scones just going to sit here all day?' she asked, fixing Abby with a blazing stare.

But Abby was looking out of the window, the image from the painting impressed on her mind. Lori had travelled more than three thousand miles: that view was something they *had* to find.

8

Abby felt a tug on the duvet cover; the sensation of it sweeping across her skin rousing her from heavy sleep. In her half-dreaming state, she thought it was Ben, moving on the mattress beside her. She turned over, rubbing her eyes – and saw her daughter's face an inch away from hers on the pillow.

'Mummyyyyyy!' Rowan squealed delightedly, oatmeal hair sticking up at the back. 'You're awake!'

I am now. Abby pushed herself upright, not quite ready for morning to begin. She glanced at the clock: just past 7 a.m. Then a shudder of shock shook her: *is it a school day?*

Her brain spooled up to speed in a split-second: *no, it is Sunday*, she realised with relief. And she wasn't at work till tomorrow. She flopped back against the bedding.

Rowan snuggled into her side and Abby squeezed her daughter's squirming body close: she wouldn't be this young forever, she thought, noticing her pig-print pyjamas were looking shorter in the arms and legs – moments like this one were numbered. She kissed the top of Rowan's sleep-mussed mop.

'What are we doing today?' Rowan asked, already wriggling out of the hug.

Abby sighed. She had laundry to do, groceries to buy, and she couldn't remember the last time she'd hoovered—

'Can we play animals?'

Rowan was crawling on all fours, pretending to be a lion or a tiger or possibly a grizzly bear. It was the kind of fun activity that Abby had, at one time, imagined Ben would participate in with unbridled exuberance. Yet he hadn't once been there to take part. But she couldn't dwell on that now, there was shopping and tidying to be done.

'Perhaps later, poppet,' said Abby, wishing she had a fraction of the energy Rowan woke up with. 'We need to go and get some food first.' There wasn't even any milk in the fridge for cereal; she'd used the last of it the previous evening to make macaroni cheese.

Rowan flung herself down flat on top of the bed, limbs spread out like a starfish.

Abby didn't know whether she was pretending to be one, continuing the guess-the-creature game, or just resisting the idea of doing mundane errands. *In that case, I know how she feels.* 'We could have dippy eggs and soldiers for supper?' she suggested, attempting to cajole her.

'Nooo,' Rowan whined, turning her face away.

'But you like them, sweetie?' Abby said soothingly, reaching out to smooth a curl from her little girl's cheek. Still Rowan stayed motionless.

Abby closed her eyes, wishing she could crawl beneath the sheets and sleep for a century.

Rowan kicked her feet back and forth repeatedly, as though sensing the loss of her mother's attention.

Abby opened her eyes. A streak of sunlight was now spilling through the curtains onto the duvet, and beyond the pane of glass was a glorious autumn day. She pushed back the covers and went to stand by the window. The clouds that usually crowded the Cumbrian skies were nowhere to be seen, and instead a vast expanse of blue greeted her, brilliant and rare. Abby felt an unignorable yearning to be outside, free from Little Garth's four stone walls, as though the wild swimming excursion had awoken within her a desire to be surrounded by wide horizons again. The morning was clear and crisp – and just couldn't be spent in the Co-op or cleaning. She looked over her shoulder at Rowan, whose fingers were outstretched in the shard of sunshine, entranced by the shadow-shapes she could create.

Abby put both her hands together to cast a bird silhouette on the bed.

Rowan giggled.

My favourite sound, thought Abby, letting out a deep breath. 'I'm going to make some toast,' she announced. 'But if you don't like soldiers any more, then I guess that means you don't like bread . . .' she said to her daughter, keeping a straight face as she pulled on her dressing gown. 'So you won't be wanting any breakfast, will you . . .?'

'Yes, I do, Mummy!' Rowan shrieked, scrambling off the bed and scampering after her out of the door.

In the kitchen, Abby peeled the last freckle-speckled banana and sliced it up for her daughter while she sat, feet dangling, at the table. Mercifully, she was back in a compliant mood, happily humming a song she must have either made up or decimated from its original form.

A few moments later, Abby put a plate of hot, honey-covered toast down in front of her. But before she replaced the lid on the glass jar, she breathed in the heady scent of heather that conjured up images from long ago: sunshine-drenched walks to hidden tarns surrounded by a sea of the purple-flowered shrubs. She could almost feel the summer-warmed water sloshing around her feet as she recalled the sheer delight of discovering such a secret-seeming place. She remembered the wonder of seeing fairy-tale lily pads floating on the surface of the shimmering pool, the captivating magic of seeing a dragonfly buzzing by.

She screwed the top back on the honey, thoughts blossoming in her head. She wanted Rowan to grow up with just as many Lake District memories as she had, to have a childhood filled with all the riches of the countryside. Her daughter was part of the landscape, and it was part of her. There was a whole adventure playground out there for her, and today was a prime opportunity to explore.

Abby set about packing a picnic with whatever she had left in the house, fired up with a desire to give her daughter an exciting and different Sunday. She made cheese and pickle sandwiches, retrieved a packet of raisins for Rowan and some cereal bars, just in case, from the cupboard, filled two water bottles and found an ancient rucksack under the stairs in which to carry their supplies.

Where shall we go? pondered Abby. Somewhere she hadn't been for ages, and a place Rowan had never seen. Not too far for a shorter autumn day, but away from their usual territory of Ambleside and its environs . . .

Then an idea came to her. The perfect picnic spot surrounded by a splendid display of seasonal colours. She was going to show Rowan somewhere she hadn't been for the best part of a decade: High Pool Tarn. A place nestled up in the woodland above the old bobbin mill, just beyond the lowest point of the longest lake, Windermere.

The drive there in itself was spectacular, and Rowan was rapt for the duration. Abby felt a buzz of happiness that Rowan wasn't old enough yet to take this magical place for granted. They trundled the length of Windermere, the water stretching out alongside them like a constant companion.

'Boats, Mummy!' Rowan beamed from the back seat. Abby glanced at her grinning face in the rear-view mirror: she was transfixed by what she saw on the other side of the car window, fingers of one hand splayed against the glass in awe.

'Ducks!' she cried.

Windermere revelled in her attention, sparkling and showing off in the bright September sunlight.

They approached Fell Foot, at the very bottom of the lake, and Abby almost indicated off the road to stop there instead, overcome with a need to show Rowan the rolling parkland and picturesque paddling spot at the southernmost tip of the water. But she could save it for another day – or perhaps they could call in on the way back, get a drink at the café.

'Mummyyy . . .' said Rowan at the exact second the sign for Fell Foot disappeared from the back windscreen.

Oh no. Abby suppressed a sigh. She knew the rest of the sentence before Rowan spoke it aloud, could tell the meaning from her daughter's intonation alone: she needed the loo. Abby continued on till she could turn round, then doubled back and pulled into the car park.

She should have known it would be busy; it was a popular place and was bound to be packed with people wandering in the meadowland and soaking in the lakeside views, eager to grasp the last vestiges of good weather before autumn blazed to an end. A swarm of vehicles glistened like over-sized beetles and she struggled to find a space amongst the rows of shiny shells.

She stepped out of the car and swallowed at the sight of a father swinging his young son up onto his shoulders, to the sound of the boy's thrilled peals of laughter. *I should have known not to come here*, she thought. She didn't need to see perfect families on idyllic days out. But it couldn't be helped, she reminded herself. Rowan had needed to stop. She looked at her daughter, straining to be free of her safety belt, but seemingly oblivious to her lack of a dad. *Thank goodness.* She unfastened Rowan, who leaped out of her seat, desperate to explore the unknown and intriguing new place she'd arrived in.

Abby gripped Rowan's restless fingers as she skipped along the path in the direction of the converted boathouse.

'What's that, Mummy?' the little girl asked on the return journey, as they walked along the lakeshore track.

Abby squinted as she followed her four-year-old's line of sight. Was Rowan pointing at the canoeists coming up from the River Leven? The bow of their open boat cut through the water with impressive speed, the blades of their oars in perfect synchrony as they propelled the vessel seamlessly upstream. They were a proper team, thought Abby, as she watched the pair steer a smooth course across the water, and they proved the power of a dual effort . . .

'There!' said her daughter, pulling on her arm.

Abby crouched down. What *was* she looking at? It had to be one of the brightly coloured buoys that bobbed about in the water, she decided, as Rowan's forefinger stayed outstretched, apparently trained on one of the red spheres nodding on the surface. *How am I going to explain that the word sounds the same as 'boy' without confusing her?* wondered Abby. She could feel the faint thump of a headache beginning, like a thunderstorm forming on the horizon. 'They're safety markers,' she started to say, doing her best to navigate the subject. 'I think these ones show which parts of the water are very shallow, so boats know to avoid them.' *That was right, wasn't it?* 'It's not very deep at this bit of the lake . . .' She petered out, feeling the pressure of sole parental responsibility pushing her down into the pebble-covered path.

'Why is it *moving*?' asked Rowan.

What? Abby frowned. She peered at the red orb; it was joggling up and down on the wavelets created by the Canadian canoe but that was all—

Then she saw it – the object Rowan must have spotted – an oval orange float drifting along in between the tethered ball-shaped buoys. She scanned the surface of the water, back in the direction of the boathouse, sure there was bound to be more than one about, and sure enough a second was visible, not far behind the first.

Wild swimmers.

Now Abby could see a third person was bringing up the rear. They were using tow floats, to signal their presence to passing boats.

As they got closer, she saw their black-clad elbows emerging from the lake like dark shark fins slicing through the water.

Rowan squeezed her hand.

'What are they, Mummy?' murmured Rowan, as the figures carved their way towards them. Her daughter was scared, realised Abby: the stretchy second skins and sleek silicone caps they were wearing made the swimmers look like lake monsters.

Abby blinked as the leader of the group raised her head to take a breath. Her face was turned towards the shore, her body now parallel with them in the water. *Yes, there was no mistaking it . . . those features belonged to Clarissa.*

'The Wildwater Women,' whispered Abby.

Rowan stood rooted to the spot.

'Come on, sweetheart,' encouraged Abby, gently pulling on her hand. 'They're just people swimming, like you and me.'

Rowan looked unconvinced. 'I don't want to go any closer.' She shook her head.

'It's okay, poppet.' Abby paused. 'Mummy knows that lady at the front.'

Rowan took a single step forwards along the path.

'Please keep walking, darling,' pleaded Abby.

Rowan cautiously began to follow her mother along the track, which curved round and sloped down to the stony shore.

Abby couldn't help being drawn towards the swimmers as a question unfurled inside her: were Lori and Rebecca there? She felt curiously like she was missing out, and the notion surprised her.

Rowan stopped stock-still as she saw the swimmers start to wade out from the shallows.

'See?' said Abby, bending down to kiss her cheek. 'Just like you and me.'

Except they didn't look so similar now she was staring straight at them: all three looked full of glee, their chilled cheeks bearing joyous grins. Abby gazed at their glowing faces as their laughter-sprinkled exclamations echoed round the sheltered shore.

She didn't recognise the folk in Clarissa's charge, only the characteristic aura of euphoria surrounding them, and the elated expressions they wore.

Rowan watched the trio with wide eyes.

Others were doing the same; a smattering of intrigued onlookers lined the edge of the lake as though the bold swimmers were local celebrities or super-human beings from another world.

But I've done it too, realised Abby, with a small burst of self-confidence that startled her.

She opened her mouth to tell her daughter, but then changed her mind. She'd only been once, after all. 'Ready to go, darling?' she said instead.

But Rowan was now reluctant to leave. She stood rigid in reverie.

Then Abby saw Clarissa coming towards them, carrying her tow float, and calling instructions to her group, so she coaxed Rowan in the opposite direction, keen not to attract the instructor's attention. She'd gone to a single free swim session, hadn't supported Swim Wild, hadn't even set foot in the shop . . . She felt a flash of hot embarrassment. 'Come on, sweetheart, we've got the rest of our Sunday in store,' she said, leading Rowan up the grassy bank.

They meandered through the meadowland, took a lingering last look at the lake in all its glitter-rippled glory, and then set off for the next part of their adventure: High Pool Tarn.

'Mummy, I'm hungry,' announced Rowan, as soon as she was strapped back in the car and Abby had started the engine. The bag with the sandwiches was in the boot, and a man in a Mercedes SUV was waiting for their space.

'You're going to have to hang on, please, darling,' said Abby, reversing out of the parking bay. Their destination was only ten minutes down the lane.

Abby pulled in when she reached the lay-by at the bottom of the wiggly woodland trail that led up to the tarn. She dug out the box of raisins from the rucksack. She wanted the picnic itself to take place in a scenic spot on the edge of the water, but she handed Rowan the snack and swung the knapsack on her back.

'What's that, Mummy?' Her daughter was looking at the old bobbin mill, just beyond the fringe of the forest.

Abby yanked down on the rucksack's straps, as though buckling herself in. She took in the ancient building with its tall chimney and silvery stone walls, and then scratched her head, as though summoning any information she'd retained about it to the surface of her brain. She'd learned about the place a long time ago on a school trip as a child, and in that moment part of her wished Rowan's questions could wait till she visited, and could ask expert guides for answers. But then she felt a pang of guilt that the thought had even crossed her mind. 'Er . . . it's . . . um . . .' she stumbled.

Rowan stared up at her.

Abby knew Stott Park was special, the only working mill of its kind left in the entire world, but she was floundering trying to put it into words for her four-year-old. 'It's a museum, sweetheart.' *Is that the best you can do?* said a voice inside her head.

'It shows what life was like here hundreds of years ago,' Abby added, feeling the burden of accuracy with two little eyes looking up at her. She glanced down at her daughter.

But Rowan's focus was elsewhere, her fingers wrestling wrinkly round raisins out of their packet. 'Where are we going now, Mummy?' she asked.

Abby put her hand on her head. 'I'm going to show you somewhere wonderful.' She bit her lip. She wanted to say, '*Your daddy brought me here for the first time, and now I'm taking you.*' But she couldn't bring herself to. She knew Rowan would soon start asking where her father was, especially now she'd seen classmates with families that looked different to hers, but how to explain about Ben was a challenge Abby didn't yet have the strength to face.

They began to climb the path, a kaleidoscopic patchwork of compacted oak leaves. A stream chattered and gurgled alongside as they wound their way through the towering trees.

'Look at this, sweetheart,' said Abby, stopping to point out the pink-tinged skin of a Silver Birch's luminous trunk to her daughter.

Then High Pool Tarn appeared like a mirage, semi-hidden by the surrounding coppice and utterly mesmeric. When Rowan first glimpsed the glistening pool, she stopped in her tracks.

'Isn't it beautiful?' breathed Abby, bending down to her daughter's eye level.

Rowan nodded.

It was too early for lunch yet, thought Abby, and the dappled sunlight seemed to be luring them to the other side of the water, as though persuading her to look from a different perspective. She led the way along the track, Rowan alternately walking a few paces and then squatting to inspect a leaf or collect a particular twig.

Abby smiled to herself. Enveloped on all sides by views of nature at its finest, she actually felt *contented*.

They did a full loop of the tarn, with the birds singing a cheerful accompaniment from the branches above, and then Abby let Rowan pick the precise spot where she wanted to stop.

'Here!' declared her daughter, plonking down beneath a Scots Pine.

Abby unwrapped the cheese and pickle sandwiches and handed one to Rowan. She took a bite of her own, resting her back against the rough grooves of the cracked tree bark. Somehow, in such a splendid setting, and after the exertion of the walk, the food tasted better; their simple picnic seemed like a feast.

After they'd eaten, they stayed by the side of the tarn half-snoozing. The sun had moved in the sky to shine a spotlight on their little section of earth. Abby tilted her face to feel its warmth on her skin, and Rowan cuddled into her with her head on her lap.

They must have both fallen asleep, because the next thing she knew, Abby jolted awake as a shriek reverberated across the water.

Rowan shot upright. 'What was that, Mummy?'

Abby rubbed her eyes, looking for the source of the sound. Then she saw them. There, on the other side of the bank, was a group of people right on the edge of the pool. *More of them?* thought Abby. There was that sensation in her stomach again – the strange longing to be included.

A hum of happiness seemed to be vibrating across the tarn. There was another squawk of jollity, followed by a distinctive American accent.

Lori?

Abby got to her feet. *Yes, it had to be.* And she could see Clarissa's shock of slate-shade hair skimming the surface as she swam out into the water, on what was at least her second class of the day. It even looked like it was *Rebecca* who was standing knee-deep in the shallows – *gosh, that is progress.*

She stuffed the picnic things back into her rucksack, not quite sure what she planned to do: she half-wanted to go and say hello, but then again she didn't want to distract them from their session. Perhaps if she and Rowan wandered round to the other side of the tarn she'd be able to catch them afterwards. *But what for?*

Rowan was playing in the pillow-pile clumps of moss that carpeted the ground between the trees.

Abby glanced back at the figures on the other side of the tarn; she longed for that powerful after-swim feeling again, that sense she had in the water that she was supported, free, that she could do *anything*. She went to stand on the brink of the bank, watched her reflection wavering in the wind-ruffled water. It was as though, that day when she'd gone to Rydal with the other Wildwater Women, she'd rediscovered a little of herself. She'd never felt more awake and aware, and for those few minutes, she'd been *Abby* – not Mummy or a member of staff at Plum Pie Bakery. Just herself, entirely immersed in the simple act of having a swim surrounded by the landscape where she'd spent her whole life. She gazed up at Gummer's How, presiding over them all in the distance, as though asking the hill for guidance.

'Come on, sweetheart,' she shouted over to Rowan. 'Let's go.'

Her daughter scampered over, clutching a souvenir pine-cone in her small fist. They set off along the path and then crossed the slatted footbridge that spanned the stream; water cascaded down from the tarn in an effervescent waterfall and they spent a moment watching it bubble and roil before continuing on to the point where they'd first laid eyes on High Pool.

Here, Abby had a choice: turn right down the slope through the coppice wood, or left to carry on round to where she'd encounter the Wildwater Women. She took a step towards the woodland path that led to the car park, just as a bird cried out from the canopy above, as though calling her back. She stopped, and then decided to change direction. What was there to lose in walking past the others? She wanted to congratulate Rebecca on the headway she'd made, and it would be good to see some familiar faces in an otherwise unsociable Sunday, she thought to herself. She certainly wasn't desperate to hurry home; the sun was still high in the sky and she was well aware of the fact the forecast said rain was due to set in for the following week. Rowan skipped alongside her, clearly in no rush to leave the hidden oasis of High Pool Tarn either.

They soon rounded a rocky mound which rose from the ground behind the swimming spot as though specifically designed to shelter those who came here seeking respite.

It was Rebecca who noticed her first; she was once again standing on solid land, and closest to the footpath.

'Abby!' she shouted, waving a gloved hand.

'Hi!' she replied with a smile. A warmth spread through her chest; a sensation that was only sparked by seeing a kindred spirit. Perhaps she was drawn to these people because they shared similarities with her in some respects, thought Abby. Maybe they too had assumed the outdoors was for others who were stronger and sportier. What were their reasons for being here? she wondered. Were they really just embracing the experience of throwing themselves into something new and challenging? Maybe they felt the same way as her, that within the group they could just be themselves, without any pretence. The women weren't aware of her story, and it afforded her a sense of freedom she hadn't realised she missed.

'Hello!' said Rebecca, bending down to greet Rowan – who clutched Abby's thigh shyly.

'This is my daughter, Rowan,' explained Abby. She smoothed the top of her little girl's hair. 'I saw you had your feet in the water,' she added, turning back to Rebecca. 'Well done!' She grinned.

'Oh, thanks,' said Rebecca, with a bashful shrug. 'Still got a long way to go . . .'

Abby saw her jaw tense as she bit back a wave of anxiety. 'But you've come a long way already,' she said with a smile.

Rebecca gave a small nod. 'Did you not fancy coming again?' she asked, shifting the subject away from herself.

'Ah, well . . . I've got the little one . . .' Abby started to say, but she couldn't ignore the fact that she *did* want to give it another go, with an intensity she'd been doing her best to disregard. The experience seemed to have stayed with her, and there was no escaping the truth that she yearned for the liberated feeling she'd had after her first wild swim.

'Hey!' called a familiar voice. 'We missed you, doll!'

Rowan let go of Abby's leg when she recognised Lori's face.

'Hello! How was it the second time?' asked Abby, refusing to nurture the seed of envy that seemed to have sprung to life inside her. She craved that soul-cleansing, fortified feeling the others had. Lori looked *radiant*. Her eyes shone and her smile seemed extra broad.

Clarissa raised a hand in acknowledgement. 'Abigail,' she said, in the manner of someone giving an answer in a memory test. 'I trust you're well?'

Abby nodded.

Rowan held out her pinecone treasure to Lori, who accepted her gift graciously. 'Wow! Is that for me, sweetie?' she exclaimed. 'Thank you!'

Abby smiled at her gratefully. 'We just wanted to say hi. We'll leave you to it,' she said, taking Rowan's hand, conscious of the fact the swimmers were dripping wet and needed to get changed. 'Lovely to see you all.' It *had* been. They had a connection, a kinship, that had been forged on the shore of a freezing lake earlier in the week and had refused to melt away since.

'You're welcome to stay, have a slice of sand cake,' said Clarissa, already fully clothed and fleece clad.

'What's sand cake?' asked Rowan.

'Erm . . . I'm not sure, darling,' began Abby, feeling a blush creep into her cheeks. *How can you work in a bakery and not know?*

'It's a Cumbrian recipe,' explained Clarissa, crouching beside her rucksack. 'A sponge cake made without flour.' She produced a scrumptious-looking sand-dune-coloured cake.

Rowan clapped at the sight of it, as though she had a front-row seat at a magic show.

'I have some spare mugs too,' Clarissa added, conjuring another couple of clinking cups from her rucksack.

She is remarkable, thought Abby. 'It's very kind of you but I don't want to intrude . . .'

'The countryside belongs to all, yet none,' said Clarissa matter of factly.

'Thank you, then,' Abby replied, despite the niggling feeling she didn't really deserve to be there.

'You're more than welcome,' replied Clarissa, as though sensing her train of thought.

'You make this too?' Lori asked Clarissa once she was dry and dressed, her eyes like saucers.

'Yes,' said Clarissa, cutting her a generous wedge.

'Is there anything this girl can't do?' declared Lori to the group.

Clarissa carried on dispensing slices of Cumbrian sand cake, but Abby saw a slight smile on her face, and suspected it was a long time since anyone had called her a 'girl'.

'Oh, *shoot*, I wanted to ask you something, actually,' added Lori, looking at their leader.

Clarissa raised her eyebrows.

'But I forgot my whatsaname,' explained Lori. 'Darn it!'

Clarissa frowned as she took a bite of her baking herself, last of everyone.

'You know, my computer thing.' She waggled a hand.

'Tablet?' suggested Abby, remembering Lori showing her an image on her iPad when she'd come into the Plum Pie bakery.

'That's it!' Lori jabbed a finger in the air as though selecting the word from an invisible dictionary.

'What on earth do you need one of those for out here?' asked Clarissa, palms upturned.

'I just had a picture on it, that's all!' protested Lori like a student squirming out of a black mark. 'I wanted to ask if you knew where the place was.'

'A photo?' clarified Clarissa.

'Yes. Of a painting my grandpa had.'

'Oh.' Clarissa's barely concealed disapproval had morphed into intrigue.

'I got family history here, ya know,' added Lori. 'Grandpop was British, and he brought the watercolour over to New York with him. It's kinda what got me interested in art . . . anyways, I wanted to find the spot in the picture. I thought you might have an idea seeing as you're such an amazing guide . . .'

'I'll certainly take a look if you show me,' said Clarissa humbly, shaking crumbs from her jumper.

'Was it the painting that inspired you to visit the Lakes?' asked Rebecca, eyes wide with wonder.

'Uh-huh, you bet,' said Lori. 'And it's every bit as beautiful here as I thought it would be.' She turned to Clarissa. 'I'll bring the photo next time.'

Clarissa nodded.

Abby marvelled at Lori's unselfconscious ability to ask for help when she needed it. *I wish I was more like that.* Why did she find it so hard to speak her mind? She could do with a sprinkle of Lori's confidence; perhaps it would seep through the wall of Silver Ghyll and by the time it came to the end of her neighbour's stay, she'd have a little of her assertiveness. *Fingers crossed.* Abby nibbled her sand cake, savouring the refreshing hint of lemon zest and the treat-sweetness of the icing sugar dissolving on her tongue. She glanced at Rowan, cross-legged beside her, absorbed in demolishing her own piece.

'Are you an artist yourself, Lori?' asked Rebecca, taking a sip of steaming coffee from her cup.

Abby stopped chewing; she had no idea what Lori did for a living. If she was a successful painter that would certainly explain her keen eye for detail – she'd even realised Rowan's primary-school-level picture was of her namesake tree, the one that stood guard outside Little Garth like a red-berry-decorated sentry.

'No, I'm not,' said Lori, shaking her head.

Oh, thought Abby, slightly disappointed. She'd envisaged Lori socialising in glamorous circles, living in a penthouse apartment with a cityscape view, all open-plan and floor-length glass, like the ones you saw in American films. She was always bursting with energy, fizzing with enthusiasm for the world around her. *Unlike me . . .*

'I actually have a gallery in Manhattan,' said Lori.

'Wow,' breathed Abby. *That is equally impressive!*

'Gosh,' said Rebecca. 'That's exciting!'

'Thanks,' said Lori. 'It's my total passion.' She clasped a hand to her heart. 'I love it.'

Abby blinked back at her in admiration. Lori was so full of *life. And I spend my days in the bakery being Joy's slave.* It was as though spending time with these strong, capable women was opening up her eyes.

'I don't mean to interrupt, but I've got to get moving,' said Clarissa, standing up.

Abby scrambled to her feet, scooping up a suddenly sleepy Rowan.

'Are you staying or walking back down with us?' asked Rebecca.

Abby's stomach lurched: she didn't relish the idea of going back home, being alone with her ever-longer to-do list. She looked at her daughter, whose limbs were floppy with drowsiness. 'We might sit here for a few more minutes.' Rowan didn't look like she'd willingly walk all the way to the car park without an inordinate amount of encouragement.

'I don't blame you,' said Rebecca. 'Soak up some sun before work tomorrow,' she added with a smile.

Abby almost got the impression they might have stayed there chatting a while if it wasn't for having to drop back their borrowed wetsuits. *But why would they want to spend their Sunday with an almost-stranger and her four-year-old? Don't be ridiculous.*

'We'd better catch Clarissa up,' said Rebecca, with a jerk of her head.

'Yes, sure,' said Abby.

The top of Clarissa's hair was already disappearing as she descended the track in the distance.

'See you around!' said Lori with a wave. 'Bye, sweetie,' she whispered to Rowan.

'We're going swimming again on Wednesday,' shouted Rebecca hurriedly. 'Or at least I'm going to try to. If you fancy it?'

Abby bit her lip.

Lori was nodding. 'Why not? You loved it the first time!'

Abby's face broke into a smile at the memory. She craved that feeling of cold water on her skin, the rush of endorphins afterwards.

'I can give you a lift; I'm picking up Lori,' explained Rebecca.

'Okay,' called Abby. She grinned back at them as they scurried along the path. 'I'll look forward to it.'

And as she turned back towards the twinkling tarn, she realised she already was.

9

Abby sat down on the sofa after tucking Rowan into bed and stared at the switched-off television screen absently. She didn't even have the strength left to watch a mindless Sunday night show till it was time to crawl into bed. She slid down so she was horizontal, and huddled against the cushions as though she was sheltering from the world in the curve of the settee. The cottage had always used to seem cosy, not claustrophobic, but as she lay there curled up like a foetus, she felt the first stifling tentacles of silence start to wrap round her, squeezing her throat and threatening to strangle her.

Then she thought she heard a tentative tap on the front door.

She shot upright, listening out for any further noise.

Perhaps she'd been mistaken?

But then there it was again – a gentle knocking.

Abby walked into the hall. Beyond the small square pane of blurred glass, she could just make out the hazy shape of Lori's face in the dusk light. *What did she need at this time of night?* She hastily swiped the sleeve of her cardigan across her eyes and spread on a smile before opening the door.

'Hey,' whispered Lori, hunching her shoulders as she spoke, as though that made her voice quieter. Was that for Rowan's sake, seeing as it was past her bedtime, or because she wanted to get across that she didn't intend to be a nuisance?

'Hi,' said Abby. 'Are you okay?'

'Er . . .' Lori's breath clouded in the early evening air. She shifted her feet on the front step.

'Has something happened?' asked Abby, instinctively glancing towards Silver Ghyll's entrance next door.

'No . . . I . . . um . . .'

Abby had only known her neighbour a short while, but in the time she'd spent with her, she'd never seen her stuck for words like this. She frowned, wondering why Lori didn't just come out and say whatever it was she needed help with.

'Look, just say if you're busy . . .'

Abby bit her lip; if she was honest, she hadn't got a whole lot of brain power left after doing the housework that had been mounting up all week and making sure Rowan was sorted for school. Whatever Lori needed, she hoped it was something easy.

'It's, er, actually my birthday today,' Lori finally blurted out.

'Oh, gosh! Is it?' said Abby.

'Yeah.' Lori gave a tinkling laugh, like she couldn't really believe it. 'Fifty-nine years young.'

'Happy Birthday!' said Abby, awkwardly lifting her arms up and down like a penguin flapping its congratulations. *What am I doing?*

'Thanks. Um, I wondered . . . you wanna have a glass of wine?' Lori winced as soon as she'd said the sentence, and started jiggling her hands as though she could erase what she'd just said, snatch the sentence back from the atmosphere.

'You mean now?' Abby raised her eyebrows in surprise.

'No worries if not. I just bought a bottle and it seemed a shame not to share it . . .'

'Right! Of course.' Abby stepped aside. 'You can't spend your birthday evening alone.'

'Sure I can, hon, I've come this far by myself.' Lori shrugged. 'I've been for dinner in town.' She smiled, as if that proved she was completely comfortable in her own company. 'I just thought I'd see if you wanted a nightcap on the way back.'

'That would be lovely then,' Abby replied. It'd only just gone seven o'clock after all, and she was touched that Lori had even thought of her – and felt they were on friendly enough terms that she could call by. 'Come in.'

Lori bent to pick something up and only then did Abby notice the foil-covered top of a fancy champagne bottle peeping out of the canvas tote bag sitting by her feet. She looked down at her leggings and cardigan combo, and wondered if she was the kind of consumer the champagne house had had in mind . . . She ushered Lori inside, pleased that Little Garth was now in a reasonable state to welcome guests.

'Take a seat,' she said, shuffling into the kitchen in her shamefully shabby slippers to search for some glasses. She'd shoved the wedding present set of Cumbria Crystal flutes to the back of a shelf in a bottom cupboard. The last time she'd used them was the birthday before she'd found out Rowan was on her way. But shortly after that she'd started to realise that something was wrong; Ben wasn't the same . . . And since then, special occasions seemed flatter, as though they'd lost their fizz in his absence, like sparkling wine left out to spoil.

'I'll pop it real quietly so we don't wake the little one, hey,' said Lori, lifting up the bottle from where she stood by the sofa.

Abby smiled.

Once they both had a glass of honeysuckle-scented champagne, she proposed a birthday toast. 'And may your stay in the Lakes be a fabulous one,' she finished, chinking her drink against Lori's.

'Thanks!' Lori glanced up at the ceiling as she took a gulp.

Abby saw the sheen in her eyes as she did so, and wondered for the first time whether the zestful front Lori always displayed might disguise an undertow of sorrow . . . Why was she here, on the other side of the world, spending her birthday away from everyone she knew back home?

'So, where did you get to this afternoon?' she asked when Lori remained absorbed in her thoughts. 'Did you come back to Ambleside or explore anywhere else?'

'Oh, er . . . I went someplace . . .' Lori pressed her forefinger to her chin. 'Now, where was it . . .?'

'Near here?' prompted Abby.

'Um, lemme think . . . I got dropped off by, er . . .'

'Rebecca?'

'Yeah, she's the sweetest! And then . . .' Lori's face fell slightly. 'I, um . . .'

Abby took a sip of her drink while she waited for Lori to think. 'It's hard to remember the names of everywhere when you're on holiday, isn't it?'

'Sure is!' Lori smiled. 'I keep mispronouncing them all too and getting corrected by locals. What's that town I said wrong today – it was on a leaflet . . .' She dug around in her bag and produced a flyer. 'Kez-wick,' she announced.

'Yes, it's a silent w,' said Abby.

'Whatever!' Lori batted the air with her hand and they both laughed.

'This place is amazing, but also pretty nuts.' She held up the pamphlet. 'You guys have a *pencil* museum!'

Abby guffawed; she'd never considered it the least bit odd, but now, seeing it through Lori's eyes, it did seem rather strange. 'It's a good day out!' she protested.

Lori gave an exaggerated sigh of disbelief and shoved the flyer back in her bag. 'Oh yeah,' she said. 'That's what else I did today – I tried to find the lake from here . . .'

'Rydal?' asked Abby.

'Uh-huh, with the instructions—'

'The directions I gave you?'

Lori nodded. 'But I ended up getting a little lost.' She gave a laugh, but Abby could tell it was laced with sadness this time. 'Seems to be a bit of a theme with me . . .'

'Oh dear, I probably should've been clearer!' Abby grimaced apologetically. 'I bet I scribbled them down in such a rush it was all a bit confusing, sorry.' She frowned.

'Aw, no, I got there fine!' replied Lori. 'Just couldn't seem to find my way back.' She chuckled again, but the trace of despair was still there.

'Well, all the tracks look so similar round here,' said Abby.

'I guess.' Lori watched the champagne glint in her glass.

'Are you all right?' Abby dipped her head, trying to decode Lori's expression.

'Oh, yeah! Home now, hey.' She looked up and raised her flute, but the light had dimmed in her eyes.

'How did you . . .?'

'Some hikers stopped. They were super nice.' Lori rubbed her temple. 'Said I could follow them back to town . . .' All of a sudden, she broke into a sob. 'I shouldn't have come here on my own.'

'Hey, hey.' Abby put her hand on her back.

Lori rooted about for a tissue in her bag. 'Pardon me,' she said, blowing her nose; her burst of emotion seemed to have surprised them both.

'Don't be silly. I can imagine it was stressful,' said Abby sympathetically. 'But don't beat yourself up about it – how can you expect to know your way round every path and ginnel?'

Lori giggled, and Abby was pleased to hear a lightness had returned to her voice. 'I can't get enough of these words. What's a *ginnel*?'

Abby grinned at her. 'You know, like a little passageway – an alley.'

'Got it!' Lori nodded. 'Look, I apologise. Guess it's kinda hit me being away from everyone, and headin' towards old age—'

'You're still young!' exclaimed Abby, squeezing Lori's arm, but instead of reassuring her, it seemed to make her falter. She scrabbled for something else to say. 'I wish I was *half* as adventurous as you.'

'What, going on vacation?' Lori dabbed her eyes.

'And throwing yourself into everything – like the wild swimming.'

A muffled ringing sound started up from the inside of Lori's bag.

'Oh, jeez, this'll be my daughter on her lunch break. Lemme just tell her I got company.' Lori found the phone, and Abby caught sight of the caller ID photo as she fumbled to answer it: a close-up of a woman's face filled the screen. She was stunning, with flawless skin the colour of fudge and a mass of dark curls.

'Hey, darlin', Lori said into the receiver.

Abby stood up and wandered over to the kitchen to give her what little privacy the cottage's interior could afford. She hadn't known Lori had kids. None had ever been mentioned. But then she supposed there was plenty that she hadn't divulged either . . .

'Sorry about that,' said Lori over her shoulder once she'd finished her conversation.

'Not at all.' Abby smiled back. 'I didn't realise you had children.'

'Well, she's all grown up this one,' replied Lori. 'Certainly knows how to speak her mind!' She gave a laugh and took a large sip of her drink. 'I already spoke to her earlier,' she said with a smile that said how much she'd appreciated the second call. 'I don't want her to worry about me. Feel she has to keep checking in . . .' Lori trailed off, then drained the last of her champagne.

'Top up?' asked Abby, trying to be a hospitable host and also sensing that Lori wanted to stay a little longer yet.

'Why not?' replied Lori.

Abby retrieved the bottle from the fridge.

'But don't feel obligated,' Lori added. 'Honestly, if you want to hit the hay then just say.'

'I'm not going to bed yet,' said Abby, thinking what a pleasant change it was to have someone to spend her evening with.

'Alrighty then!' Lori grinned from the living-room area, shaking her glass from side to side in anticipation of her refill.

Abby poured them each some more champagne, then sat down again.

'My daughter – Ashanti,' said Lori, showing her the screensaver.

'She's gorgeous. And what a beautiful name,' said Abby.

'Thank you, my husband's Ghanaian,' explained Lori, the alcohol encouraging details of her homelife to flow from her lips. 'It was his suggestion,' she added with a sideways glance.

Abby smiled and took a sip of her drink. She'd assumed she was single. *Why has Lori left her family behind and come on holiday alone?* she wondered. If she drank much more wine she might have enough courage to come straight out and ask.

'And what does he do?' asked Abby, curious to know more.

'He has a gallery too, just a couple blocks from mine. Joe Boateng, it's called.'

'Is that his name?'

'Sure is,' replied Lori. 'We met at an exhibition he had, and I fell head over heels.' She rolled her eyes.

Abby pictured a glamorous scene: all cocktail dresses, canapés and scintillating discussion. Lori came from such an exciting, cosmopolitan world, while she'd only seen New York on the cinema screen.

'Seems like a different life now . . .' said Lori, her smile subsiding into a sigh.

'Have you and your family been to the UK before?' asked Abby, emboldened by the champagne and intrigued to know what had brought Lori here on her own.

'Uh-uh. We've been to London, but not here. They're *very* jealous. I showed 'em the photos I got today and they couldn't believe it! Looks like a backdrop in a movie, huh, that place we went?'

'High Pool Tarn,' said Abby. 'It's gorgeous up there. Ben – Abby's dad – first took me years ago —' She broke off, surprised at herself for sharing such intimate information with Lori.

'You miss him, hey?' said Lori, tilting her head to one side. Abby nodded.

'You wanna talk about it?'

Abby swallowed. 'Not so much.'

Lori laid a hand on her arm. 'Some things you never get over, but you do learn to live with them,' she whispered.

Abby rubbed her eyes and took a steadying breath. 'Did you tell your daughter you'd been wild swimming?' she asked, switching the topic.

'Oh yeah. She thinks it's bananas,' said Lori.

'It is, really,' agreed Abby and they both giggled.

'You're gonna come this week, right?' asked Lori.

'Yes, I can't wait,' replied Abby, without hesitating, the champagne spurring her on to speak from her heart.

'Great!' Lori grinned. 'I have the details somewhere . . .' She picked up her phone and scrolled for a few seconds. 'Ah, here we are' – she glanced up – 'Coniston lake at six o'clock.'

'Water.'

'Pardon me?'

'Water,' repeated Abby.

'Oh, I'm good with wine, thanks.'

'No – it's Coniston *Water*, not Lake.'

Lori wiggled her head rapidly from side to side. '*What?*'

'Here's a riddle for you,' said Abby with a giggle. 'How many lakes are there in the Lake District?'

'Jeez, so this is a trick question . . .' Lori narrowed her eyes. 'I've had too much wine for these kinda brain-twisters.'

'One – Bassenthwaite Lake,' said Abby. 'Well, they all are, *really*,' she added when Lori looked baffled, 'but that's the only one we *call* a lake.'

'Alrighty.' Lori rubbed her forehead. 'And the others?'

'They're meres and waters,' Abby explained.

'Gotcha,' replied Lori.

Abby grinned. 'Just so you know, in front of the locals.'

Lori saluted. 'Noted,' she said with a laugh.

'So, Rebecca's collecting us on Wednesday?' asked Abby, now her lesson in lake names was over.

'Uh-huh. A half hour before.'

Abby nodded.

Lori clasped her hands together. 'This week it might be the place in my grandpop's painting!' she said, her eyes alight with optimism.

Abby took another mouthful of wine, unable to bring herself to dispel Lori's hope. The trio of hills at the head of the lake in the painting were as distinctive as they were unfamiliar. She knew the picture wasn't of Coniston; the view of the water surrounded by mountains didn't correspond with the landscape they'd see on their wild swim that Wednesday.

'It's not, is it,' said Lori, reading her silence exactly.

Abby shook her head. 'Sorry.'

'Will you quit apologising for stuff that is *not* your fault!' said Lori.

'Sor—'

Lori gave her a stern look, her glass paused halfway to her lips.

Abby gave a small smile.

'The search goes on!' said Lori, slapping her thigh.

'So, that's *really* why you came all this way?' asked Abby. 'You wanted to see the spot in the picture for real?'

'Sure! Sort of had the idea in my head for a while . . .' Lori drained her glass and slid it onto the coffee table, then gave a sigh as though the detailed reasoning behind her decision to come to the Lakes solo was buried so deep inside her it would take more effort than she currently had to uncover it. 'I guess I've always wanted to, since I was a girl,' she said, and Abby suspected it was too tiresome a task for the truth to be excavated at this time of night, so she left her questioning at that.

But Lori continued talking of her own accord, as though taking comfort from remembering things she'd been told about the past, and her family history.

'The picture hung in my bedroom when I was a child. Now it's on the wall of the guest room in my apartment. I wanted to see where my grandpop was from, before I'm too ancient and frail.' She laughed.

Abby flicked her wrist as though she refused to hear Lori describe herself that way.

'You know what I mean,' murmured Lori, fiddling with the hem of her cardigan. 'Anyways, I used to wonder what the story was behind it,' she carried on.

'Why your grandad had it, you mean? Or who painted it?' asked Abby.

'Both.'

'Was he from Cumbria, your grandad?' said Abby, putting down her glass, the last traces of the toasted-nut taste of the champagne fading on her tongue. 'I suppose it wouldn't have been called that back then, though.'

'Uh-huh, he sure was. Cumber-land, I believe,' replied Lori, making the ancient county name sound like two words instead of one. 'Like the sausage, huh?' She chuckled and Abby nodded. 'He emigrated to New York in the nineteen twenties.'

'Wow.' Abby settled back onto the sofa again. 'Went to make his fortune?'

'Oh, I dunno about that! But he went over to find work, anyways.'

'So he wasn't an artist, then? He didn't do the painting himself?'

'God, no! A joiner, in fact.' Lori widened her eyes as though having such a practical-minded family member was a surprise. 'But he used to tell me tales of the countryside back home.'

'Of round here?'

'Oh yeah. All about the mountains and the colours and the way the lakes almost had their own different personalities . . . He'd say the scenery was like nowhere else in the world.'

Abby didn't speak for a moment; she let Lori's words sink in instead, as though they could form a kind of rich and fertile soil inside her from which gratitude for the life she had could grow. What Lori's grandfather said was right, and she suddenly felt a profound sense of appreciation for the place she called home.

'My mom asked about the painting a couple times,' Lori carried on. 'But she got the feeling it was hard for him to talk about. He just said it was a present from someone he'd known in the past.' She frowned. 'Funny how when you get older, you realise your parents are just people like you, with their own battle scars and heartaches.'

Abby nodded.

'But secrets are strange things, they seem to know when they want to be shared.'

Abby bit her lip. 'What do you mean?'

'Oh, just that they always come out in the end, don't you think?' Lori smiled, but her eyes were shining again. 'I'm heading off track here . . . where was I . . . oh, yeah, so I grew up with that painting and Grandpop left it to me because I loved it so much.'

Abby had only glimpsed it once, but the image had stayed with her; like she'd stood looking at the panorama herself. 'It's charming.'

'It sure is. It's not like anything else I've seen before,' said Lori. 'And I've looked at a whole lot of art.'

'Where do you think it came from?'

'My theory,' – Lori shot Abby a conspiratorial glance – 'is that it's not by a professional artist at all.'

Abby frowned as she waited for Lori to explain.

'I believe it was painted by a sweetheart.'

Abby raised her eyebrows. 'As a keepsake?'

'Exactly. A token of love.'

'You can tell that kind of thing just by looking at the brushstrokes?' asked Abby in amazement.

'No, but I'm flattered you think I have that much talent.' Lori laughed. 'I found a note when I got the picture reframed for my spare room. Hidden between the back board and the painting.' Lori pressed her palms together to illustrate the space between.

'What did it say?' breathed Abby. Concealed messages were the stuff of screenplays.

'It was a farewell,' said Lori. 'From a woman who promised she'd love him for ever. It said, "wherever you go in the world, you'll have this view with you".'

Abby put her hand to her mouth. 'Why couldn't they be together?'

'I don't know.' Lori gave a small shrug. 'It was different times back then. Maybe my grandpop was seen as unsuitable.'

'What, like if she was well-to-do and her family disapproved?'

Lori nodded. 'My theory is he left here because he was heartbroken.'

Abby bit her thumbnail. 'It would make sense, I suppose.'

'Sad, though, right?' said Lori.

'But he must have met your grandma, built a new life,' replied Abby.

'He sure did, but I guess he left a part of his heart here.' Lori nodded slowly. 'And I totally get why, now.' She smiled, as though, having seen the Lake District landscape with her own eyes, she'd found some missing pieces of a jigsaw puzzle she'd been trying to complete. 'He loved this place, and talked about it his whole life.'

'So, you wanted to know where he came from?'

'Absolutely,' whispered Lori. 'It's my history.'

Abby met her gaze. There was raw emotion beneath Lori's champagne-glazed expression, and she couldn't help but wonder if she was here to understand more about herself than her grandfather's past.

10

'Crummockwater,' declared Clarissa, a fraction of a second after Lori flipped the photo of her grandfather's painting onto her iPad's screen.

'For real? You know that already?' Lori replied, looking at their swimming instructor in disbelief.

'No doubt about it,' said Clarissa, who was buckling herself into her rucksack in readiness for the short walk to Coniston's shore. 'Utterly positive.'

'Right on!' replied Lori. 'Thank you!'

'No problem,' said Clarissa, closing the back doors of the Defender.

'You see that?' Lori asked Abby, jerking her head at their leader. 'How quick that was?'

Abby nodded and gave a laugh. 'Mystery solved, then! All that remains is to make sure you go and see the spot before you have to head home.'

Lori walked back towards where Rebecca was standing beside her little red car.

'Is that the painting you were talking about when we were at High Pool Tarn?' Rebecca asked, grabbing her swimming bag from the open boot and turning to look over Lori's shoulder.

'Uh-huh,' she replied, tilting the tablet towards her.

Abby came to stand by Lori's other side, to glimpse the picture once again. The watercolour was of three fells standing at the head of the lake, Crummockwater, like close friends. *Lori, Rebecca and me.*

'This way!' called Clarissa all of a sudden, cutting into her thoughts.

'Just need to pop this in the trunk,' said Lori, stowing her iPad away safely in the boot of the car, before Rebecca slammed it shut and locked it.

The three of them hurried to catch Clarissa up. They crossed the lane beyond the clearing of the car park to the pebble-covered bank where Clarissa was already standing, on the edge of the water.

'Are you going all the way today?' Lori asked Rebecca, setting her bag down on the shore.

'I'll try,' replied Rebecca, starting to wriggle out of her raspberry-coloured jacket.

Abby stood stock-still, spellbound by the sight of a shaft of soft sunshine like a spotlight on the summit of Coniston Old Man on the opposite side of the lake.

This was the location shown on the front of the wild swimming leaflet, she realised. A landing stage stretched out before her, its wooden posts reflected in the lake so it looked like it was on stilts, floating far above the surface.

'No jumping off the jetty,' quipped Lori, looking at Rebecca, who laughed at her attempt to lighten the mood.

But their instructor didn't seem to appreciate the joke. 'That would be *extremely* foolhardy,' said Clarissa, by now sporting just her black swimming costume. 'This might be a pertinent opportunity to tell you about the umbles.'

'Pardon me?' said Lori, squinting at their instructor as she tugged on her wetsuit. She glanced at Rebecca, who appeared equally clueless, and then Abby, who shook her head back at her. 'I've no idea,' she mouthed.

'If you see any signs of them,' continued Clarissa, 'you must act fast.'

'Oh, jeez,' said Lori, looking suddenly unsettled. 'They're not some sort of *predator*?' she asked, peering past the little pier with a perturbed frown on her face.

'No, but they can be deadly,' said Clarissa.

Rebecca plonked down on the stony ground.

'There's no need to worry unduly,' said Clarissa, giving her a reassuring smile, 'it's just best to be prepared, now some of you are working up to staying in the water for longer.'

Lori sat down on the pebbles too, and put on a pair of new neoprene shoes.

Abby looked at Rebecca's feet – she was wearing similar ones too. God, she had none of the gear. She sank down beside the others to listen to Clarissa's warning.

Clarissa, standing with her back to the blue-grey water, glanced at them all in turn to ensure she had their full attention. 'You must always watch out for the umbles and take care of each other.'

Abby blinked up at her, saw the seriousness in her eyes.

'Oh god, please just say what they are.' Lori had her palms pressed to her cheeks.

Rebecca had crept back into her quilted coat cocoon.

'There's no need for alarm,' continued Clarissa, hands held up like a conductor of calm, 'it's just important to be aware.'

'Of *what*, though?' said Lori, hands now on top of her hair.

Abby pulled on her woolly bobble hat, as though it were a helmet.

'The umbles show changes in motor coordination and consciousness.'

'Wait, can we have that in English, please?' replied Lori, arms folded on top of her knees.

'They're the signals that show your core temperature is dropping, and hypothermia is starting to set in,' said Clarissa sombrely.

Abby sat bolt upright with surprise as Rebecca swore.

'An excellent illustration of the first stage: the *grumbles*,' Clarissa said, pointing at Rebecca. 'So we're talking a change in behaviour, a bit of whinging, a negative attitude.'

Rebecca buried her chin in the collar of her jacket.

'Then, we have the *fumbles*.' Clarissa flexed her fingers. 'Loss of dexterity.'

Abby remembered the searing pain that had initially needled her extremities, and could easily imagine it developing into dangerous numbness.

'This is slow reaction time, dropping things, and poor coordination,' said Clarissa, counting off the symptoms on her hand. 'But you'd still be able to walk and talk at this point.'

'Jeez, what's next?' muttered Lori.

'Then there's the *mumbles*,' Clarissa carried on.

'God, I think I have that all the time,' Abby heard Lori say underneath her breath.

'Slow, slurred or confused speech,' clarified Clarissa. 'You *must* get out of the water if this happens.'

Abby felt a frisson of fear.

'There's nothing to be afraid of,' said Clarissa, as though she could sense it. 'Because you know what to look out for,' she continued. 'You learned to acclimatise yourselves to the water first of all, and this is just the following step – knowing when your body's had enough and needs to get warm again.' Her words were sound and her tone was matter of fact, as though to demonstrate that logic was the surest cure for panic.

The three of them nodded back at her.

'Now come the *stumbles*, and that's when it gets really critical' – Clarissa put her hands on her hips for emphasis – 'you should be well out of the water by this time. Movement becomes difficult, it's a struggle to walk in a straight line. Violent shivering.'

The trio of swimmers was totally silent as they absorbed what she was saying, and envisaged such a frightening scenario.

'And lastly,' said Clarissa.

'Oh my god, there's more,' murmured Lori.

'The *crumbles*,' Clarissa announced.

Rebecca gave a gasp and Abby reached a hand out to touch her arm.

'Severe hypothermia. The body starts to shut down, even shivering stops. Someone in this situation needs to be got out of the cold immediately. They need to be wrapped up in dry clothes and kept still. Call an ambulance.' Clarissa clapped her hands together as though it would seal all she'd said into their brains. 'Any questions?'

'Are we still going swimming after that?' said Lori.

'Of course,' said Clarissa, indicating they should get to their feet with a brisk flick of her wrists. 'You're now better prepared than ever.'

'Alrighty,' muttered Lori, standing up and shaking out her limbs.

Abby scrambled upright and held out her hands to pull Rebecca up too. 'We're in safe hands with Clarissa,' she said, but the colour had scarpered from Rebecca's cheeks.

'Regulate that breathing!' called their instructor, already up to her midriff in the lake.

Coniston beckoned them; a burst of brilliant sunlight blazed across the glass-smooth surface. The Old Man stood sentinel in the distance.

Clarissa looked as comfortable as if she were in a hot tub on a scorching summer's day, thought Abby. 'When you're waist deep like this—' shouted their leader.

'I haven't even got my big toe in yet!' yelled Lori.

'—Take a big breath, drop in and float for a minute to get used to the temperature,' continued Clarissa, reclining like she was about to switch the lake's jacuzzi setting on.

Rebecca began to peel off her coat with all the speed of a crab shedding its shell.

Abby paddled out till she was up to her ankles in ice-cold water. Spikes of agony stabbed her bare skin. She felt a gust of wind buffet her back, as though urging her on. She took a few more steps forward, pain surging through her body despite the sealskin-like wetsuit she wore. The lake lapped round her legs, pinching at her thighs, reminding her she could feel, that she was alive.

Lori came to stand beside her, arms stuck out like a chillsome scarecrow.

Abby looked back at Rebecca, frozen to the spot on the shore. 'You can do it!' she called with an encouraging nod. 'I saw you at High Pool Tarn – you're so nearly there now!'

Lori cupped her hands round her mouth to shout, 'You got this, girl!' at the top of her lungs.

A black-headed gull squawked from its perch on one of the jetty posts, as though joining in the cheering, before flapping its wings and taking flight to leave them to it.

Rebecca waded a little way into the shallows.

'Don't linger too long or you'll lose heat standing there!' Clarissa called.

'Come with us, we'll do it together,' said Abby over her shoulder. She sploshed to the side to make a space between her and Lori, as though they were two bookends designed to support Rebecca's story.

Rebecca splashed towards them till they were standing in a straight line facing away from the shore, and the image of the three fells on the edge of the lake in Lori's grandfather's painting swam into Abby's mind. She sucked in a deep breath of cool autumn air and blew it steadily from her lips as she trailed her fingers across Coniston's surface, for once feeling completely in the moment, truly present.

'Ready?' she said to Rebecca.

She gave a tentative nod back.

'One . . .' Lori began counting.

Abby reached out and took Rebecca's hand.

'Two . . .' Lori did the same, grasping hold of her other one.

'Three!' She and Abby chorused together, and they all bobbed down into the water as one.

'Float for a minute!' called Clarissa, doing front crawl alongside them. 'Keep that breathing going!'

Abby's face broke into a grin; she could feel her cheeks burning as though she'd found her inner fire again. 'You're in!' she said to Rebecca, who was beaming at her in disbelief.

'I am!' she spluttered, eyes wide with surprise.

'Great job!' exclaimed Lori, with a broad smile.

'Well done!' said Clarissa, as the trio dissolved into delighted laughter. 'Good to see you looking after each other,' she added with a nod of approval. 'Now, when you're ready, start to swim with slow, steady movements.'

Abby swept her arms through the water as she began to do breaststroke, felt the satisfying sensation of her muscles tensing and releasing. The nape of her neck smarted like she was wearing a scarf made of hogweed, and her fingers stung like she'd knitted it herself. But her body hurt much less than it had the first time. *I'm getting better at this*, she thought to herself as she pushed forward, *more used to it*. If she'd made this tiny bit of progress, having only been twice, then what was possible if she kept going?

She swam close to the shore, separating away from the others slightly to marvel at the gnarly knotted tree roots that twisted thirstily towards the water, and the way the sunlight filtered through the lacelike leaves, casting delicate mottled shapes on the stones below.

'Braithwaite!' came a booming shout from behind her, all of a sudden. A male voice: bold, unfamiliar – and calling Rebecca's surname. Abby turned round and started treading water while she tried to make sense of what was going on. She saw Rebecca, standing up again in the shallows, face to face with a man in a kayak, his paddle poised to splash her in what she supposed was intended to be a playful manner. He was smiling at Rebecca, but she looked far from amused.

'Fancy seeing you here!' Abby heard him say, then he pretended to slice the blade of his paddle across the lake with a sudden jerking movement, just to make Rebecca jump. 'I hardly recognised you out of your uniform!'

'Go away, Guy!' Rebecca shouted in return, stumbling on the pebbled ground as she sloshed her way out of the lake.

Clarissa was circling back towards her like a protective mother duck.

Lori, who'd been lying on her back, looking like her invisible lilo had sunk, flipped onto her front, a frown fixed on her forehead and her eyes trained on the situation unfolding before them. 'Hey!' she yelled at Guy. 'Leave her alone!'

Abby swam towards the figure retreating from the water; Rebecca's shoulders were hunched, her head bowed.

'Aw, Braithwaite!' Guy called after Rebecca. 'Where are you going?' he asked, his tone teasing, as he paddled after her into the shallows, splashing her for real this time. 'You've only just got in!'

Rebecca's head snapped round. 'Get lost, Guy!' she shouted. 'It's not funny, okay?' Her arms were rigid, her fists clenched by her sides.

'Woah, woah, calm down!' he replied, resting his paddle across the spray deck of his kayak. 'I only came over to say hello. It's nice to see you in the wild – I didn't know you ever left the reception desk.'

Is he an obnoxious hotel guest, or perhaps someone Rebecca worked with? wondered Abby.

'Well, it's not good to see *you*,' said Rebecca, glaring at him.

He frowned, pulling a mock-affronted expression. 'So that's it, you're off? You haven't even swum! Want me to show you how it's done?' He grinned at her, eyes glinting in the late-afternoon light.

'No I don't, thank you very much!' snapped Rebecca, wrapping her towel around her shoulders, back on solid ground.

'You don't need a wetsuit by the way, it's *warm* today!' Guy goaded her.

'That's easy for you to say, sitting in your little canoe!' retorted Lori.

Clarissa torpedoed through the water faster than a rainbow trout. 'Can you please keep a respectful distance from these swimmers!' she shouted, looming up out of the lake formidably.

'All right, all right,' said Guy, flicking his damp, dark hair from his forehead, out of his eyes, before picking up his paddle. 'See you soon, Braithwaite!' he shouted, shooting Rebecca a mischievous smile and then gliding off towards Coniston Old Hall, further up the lake on the opposite side.

Abby staggered over the stones towards Rebecca. 'Are you okay?' she asked, shivering as the breeze whipped her exposed skin.

'Yeah, I'm fine,' she replied, rubbing her face furiously with her towel. 'Argh!' she shrieked, her whole body shuddering. 'He's *so* annoying! I was actually in before he showed up.'

'Don't let him bother you,' said Abby, trying to yank off her soaking wetsuit with frozen fingers. 'You did so well,' she added with a smile.

'What, not to punch him?' Rebecca joked.

Abby laughed. 'I meant being in the water – you were fully in, properly swimming.'

'*Drifting*, more like,' replied Rebecca, wriggling out of her costume beneath a towel-tent she'd constructed to hide her modesty.

'You did it, girl!' hollered Lori as she waded towards them out of the lake, diamond-like droplets dripping from her limbs as she did so.

'A great improvement, Rebecca,' said Clarissa from behind Abby; she turned to see her dressed in full Herdwick-inspired attire of grey fleece, taupe trousers and sturdy shoes before the rest of them had managed to struggle out of their swimwear.

Rebecca grinned back; her cheeks flushed with success despite her encounter with the cocky kayaker.

'So, who was *that*?' asked Lori, eyes sparkling in the soft September light.

'Ugh,' said Rebecca, sitting down on the stones to tug on her trainers. 'Guy Loveland.' She blew out a sigh so deep it signalled there was a back story that she couldn't be bothered to tell.

'And he is . . .?' said Lori, slowly peeling off her wetsuit to unveil the ruffled top of her impractical swimming costume beneath, like she was demonstrating how to reveal a secret.

'*God*,' said Rebecca with another huff.

'Certainly looks like he *thinks* he is,' quipped Abby.

The others – bar Clarissa, whose head was buried in her backpack – guffawed with laughter.

'He's *insufferable*,' said Rebecca, fastening her jacket all the way to her chin, as though she wanted to zip up her lips and never speak his name again.

But Abby's laughter subsided when she realised who Guy had to be, with a last name like his—

'He's the owner of the Loveland Hotel,' said Rebecca. 'Well, heir to it, at any rate,' she explained. 'His parents run it, but everyone knows they want him to take over their empire.'

Abby choked back memories of a fleeting meeting with Martin and Amelia Loveland on one of her and Ben's wedding planning trips; the couple had appeared to be as charming as they were well groomed, but she more than anyone knew that people were capable of putting on a front . . .

'But Guy doesn't ever do any actual work, he just likes to swan about *as if* he owns the place,' Rebecca carried on.

Abby remembered feeling a little that way herself, on her special day – she'd guess the hotel tended to have that effect on its residents. There she'd been, dressed as a princess, and the Loveland had seemed like a palace, the setting for a fairy tale. She could forgive Guy for thinking it wasn't a place rooted in real life . . .

'Anyway, that's enough,' said Rebecca and Abby pushed aside her nostalgia. 'I have to deal with Guy most days as it is and that's *plenty* for me,' she added, scrabbling to her feet and brushing herself off as though she were sweeping away any remaining thoughts of him.

'Oh my god!' exclaimed Lori, and Abby's attention snapped back to the present; she followed Lori's line of sight and drew in a sharp breath.

Clarissa had constructed a camping stove and was cooking something right there by the lakeside.

'Are those pancakes?' asked Lori, bending down to examine the contents of the skillet.

'Drop scones,' announced Clarissa, pouring a couple of dollops of liquid mixture into the pan from a sports bottle. 'Very similar,' she conceded.

The smell of buttery batter beginning to bubble on the bottom of the saucepan filled Abby's nostrils. She hadn't had drop scones since she was little; she remembered her grandmother making them, and the childlike wonder of seeing simple ingredients transformed into a tea-time treat in an instant. But she'd never known anyone make them outdoors, with only the most basic equipment to hand. She gazed at Clarissa in awe: she was crouching next to the stove, head cocked to one side as she waited for exactly the right moment to turn the drop scones over. She flipped the first one, and it was a perfect golden brown like the autumn leaves that scattered the ground.

'Wow,' breathed Rebecca, beside her.

'Are you some kinda magician?' said Lori, as Clarissa tossed the other scone with expert precision.

Clarissa's mouth was upturned into a modest smile. 'These two should be ready now,' she said, scooping out the contents of the pan onto serving plates that had seemingly appeared from nowhere. 'They're at their best straight from the stove, so dig in.'

'You don't need to tell me twice,' said Lori, leaning down to marvel at the sweet-scented steaming cakes. 'They look *gorgeous*,' she exclaimed, picking up a plate.

'Someone take the other,' said Clarissa. 'More coming up in just a minute,' she added, unscrewing the top of the batter bottle with a few quick twists of her wrist.

Abby smiled at Rebecca. 'Go ahead, you deserve it!'

'Are you sure?' Rebecca replied, reaching for the drop scone like it was a gift made of real gold.

Abby nodded.

'Help yourselves to honey and jam,' said Clarissa, producing jars and spoons from a side pocket of her bag.

How could she possibly cater for each of her wild swimming groups so effortlessly, wondered Abby, when she herself felt overwhelmed just cooking for herself and a four-year-old. *And why does she do it?* Everything was generously given, each morsel handmade, laden with comfort and meant as a gesture of care.

Once the second batch of scones was hissing in the pan, sending another wave of the homely aroma into the atmosphere, Clarissa pulled a flask of hot coffee from her rucksack and divided it equally into four mugs with consummate efficiency. 'A warm drink for you all,' she announced, but her voice was drowned out by words of praise.

'Oh my god!' Lori said through a mouthful of drop scone. 'This tastes *unreal*!'

'*Mmm*,' said Rebecca as she took a bite of hers, a smile bursting across her face. 'It's like *heaven*.'

'Yeah, if you're not a magician, you're an angel, that's for sure!' said Lori, searching for any crumbs she might have missed on her plate.

'I've enough for seconds, if anyone wants one,' said Clarissa, handing a bronzed drop scone to Abby, who beamed back at her as she sat cross-legged on the pebble-carpeted shore to drizzle honey on top of it.

'Oh yes please, ma'am,' said Lori, holding out her plate. 'I'mma have to step up my swimming game though if I'm not going home fifty pounds heavier.' She laughed and the others joined in.

'It's nice to cook for people who appreciate it,' said Clarissa with a Herdwick-style smile.

'It sure is,' said Lori, shifting position on the stony ground. 'Hey, I'm just being spontaneous here,' – she drew circles with her hand in the cool evening air – 'but, er, you guys are welcome to come to my cottage for a bite to eat.' As soon as she'd spoken the sentence aloud, she seemed to think better of it; her hand was wafting side to side now as though to encourage the breeze to carry it away. 'You probably have plans or someplace more exciting to be . . .' She trailed off, turned to face the scones sizzling on the stove.

'You mean tonight?' clarified Abby, licking the last honey-stickiness from her lips.

'Yeah, whenever.' Lori shrugged.

'I'd love to, but I have to collect Rowan.'

'Oh, sure you do.' Lori batted the air again.

'How long are you here for?' asked Rebecca, as Clarissa slid a second scone onto her plate.

'Um, well . . .' Lori seemed to stumble over the question, visibly wrangling with her answer. 'I . . . er . . .'

Abby eyed her expression with curiosity, could have sworn she saw Lori swallow down the truth. She'd initially said she was staying at Silver Ghyll for a fortnight, but that would mean her holiday was up at the end of that week. Yet she'd issued an open-ended dinner invitation. Something didn't add up. She thought about the husband Lori barely mentioned. Maybe there was trouble at home. Was this the trip of a lifetime or a trial separation, she wondered.

'I wanted to keep things kinda flexible, ya know?' said Lori, draining the last of her coffee as though her mouth was suddenly dry. 'I haven't had a proper vacation in years . . .'

'Tell me about it,' said Rebecca with a sympathetic smile. 'I'd love to take off to the other side of the world for a bit, escape work for a while.'

'Uh-huh, right?' said Lori with nod.

Abby began to stack up the plates, noticing Clarissa was repacking her rucksack.

'Well, we could do this weekend, girls?' Lori smiled at the circle of Wildwater Women. 'Are you free Friday, C?' she said to Clarissa, who appeared not to have realised she was included in the offer.

'Oh,' she said, stopping slotting objects back in her bag. 'That's very kind. I've currently nothing in my calendar.'

'Alrighty!' replied Lori with a delighted clap of her hands. 'You guys?' she said, glancing at Rebecca and Abby.

'My shift'll finish at six,' said Rebecca, looking at Abby as though seeking confirmation of whether she was coming too, bringing her quota of the younger contingent, before she committed. Abby was touched, and a rush of warmth spread across her chest, as though she could feel a friendship physically being forged between them.

'That would be lovely,' replied Abby, smiling at Lori first and then the others. 'I'll ask if Rowan's grandma wouldn't mind babysitting.'

'Right on!' said Lori. 'I guess I'll have to work on my cooking skills,' she added with a grimace. 'Those pancakes were *sooo good*,' she said, eyes closing in satisfaction.

'Drop scones,' Clarissa corrected her.

'Whatever you say!' said Lori with a chuckle.

'Glad you enjoyed them,' said Clarissa, standing up and swinging her rucksack onto her back.

The rest of the group received the signal; it was time to leave the lake shore. They walked the short way to the car park as the last of the sun streaked towards the horizon in a blazing spectrum of copper-orange.

'Thank you so much,' Abby said to Clarissa as she put her wetsuit in the back of her Defender and the others followed her lead.

'And thanks for telling me the name of the place in the picture!' said Lori. She gave Clarissa a broad grin, but then it faded from her face like the final rays of light from the sky at nightfall.

'Crummockwater,' confirmed Clarissa, as she closed the rear door of her four-by-four. There was never a word wasted

from their leader. Never a question asked, or a story sought –
but Abby guessed Clarissa Dimplethorpe was entrusted
with a great many secrets – precisely because of that.

Abby turned and saw Lori's eyes shining in the low evening
light, but then all of a sudden her smile was back in place,
bright as a new day at dawn.

'That's it!' she replied. 'Anyone want to take a road trip
there with me?' she asked. 'I'm gonna check it out this
weekend.'

'Do you mean go swimming there?' said Rebecca, jamming
her hands in her coat pockets as she hovered halfway to
her car.

'Why not?' replied Lori.

Rebecca hesitated.

'You know you can do it too now – you proved that today,'
said Clarissa encouragingly, as she walked round to the driver's side of her car.

'I could do Sunday, I suppose.' Rebecca chewed her lip.

Lori looked at Abby. 'Gonna join us?' She spread her
arms wide. 'Oh, you got the little one, huh,' she answered
for her.

Abby nodded. 'But I'll see you all on Friday night anyway.'
She smiled.

'Sure thing,' replied Lori.

'Right, must dash,' called Clarissa, clambering into her
Defender. 'Let me know what to bring on Friday – you
have my details – and if you want to swim in Crummockwater on Sunday, say the word,' she said, before starting the
engine.

'Perfect!' said Lori, clasping her hands together as though
to lock the plans in place.

'You could always bring your daughter, too,' suggested Rebecca, leading the way to her car. 'Have the walk there, at least.'

'Okay.' She never had anything to look forward to in the diary, now she had two arrangements set for one weekend. Abby smiled as a surge of happiness bubbled up through her body.

11

'It's a mystery to me,' said Tom with a bemused pout. He held out the cake stand containing the still-intact lemon meringue pie he'd made first thing that morning.

'I'll add it to the greatest unsolved questions of all time, along with "is there really a Bownessie monster in Windermere?" and "why on earth is our boss called *Joy*?"'

Abby giggled, then slapped a hand over her mouth in case the latter appeared. She peered at the crisp whipped peaks of the pie; it resembled a snow-topped mountain gilded with winter sunshine. 'It looks delicious,' she declared, leaning an elbow on the top of the glass cabinet.

'But it hasn't sold. Not one slice,' Tom said, setting the stand down on top of the counter.

'Well, there's so much choice, and *everything* you bake is amazing,' said Abby with a smile. 'It's hard for people to choose!'

'More difficult to predict what they'll pick,' replied Tom.

Abby walked over to flip the sign on the door; it was four-thirty, and the shop was finally closed.

She returned to where Tom was standing behind the counter, back resting against the worktop.

'Depends which customers come in, I suppose,' she said. 'I know everyone who's tasted it *always* raves.'

'Yeah, I guess,' Tom said, folding his arms. He caught her gaze. 'You seem a bit . . . different, Abs,' he said with a half-smile.

She stopped still beside the till. 'Do I? How?'

Tom put his forefinger on his chin. 'Dunno . . .'

Abby laughed and carried on covering up the cakes in the display cabinet, as she had been doing before her colleague came through for a quick catch up before he clocked off for the night.

'D'you want a hand with that?' Tom asked.

'I can do it,' said Abby, without looking up.

'I know you can,' he replied. 'I wasn't questioning that.' He bent down to help her, picking up a pair of metal tongs and starting to transfer the tray bakes from the top shelf into airtight containers.

'Thanks,' she said, with a grateful grin.

'Don't take this the wrong way . . .' said Tom as he clicked the lid in place on a Tupperware of gooey flapjack.

'Oh god, what are you going to say?' said Abby, straightening up and wiping her hands on her apron.

'You seem a bit . . . *happier,*' said Tom, raising his eyebrows.

Abby rubbed her forehead. 'I've been trying to take some of your advice,' she admitted.

'Oh, really?' replied Tom, putting his hands on his hips. 'You're telling me I've said something *useful*? I'm sure both the boss and the missus won't agree with you there.' He chuckled to himself.

Abby held her palms up. 'I'm serious, I took what you said on board.'

Tom's eyes were wide as he waited for her to explain.

'I've started doing something for me. I've started swimming,' she said, heat flooding her cheeks as she realised he was the only person who knew, outside of the Wildwater Women.

'That's grand!' Tom beamed at her. 'It certainly seems to be doing the trick,' he added, before pursing his lips as though he might have risked offending her.

Abby came to stand beside him, arms braced against the worktop as though it were holding her up, giving her the strength to be honest. 'Yeah, I was seeing each day as something just to get through rather than enjoy. But even though I've only been a couple of times, it's making a big difference already,' she murmured, then blew out a breath.

'I'm glad to hear it.' Tom gave a nod. 'So where do you go swimming, then? I didn't think there was a pool near here.' He scratched his head.

Abby opened her mouth, then closed it again.

'There's the health club at the Loveland Hotel, but that must be—' Tom blushed, as though he suspected Abby could piece together his train of thought.

'– *expensive*,' she said, finishing the sentence for him. 'I'm not a member there, you're right,' she added, nudging his arm fondly.

Tom bit his lip as though he wished he could chew up the words he'd just spoken. 'I'm not either,' he mumbled with a sheepish smile. 'When we win the EuroMillions and buy our own bakery, we'll join up then.'

'Deal,' said Abby.

They both laughed.

'I've actually joined a wild swimming group,' confessed Abby, grimacing as though she were admitting a guilty secret.

'A wild what?' asked Tom, his forehead creased.

'Swimming club,' said Abby.

'In the lakes? At this time of year?'

Abby nodded. 'A few of us meet up . . . and go to different places—'

'And act wild?' teased Tom, making his fingers into claws.

Abby bit her lip. 'I know it sounds silly . . .'

'I'm only messing!' Tom put his hands by his sides, imitating a soldier instead of a tiger this time. 'It doesn't at all!' His face turned serious all of a sudden. 'I'm just glad you're feeling better, Abs.'

'Thank you,' she replied.

'No worries. I'm always here for you – and Row – you know that.' Tom rammed his hands in his pockets as though he might've been moved to hug her if his limbs were free to act of their own accord. 'Righto,' he said, all of a sudden, as though signalling a change of subject.

'You get going,' said Abby, 'I can finish the rest.'

'Yes. Okay. Better had,' replied Tom, snapping into action and disappearing off into the back room to retrieve his coat.

Abby started to sweep up crumbs from the worksurface.

'Oh, you should take this,' said Tom, popping out onto the shop floor again.

'What?' said Abby, glancing up at him.

He tapped the countertop next to the sumptuous-looking lemon meringue pie that was still standing on the side. 'It won't keep till after the weekend.'

'Oh, no, I couldn't,' said Abby.

'Why not? Don't you like lemon meringue?'

132

'You've put all that work into it—'

'Exactly – so it's a shame for it to go to waste,' said Tom.

'Of course – but *you* made it. You take it home.'

'We won't be there to eat it. We're going away.'

'Ah,' said Abby, and a sigh escaped her lungs. She wondered what it was like to have a mini-break somewhere as a family, perhaps a log cabin further north, she imagined, before squashing the gnawing sensation in her stomach. 'Okay, then.'

Tom shot her a smile. 'Have you got any plans for the weekend?' he asked as he shrugged on his jacket.

For once, I actually have, realised Abby. 'Yes,' she said, a grin spreading across her face as she pictured her newfound friends. 'I'm going out for dinner tonight.'

She noticed Tom's fingers let go of his coat zip.

'And I'm off up to Crummockwater on Sunday,' she added.

'Grand,' he replied, deciding to leave his jacket undone. 'Well, have a good one!' he said, before scooting out of the door.

Abby raised a hand in a wave and watched him hurry off down the street, then turned back to the counter. She stared at the pie in the silence of the empty shop. *I could take it tonight, share it with the girls*, she thought with a shrug. *Why not?* as Lori would say. That was dessert sorted. Now, for starters, she had to close up the bakery and get scrubbed up for her first Friday night out in what seemed like forever.

Abby walked the short distance from Little Garth to the holiday cottage next door, feeling immediately foolish once she stepped out into the street. Each item of clothing she'd tried on had felt inappropriate, as though she didn't even know what to wear any more, let alone who she was as a person. She'd eventually put on a long-sleeved black jersey dress that up until twenty minutes ago had still had the tag in, and a pair of ankle boots she'd bought years ago but never had the heart to wear in more recent times – back in her bedroom they had appeared to accompany her frock fairly well, but now she'd left home, her entire outfit seemed ridiculous. She felt like she was impersonating someone else: she wasn't a woman who dressed up in evening clothes and wore mascara and lipstick. She'd stared at her bare face in the bathroom mirror for several minutes before she'd attempted to apply subtle makeup, but now she felt clown-faced. *What was I thinking?*

'Hey there!' said Lori, throwing her arms wide in greeting as she opened the door to Silver Ghyll. 'You look *amazing!*' she added, gazing from Abby's eyes to her boots and back again in an exaggerated gesture of admiration.

'Thanks,' said Abby, clutching the container of lemon meringue pie to her chest with one hand and the neck of a bottle of Sauvignon Blanc in the other. 'I think it's the accessories that make it,' she quipped, nodding at the cake box and holding up the wine.

Lori laughed and waved her inside. 'It's good to see you smiling!'

'Am I the first one here?' asked Abby, glancing round; Lori had lit glowing rows of tea lights in the centre of the dining table and across the top of the mantelpiece in the living room and the candles winked at her in welcome. The cottage looked *enchanting.*

'You are, hon, but I guess you lucked out with your journey time, huh?' replied Lori with a chuckle.

Abby grinned. It was true: the others would have to travel *slightly* further than the few short steps she had from the house next door.

'Clarissa's picking Rebecca up; they should be here any second now,' said Lori, looking for glasses in the kitchen cupboards.

'You've made it look magical in here,' said Abby, jerking her head towards the living room as she slid the cake box onto the side.

'Gee, thanks!' said Lori. 'Good to know I haven't lost my artistic side yet, hey.' She went to open the fridge door, glanced inside, then shut it again as though she couldn't remember what she was looking for.

'I brought this,' said Abby, handing her the bottle of wine.

'Oh, you're a doll!' said Lori, her face lighting up as though Abby had answered an unspoken question. 'What can I get you?' She flung open the door to the fridge once more. 'You wanna glass of this?' she asked, holding up Abby's gift. 'Or I have champagne, vodka, juice . . .'

'You've gone to so much trouble!' said Abby, taking in all the options Lori had listed.

'Not at all!' Lori flapped a hand. 'It's girls' night! We're having a party, right?'

Abby smiled. *When did I last have a drink before I met Lori?* She cast her mind back, making sure to stop in time before she spooled too far and hit the most painful parts of her past. After Rowan had been born, and she was allowed to have alcohol again, she'd turned to wine sometimes, choosing a blurred dream about Ben over drowning in his absence sober. But that had been at the beginning, before she realised that drunken imaginings couldn't bring her husband home—

'You okay, doll?' asked Lori, dipping her head to catch her eye.

135

'Yes! Sorry,' replied Abby, shivering in the blast of fridge-chilled air that lingered like a ghost. 'Wine would be lovely,' she said, painting the smile back on her face as though she was simply reapplying lipstick.

'Coming up!' called Lori, going off to hunt for a bottle-opener. 'Siddown! Relax!' she shouted over her shoulder.

As Abby moved towards the sofa, she spotted a collection of chunkier candles in the hearth, cylindrical blocks of cream-coloured wax in varying sizes, their flames fluttered as one to produce a fire-like illusion. Together, they produced a noticeable heat, and Abby felt the tension in her body start to melt like she too was made of the same malleable material.

'Cheers!' said Lori, passing her a generous goblet of wine.

Abby took a sip and the citrus-and-grass flavours seemed to celebrate on her tongue.

'This is good,' declared Lori, swirling the liquid in her glass.

Headlights flickered across the window as Clarissa's Defender pulled up outside in the dusk dimness, like a creature drawn by the rosy warmth radiating from Silver Ghyll's interior.

Lori jumped up.

Abby followed her into the hall.

'Good evening, one and all,' said Clarissa; she was wearing a smarter, woollier version of her usual monochrome uniform; a soft grey poncho over tapered trousers – as though, this time, she were a sheep dressed for a special occasion.

Rebecca waved from behind her on the little garden path.

'Heeey!' said Lori, beckoning them both inside. 'Happy Friday!'

'Indeed,' replied Clarissa, producing a bottle-shaped present from the folds of her poncho and plonking it down on the table. 'Sloe gin. Homemade.'

'Erm, I brought nibbles,' said Rebecca, setting a large, square wicker basket on the side. 'Didn't want you to have all the work with the cooking.'

'Oh wow, thanks!' said Lori, trying to peek inside. 'You're an angel. I didn't get an appetiser, just a whole heap of chips.'

For a starter? wondered Abby, catching Rebecca's eye as she took another sip of wine.

'Whatcha bring?' asked Lori, lifting the corner of the tea towel that covered the basket's contents.

Rebecca playfully slapped her hand away. 'Only a few picky bits. I just need to warm them up in the oven,' she said, going to inspect the cooker.

'I haven't used that thing yet,' muttered Lori, a frown furrowing her forehead.

Clarissa was scoping out the cottage with purposeful strides, as though she were searching for the perfect place to pitch a tent. 'Grand spot, this,' she declared, coming to rest next to the sofa. 'Plenty of character,' she added with a nod of approval, hands on her hips.

'Sure is, huh?' said Lori. 'I love it here!' she added, flinging her arms wide for emphasis, and Abby got the impression she was encompassing the whole of the Lakes in her comment, not just Silver Ghyll Cottage.

'What do you wanna drink, girls?' Lori hollered, despite the cosy proportions of the house.

'I'll have a sloe gin, thanks,' said Clarissa, pacing the sitting room as though she weren't designed to sit still.

'With a mixer or on the rocks?' asked Lori, going over to marvel at the glass bottle Clarissa had brought as though it were a potion straight out of Harry Potter.

'Neat, please.'

'Go make yourself comfortable!' said Lori, glancing up at Clarissa, who looked oddly out of place confined within four walls rather than roaming the fells, as though she were a free-range animal that had found themselves fenced in a pen.

'Oh, shoot, I forgot to buy ice . . .' Lori mumbled.

'*Buy. Ice?*' repeated Clarissa under her breath, as though Lori were talking a foreign language, a bemused expression contorting her face.

Rebecca clattered a baking tray into the oven before the others could catch what it contained, and closed the cooker door.

'How about a cocktail?' suggested Lori, delving into the fridge and then brandishing the champagne. 'Sloe fizz, anyone? A shot of your gin, C, topped up with this?' she waggled the bottle of bubbly. 'It's ice cold, at least.'

'Go on then,' Clarissa replied, perching on the edge of an armchair as though she was more used to sitting on a stone on the lakeshore.

'Sounds yum!' said Rebecca, grabbing a dish of something else from her basket.

'Abby?' asked Lori, already tearing off the foil wrapping around the cork.

The lit wicks of the tabletop tea lights seemed to dance in encouragement.

'Okay,' Abby replied, realising she'd almost finished her first glass of wine. 'Yes, please.' She'd started to relax now she was surrounded by her wild swimming friends. She'd begun to get to know these three women – all so very different and from widely varied walks of life – and for the first time seemed to have found a circle of people she felt an affinity with.

'Right on!' said Lori, popping the cork and whooping with delight.

'Well, I have to say, this tastes rather good,' exclaimed Clarissa a few moments later, raising her glass of Sloe Fizz in a toast to the rest of the group.

'I want to say a few words,' said Lori, clearing her throat. 'Thank you, guys, for making me feel super welcome here . . .' Abby saw her eyes sparkle with real emotion in the candlelight as she spoke. 'It really means a lot to me,' she continued. She looked as though she'd been about to say something more, but thought better of it, and a beat later a broad grin was back on her face. 'It's great to have you all here!'

'And it's wonderful to be here,' said Abby, lifting up her glass.

'Cheers!' said Rebecca, doing the same.

'Hear, hear!' said Clarissa.

Abby savoured the combination of sweet berries and crisp champagne.

'This is my new favourite drink!' declared Lori, taking another gulp.

'Packs a punch, doesn't it!' Rebecca's eyes were watering. 'Can't have much of this or I'll burn the nibbles.' She rushed over to the cooker to check on her canapés.

'Please, take a seat!' Lori urged the others, before going to see if she could help Rebecca.

'So, whatcha cooking up?' she asked, peering over her shoulder.

'Pigs in blankets,' replied Rebecca, taking the tray out of the oven and wafting a mouth-watering aroma of roast sausages wrapped in bacon into the atmosphere.

Lori shook her head as she searched for a plate in the cupboards. 'Nah-ah.'

'*What?*' said Rebecca with a laugh. 'These are pigs in blankets!' she repeated, holding the baking sheet aloft with giant oven-gloved hands.

Lori pulled out an old-fashioned serving platter she'd found on a back shelf. 'No they're not!' she countered. 'I'll show ya!' She patted her pockets, looking for her mobile.

Clarissa and Abby came over to join the discussion, lured by the promise of hot bacon wound round succulent chipolatas.

'Smells like Christmas,' exclaimed Clarissa.

Abby's stomach suddenly rumbled.

Lori held up her phone to show them all an image on the screen.

'They're not pigs in blankets, they're sausage rolls!' chorused the rest of the group.

'Unanimous decision, I'm afraid,' declared Clarissa diplomatically.

'And just when I thought I was up to date on my Britishisms!' said Lori with a good-natured giggle, grabbing the platter and going back over to the living room. 'These look delicious, anyways,' she added, popping one in her mouth.

'I made a smoked salmon dip too,' said Rebecca, picking up a bowl from the kitchen counter.

'Perfect! It'll go with the chips,' called Lori, indicating the dish she'd set on the coffee table in anticipation of her guests' arrival.

'Crisps, you mean,' said Rebecca, plucking one out of the bowl and scooping up a dollop of dip.

'Right, I'm outta here!' joked Lori, getting to her feet and batting the air with both hands and they all burst into laughter.

Abby reached for a sausage; her cheeks hurt from smiling so much. 'Rebecca, these are *amazing*,' she said, when she'd finished chewing.

'I can't get enough of 'em, whatever you guys call 'em,' said Lori, licking her lips as she sat down again.

'They're marvellous,' said Clarissa, helping herself to a second one, before making a beeline for the smoked salmon.

'Well, you've baked so much for us,' replied Rebecca, smiling back at their swimming instructor. 'Given us all those incredible cakes,' she continued. 'You deserve a little bit back.'

Clarissa looked like a sheep caught in headlights, her hand paused halfway to her mouth with a dip-laden crisp. But her dark eyes seemed to soften in the amber glow of the candle-light. 'Pay it forward, I believe is the modern phrase,' she whispered, settling back against the cushions of her armchair.

Abby cradled her glass of champagne, thinking about Clarissa's words. The kindness all three of these women had shown her was starting to bring her back to life. She vowed to continue their spirit, looking out for those who needed a little nurturing. She took a sip of her drink, but noticed Lori's gaze had glazed over as though a foreboding cloud had cast her face in shadow, as she'd seen once before. Rebecca, too, appeared lost in contemplation. Perhaps the people sitting here beside her were equally grateful for Clarissa's guidance and care – not just when it came to their wild swimming excursions but in opening their eyes to the beauty of the world around them and the strength that could be found in their friendships. Maybe she'd been blind to the possibility that the other women might need her as much as she did them, wondered Abby, silently promising to make sure each one of them was okay.

'Oh, I forgot music!' said Lori, snapping out of her haze all of a sudden. She leaped up to fiddle with Silver Ghyll's sound system: a surprisingly state-of-the-art setup with wireless speakers. 'Lord, this looks complicated . . .'

Abby stood up to try and assist.

Lori slotted her phone onto the stand on the sideboard, pressed some buttons, and classical music started seeping from the walls. She prodded the screen on her mobile to try and make it stop. 'Oh, not that . . .' she muttered, with a sigh.

'Mozart is fabulous!' declared Clarissa.

'Not at a party!' countered Lori, finally managing to switch the playlist. 'Who wants another drink while I'm on my feet, huh?' she asked, discarding her pashmina and blowing out a deep breath.

'You relax, I'll get them,' said Abby, sensing she was flustered but not quite sure why.

'Oh, you're a saint,' said Lori, flopping down on the sofa and sweeping her hair back from her flushed face.

'I'll have a soft drink, thanks,' called Clarissa, placing a hand over the top of her glass; a mime to be understood above the upbeat tune now vibrating around the room. 'Driving,' she mouthed by way of explanation.

'It's my turn next time,' Rebecca said with a smile.

'You'll all have to come round to mine,' blurted out Abby, topping up their cocktails, the alcohol urging her on, the music rallying her, but she realised she meant it. Little Garth could do with having its spark reignited, and so, too, could she.

'Sounds great!' said Lori, taking a big swig of her sloe fizz. 'So what's the story with you and your little girl's dad, huh?' she asked.

Abby felt herself sink down in her seat like a fallen soufflé, felled by the unexpected question. She let out a lungful of air. Trying to distil her and Ben's relationship into a sentence or two that would both adequately explain what had happened and not immediately cause her to burst into tears was an impossible task. She set down her drink, doing her best to steady her drumming heart.

'Coz that guy at your work is preeeetty darn cute,' continued Lori, nudging her arm affectionately.

Abby's stomach lurched and the walls of Silver Ghyll seemed to sway.

'He didn't walk out,' she said softly, half-willing someone to change the topic of conversation, half-desperate to prove to herself she could say the words without dissolving.

Silence settled like snow as one track ended and the next song took a few seconds to start.

'He died.' Abby bit down on her bottom lip so hard she tasted the faint bitterness of blood.

'Oh, sweetie,' said Lori softly, swathing her in a cashmere-soft hug. 'Jeez, I'm so sorry.'

Abby's throat felt as dry and scratchy as if the canapés she'd consumed had been made of sand. She wanted to stand up and get herself a glass of water, but she wasn't sure her legs would support her.

Clarissa clomped across the carpet as though she recognised what was going through Abby's mind, had seen similar situations many times before.

'Thank you,' Abby croaked when she returned with an ice-cold tumbler. She drank it down in one, as though she might be able to quench her parched heart as well as her thirst.

'Shoot, I'm so sorry . . .' said Lori.

'Don't be.' Abby dabbed beneath her eyes with her finger-tips. 'It's a long time ago now – just when I speak about it, everything comes flooding back . . .' She sniffed. 'Shouldn't

143

have mixed my drinks, either,' she added with a half-smile. 'So it's my own fault for crying.'

'None of that, please,' said Clarissa with a stern shake of the head. 'Don't do yourself down.'

Abby lifted up her chin. 'Being with you guys – and getting out and feeling the stones beneath my feet, the water on my skin – has made me feel so much better. Like I *belong*, like I'm connected and I've finally found my tribe.' She sat up straighter. 'I've talked to friends and family before, of course, and they've helped. Plus, I've had to get on with things, for Rowan's sake – but I've not been *me*, been *happy*.'

The others nodded as they listened, and Abby wondered whether any of them could identify with what she was saying.

'I couldn't bear to be around happy couples. I pushed people away.' Abby swallowed. 'I was stuck in a rut before I met you all . . . but I'm beginning to break out of it. I might just be getting my life back.' She smiled. 'So, thank you.'

'You've done the hard work yourself,' said Clarissa, sitting on the very edge of her seat as though she wasn't used to the comfort of soft furnishings.

'But I couldn't have done it without you,' whispered Abby, looking at each of them in turn.

Lori squeezed her hand. 'I still feel *awful* . . . I shouldn't have asked, it was so stupid.'

Abby shook her head. 'Ben . . .' She swallowed; she still stumbled whenever she said his name, even after all these years. 'It happened before Rowan was born.'

'You don't have to tell us any more,' murmured Rebecca.

But Abby felt as though a pressure valve inside her had been released; talking about her husband in the company of the Wildwater Women had somehow freed her a little. She didn't have to keep her struggles to herself – she couldn't be amongst a more supportive group of people. Suddenly she wanted them to know what she'd gone through – or else how could they really understand who she was? Surely true friendship had to have a foundation of honesty. She took a fortifying breath. 'He . . . had these pains in his legs, and they got worse and worse . . . then . . . he only had two more weeks after the doctors told us . . . the diagnosis. Cancer.'

Rebecca gasped.

Lori slapped her palms over her mouth.

Clarissa bowed her head.

The pop song pulsing from the walls couldn't have seemed more inappropriate.

Lori got up, as though to switch it off.

'Don't,' said Abby, catching her sleeve. 'We're stopping this chat now. I'm pleased you guys know – it honestly feels good to have told you – but this isn't the time or the place to wallow.'

Clarissa nodded in approval. '*Wallowing* is something that should only ever be done in the *water*,' she said, raising a smile from the rest of the group and managing to lighten the tone.

'We're always here if you need us, you know that,' added Rebecca.

'You betcha!' said Lori.

'But you'll be jetting off back to America soon,' retorted Abby, gently prodding her in the ribs.

'Doesn't mean we can't keep in touch!' countered Lori. 'All these gadgets we got nowadays sure help with that!' – Abby sensed Lori's shoulders tense beside her – 'Anyways, I'm sticking around for a while yet.'

Abby saw her jaw clench, despite the excited pitch of her voice.

'Are you?' asked Rebecca.

'Oh, yeah!' Lori smacked her thigh. 'You're not gonna see the back of me for another couple weeks, actually – I've extended my vacation!' She had a broad grin on her face. 'There's a whole lotta stuff I still wanna do . . .' she said, as though offering up the reason before anyone asked her to explain. But she trailed off, and Abby wondered whether there was more to Lori's decision to delay going back to the USA than just the fact that she had a few more Lake District beauty spots to tick off first. She'd asked about Ben, maybe she could find a way to ask more about Joe, in case Lori just needed the prompt. But there was that faraway look in Lori's eyes again. Now wasn't the time.

'What else is on your list, apart from our trip to Crummockwater on Sunday?' said Rebecca, passing round the last of the nibbles.

'Oh, er, lemme see,' Lori said, reaching for one of the two remaining bacon-wrapped sausages. 'Well, more wild swimming, of course!' she replied, beaming at Clarissa.

'Glad to hear I haven't put you off so far,' Clarissa said.

'Oh, not at all! I love it!' exclaimed Lori, talking with her mouth full as though the words couldn't wait. 'Anyways!' She swallowed her food, like she was marking a shift in the conversation, moving the subject away from herself. 'I don't wanna put my foot in it again' – Lori grimaced comically – 'but, er, have you seen that dude in the canoe again, Rebecca?' she asked, slouching back against the sofa cushions as though shuffling out of the spotlight.

'Ugh!' groaned Rebecca, crunching down on a crisp. '*All* the time. He thinks he's God's gift, that man.' She gave an enormous sigh. 'He strolled up to Reception the day after we went to Coniston,' – she did an impression of him, bending her elbows and pushing her chest out like she was imitating a puffed-up cockerel – 'leaned on the front desk and said to me, "I could give you swimming lessons in my pool, Braithwaite!"'

'Aw, doesn't sound so bad . . .' said Lori with a giggle. 'Reminds me of that show – what was it called – with the lifeguards in the little red shorts—'

'*Baywatch*?' said Abby, suppressing a snort.

'That's it!' cried Lori.

'He might be good-looking, but he sure as hell knows it,' said Rebecca, scratching her arm as though he were able to irritate her without even being present.

'A total jerk, huh?' said Lori, her shoulders slanting. 'Well, that's not what you want at all, honey.'

'I used to teach Guy,' said Clarissa.

Rebecca's cheeks turned beetroot. 'Did you?' she asked in a small voice.

'He's got a soft centre beneath all the bravado,' Clarissa continued. 'And I don't envy him, having all that expectation piled on him.'

'But he loves it!' said Rebecca. 'Breezing in and out, telling everyone about *his* hotel – *his* pool!'

'Maybe he's just tryna impress a certain someone,' said Lori, raising her eyebrows at Rebecca.

'Oh no, I don't think so!' Rebecca shook her head like she was wafting away a wasp, but then her face subsided into a frown.

'It can't be easy for him, having his future almost mapped out by his parents,' Abby chipped in. 'Isn't that what you said, Rebecca? They've sort of teed him up to take over?'

147

Rebecca nodded.

'Have you spent any real time with him away from the hotel?' asked Clarissa, tilting her head to one side.

'No way!' replied Rebecca. 'I couldn't think of anything worse. I see him enough at work as it is.'

'I thought you said he only bobbed in and out when he felt like it?' countered Clarissa with a twinkle in her eye.

Rebecca's blush deepened.

'Did he say anything else when you saw him?' asked Lori. 'Or just asked you out on a swim date?'

'He did not!' cried Rebecca, crossing her arms.

'Did you not just tell us he invited you to his pool?' added Lori, stoking the fire of indignation that burned inside Rebecca, making her face flame.

'It does sound a little like he was testing the water, by saying that,' said Abby with a nod.

Clarissa cocked her head to the other side as she watched the conversation bat back and forth.

'He just thinks he's better than everyone else!' exclaimed Rebecca.

'Maybe, in actual fact, he wishes he had the freedom they have,' said Clarissa. 'The ability to decide his own destiny.'

'No one wants their fate handed to them on a plate,' said Lori. She heaved a sigh so loud the others all looked at her. But then she leaped up suddenly.

'Shoot – I forgot to check the entrée,' she shrieked, draining the last drops of sloe fizz from her glass and standing up. 'I hope it's okay . . .' She scooted over to the cooker. 'I'll get us takeout if not . . .' she called from the kitchen.

Abby followed. 'Well, it smells amazing!' she said as Lori opened the oven door.

'I did, like, an eggplant dish,' she replied. 'It's my husband's specialty, actually, kinda like a stew but it's real good, I promise. I didn't know if any of you girls were veggie, so . . .' She waved her hands about to disperse the steam.

'Shall I set the table?' asked Abby, glancing over her shoulder and seeing there wasn't any cutlery already laid out.

'Oh god! Yes please!' called Lori, yanking out drawers to look for the knives and forks.

Clarissa and Rebecca came over, curiosity drawing them closer to the whirlwind of chaos that Lori was creating as she went about serving the meal.

But soon they were all sitting round Silver Ghyll's dining table with the scent of spices and the sound of laughter in the air.

Abby gazed at the fragrant plate of aubergine casserole in front of her, then looked round at the women surrounding her, a broad smile stretching itself across her face. An unfamiliar sensation was fizzing in her stomach, starting to spread through her body, sparked by the combination of friendship and good food, and the fact she was finally making a fresh start. As she tasted the first forkful of the gorgeous Ghanaian stew, and the smoky-sweet paprika and hot chilli pepper exploded on her tongue, she realised the feeling was *happiness*.

12

Abby had been up since the sun first started to peep over the fell. As soon as she woke that Sunday morning, she felt a thrill of excitement zip down her spine. She was looking forward to her excursion to Crummockwater with the kind of enthusiasm that might be expected if she were off on an extravagant holiday. She shoved off her duvet and stretched her arms up towards the ceiling as though she were reaching for the sky itself, eager to welcome the day. The idea that a trip to a place only an hour away could fill her with such fizzing anticipation made her smile to herself as she pulled back the curtains and let the faint light of dawn filter in through the window.

She set off to drop Rowan at Maria's house while it was still early, and walking through the town while the rest of its residents were dozing lazily, revelling in a weekend lie-in, felt like they were the first ones to be let into a theme park just as the doors were flung open. The atmosphere was hushed and still, and a bubble of elation began to burble up inside Abby, as though she had fast-track tickets to the world in all its autumnal glory. Wansfell was crowned in a low mist, and dewdrops hung from grass lawns like priceless gemstones. Birds serenaded them in surround-sound, like she and Rowan had front-row seats at a private performance of nature's finest orchestra.

Her daughter scampered up the path to Fairfield View and stood on tiptoe to ring the bell. Maria answered the door wearing an over-sized polo-necked jumper and a huge grin.

'GRANDMA!' Rowan squealed, throwing her arms round Maria's waist, and Abby's heart squeezed as she watched the two of them greet each other with such exuberance no one would guess they'd only parted the previous day, when she'd come to pick Rowan up the morning after the dinner party.

'Morning, Maria!' Abby said with a smile. 'Thanks again for having her.'

'Oh, it's a pleasure.' Maria laughed as Rowan disappeared off down the hall, muttering the lyrics to a song she'd either learned at school or made up, as she searched for something of interest: a foodstuff or furnishing she wouldn't find at home. 'It's a treat to have her for the day.' The corners of her eyes crinkled.

'She might be a bit full of energy, without school to wear her out for you first,' said Abby with a smile.

'Oh, we'll be fine!' Maria looked over her shoulder at Rowan bounding about behind her. She turned to face Abby again, her forehead wrinkling into a thought-wrought frown. 'If ever you want . . . a whole weekend to yourself . . .' she started, her slippers shifting position on the carpet like she was trying to avoid treading on an awkward subject. 'All you have to do is say . . .'

'Oh, I'm not going to make a habit of this, don't worry!' replied Abby, tucking some stray strands of hair behind her ear. *Does she think I can't cope? She probably would if she knew I was off to plunge into a freezing pool of water – and that I'm pretty excited about it, too . . .*

'Well, it's about time you thought of yourself as well, Abby love.' Maria's lips trembled like a pair of pink caterpillars. 'You deserve some happiness; you've been through a lot . . .'

'Thank you, I know you've had a lot to deal with too...' said Abby.

'Don't feel you can't . . . you know . . .' Maria fiddled with the neck of her pullover.

What is she getting at? wondered Abby, jamming her hands in her coat pockets as though the answer might be hidden in one of them.

'You can tell me if you've started seeing someone, is all I'm saying, love,' Maria blurted out. 'Not that you have to, of course, but don't feel that you can't.' She clasped her hands together.

'*What?*' muttered Abby, taking a step back on the garden path as though Maria's garbled words had physically knocked her off her feet.

'I want the best for you – and Rowan, that goes without saying – and if you're dating again then as long as you're—'

'I don't understand.'

'Oh, love, I don't want to put you on the spot – it's come out all wrong.' Maria looked as though she wished the roll-neck of her jumper would cover her entire head. 'I just meant don't feel awkward around me if you've moved on, that's all – and I'm happy to babysit Rowan whenever you want, we've enjoyed spending some more time together, it's been special—'

'Wait a second,' interrupted Abby. 'I haven't met anyone.'

'Oh.' Maria's hands dropped to her sides. 'I just assumed . . . when you asked if Rowan could stay over on Friday . . .'

Abby shook her head. 'That was just . . . I went round to a friend's.'

'Right . . . okay. Well, I don't want to pry anyway . . .' Maria was flapping her arms.

'Honestly!' protested Abby. She paused. She might as well come out and admit what she'd really been up to, as it was far more preferable to Maria thinking she was palming Rowan off with her in order to pursue some hopeless romance. 'I've started swimming, that's all!'

Maria's kind eyes narrowed. 'What, late on Friday nights?'

Abby waved her hands. 'No, no. Friday was a dinner thing . . .'

Maria fidgeted with a fluffy cuff.

'I've joined a group! Like social swimming,' explained Abby. 'The Wildwater Women.'

'The wild *what*?' Maria laughed as though she thought Abby had concocted a cover story on the spot.

'It's the truth! I've started wild swimming.'

'What? Where? You mean in the *lakes*? Every time I see someone in there I think they must be mad!' Maria raised her eyebrows.

'Well, I'm doing it.'

'At this time of year?' Maria put her hands on her hips. 'Are you sure you're all right, Abby, love?' Her face was creased with concern.

'Absolutely!'

'D'you want to come in for a second? Quick cup of tea?' Maria was nodding as though on Abby's behalf; perhaps she now deemed her unfit to make her own decisions . . .

'No, thank you, I'd better go.' She gave a little wave goodbye. 'But, seriously, I'm starting to feel so much better.' She gazed straight at Maria. 'And I really didn't think I *ever* would,' she added with a shake of her head. And as she walked back through Ambleside, and watched the town start to stir from its slumber, she felt a smile of surprise burst across her face.

When Clarissa's Defender drew up outside Little Garth not so long after she'd got home, Abby slung her swimming bag on her back and slipped out of the door once again – but this time a fine drizzle caressed her face. She tilted her head upwards like she was receiving soft kisses, saw a kind of splendour in the swirling grey clouds.

She heard Silver Ghyll's front door slam and looked round to see Lori's expression of horror at the unexpected turn in the weather.

'We're taking a rain check, right?' she said, clutching an umbrella just in case she really *was* going to have to go the short distance from doorstep to Defender.

Abby shook her head. 'Welcome to the Lake District,' she said with a smile. 'As unpredictable as it is beautiful!'

Clarissa opened the driver's-side window. 'Are you two going to dilly-dally all day?' she called. 'It's only a bit of water, for goodness' sake!' she added.

They could see Rebecca sitting beside her in the passenger seat, coat hood still up as though she wasn't convinced they should continue with the trip either.

'Oh, what the hell!' shrieked Lori, shoving her umbrella into her tote bag. 'Guess we're gonna have to embrace it!'

'Yep!' replied Abby with a grin, and they both scurried through their garden gates and scrambled into the backseat of Clarissa's four-by-four.

'Finally!' their instructor muttered under her breath as they buckled up their safety belts. 'You do know you're going *wild swimming*?' she cried. 'And that involves getting wet!' She gave a bemused sigh.

The three women in her charge dissolved into giggles.

The scenery on the journey northwards had Abby and Rebecca equally as awestruck as Lori, despite being locals, and their faces stayed pressed close to the window for the duration.

Abby hadn't ventured up beyond Keswick since well before she'd had Rowan, and she was looking forward to drinking in the landscape the same way others would anticipate having an exotic tipple they'd once tried before on holiday – she'd had a taste, and she couldn't wait to return for more.

As they drove out of Ambleside, on to Grasmere, she noticed the trees lining the lanes had scattered confetti-like leaves on the tarmac, and that passing cars had compacted them to form a crushed-orange carpet. Beyond, patchwork squares of verdant fields surrounded by ancient stone walls created a quilt that covered the fells. Even though the rain appeared to have set in for the day, it suddenly seemed rather atmospheric.

'Do you know how many lakes we're going to see today?' asked Clarissa, glancing at Lori in particular in the rear-view mirror.

'Oh, I know this is, like, a trick, isn't it . . .?' she replied, turning to Abby beside her with a puzzled expression on her face, as though she could remember their previous conversation about there only being one *true* lake, but couldn't recall exactly what had been said.

'Seven in total,' said Clarissa with a nod at Lori's confused reflection, answering her own question as though she didn't have time to waste – despite the fact she devoted much of her life to others. *She is such an enigma*, thought Abby, as she watched their instructor navigate the narrow roads with aplomb.

'Oh, thank god, no riddles today,' muttered Lori, putting a hand to her chest in relief. 'So, which ones are we seeing, huh? Lakes or waters or whatever you guys wanna call 'em!'

'Rydal and Grasmere, of course,' said Clarissa. 'Then Thirlmere, followed by a glimpse of Bassenthwaite, then Derwentwater, Crummockwater and Buttermere.'

'Whoa!' Lori clapped her hands.

'A few new ones for you then,' said Abby with a grin.

'Coming up on the left, now, you'll see the Lion and the Lamb,' announced Clarissa, her focus unwavering from the windscreen as though she'd know the landscape around her even if she were blindfolded.

'The Lion and the Lamb?' echoed Lori in her New Yorker twang. She peered out of the glass as though she expected to spot a safari animal and a small sheep somewhere on the hillside.

'Look up,' whispered Abby, with a smile. She'd seen it before, but years ago when she was younger. *I really ought to bring Rowan one day, she'd love it*, she thought to herself.

'I got it!' shrieked Lori, gazing at the top of Helm Crag.

Rebecca's eyes, too, were trained on its summit, and the rocky outcrop that resembled a lion sitting beside a lamb. She appeared to have relaxed slightly, realised Abby, and was now sitting back in her seat, taking in the sights as they meandered towards their destination.

They passed through the old market town of Keswick, then looped back south along the shore of Derwentwater, which still looked dazzling despite the dreary weather, with its story-book-worthy islands looming from its silvery surface.

'See the jaws of Borrowdale?' said Clarissa, and Lori lurched forward to peer more closely at the lake.

'Jaws like the *shark*?' she asked, craning her neck with curiosity.

The others all laughed.

'No!' replied Clarissa. 'Up ahead, over there.'

Abby pointed a finger to guide Lori's gaze in the correct direction.

'It's the narrowing between Kings How and Castle Crag, eroded by ice over thousands of years,' explained Clarissa.

'Wow,' breathed Lori.

Rebecca had her palm pressed against the front passenger window in wonder.

They reached Honister Pass, right in the heart of the Lake District, and Lori gasped at the single-track road that wove along the mountainside.

'We're super high up now!' she cried as they wiggled and climbed.

Abby was transfixed by the dramatic panorama – every way she looked, the views were spectacular. Vast glacier-carved valleys and steep unspoilt slopes that were virtually devoid of any signs of change for centuries. Although she'd seen the lakes and hills in this part of the county before, the sheer majesty of her surroundings almost moved her to tears. *Why don't I come here more often?*

'This is *unreal*!' murmured Lori as she marvelled at the magnificent countryside stretching out in all directions. 'You guys are *so* lucky!'

They started to descend again, the steep pass lined by enormous boulders bigger than the car.

'Deposited by the glaciers,' explained Clarissa as the group marvelled at their impressive size. 'Gatesgarth beck,' she said, jabbing a finger at the stream snaking alongside them. The river gushed over rounded rocks, the clear water turning into cappuccino-top froth. Abby saw a waterfall tumbling out from the mist-hidden tips of the mountains.

Rebecca clutched the car door as they caught their first glimpse of Buttermere, far below them on the left-hand side, followed by Crummockwater beyond it in the distance.

'Almost there,' announced Clarissa.

Lori beat an excited drumroll on the tops of her thighs.

Abby reached over to squeeze Rebecca's shoulder, and she turned back to give her a grateful smile.

They parked in the picturesque hamlet of Buttermere and clambered out, eager to stretch their legs after the journey.

'Let me get this straight,' said Lori, hands on her hips. 'The village and the lake have the exact same name?' she asked.

Clarissa nodded. 'They do indeed.'

'Isn't that really confusing?' said Lori with a frown.

But their leader was already unloading swimming gear from the back of the Defender.

'It is a little,' agreed Abby, her reply muffled by the wetsuit Clarissa thrust into her arms. She glanced at Rebecca. 'Are you all right?' she asked.

'Just feel a bit far out of my comfort zone,' she said in a small voice. 'Maybe being further away from home, I don't know . . .' Her skin was pale, fear had stolen the colour from her cheeks.

Lori wrapped an arm around her. 'Don't worry, doll, we gotcha!'

'There's no pressure,' said Clarissa. 'If you want to just sit by the water, that's fine. Take it at your own pace. *Acclimatise*.'

'Okay.' Rebecca nodded. 'Thank you.' She hitched her bag onto her shoulder. 'I'll take my stuff, in case . . .'

'That's the spirit.' Clarissa gave a nod, and started to lead them down the track beside the white walls of the Fish Inn.

Abby walked alongside Lori and Rebecca in her wake. 'We're actually going to see the view in your painting!' she said, turning to face Lori, hoping a change of chat would help ease Rebecca's mind.

'I can't believe it!' Lori squealed. 'Seeing it in real life – ohmigod, it's a dream come true!' She strode out in front of the other two, excitement propelling her onwards.

Rebecca's gaze was on the rain-glazed pebbles that made up the path.

They forked right, and moments later caught sight of Crummockwater, glistening like it was made of liquid white-gold.

Lori stopped dead in the centre of the footpath. She stared at the lush green banks where the land met the lake, then her eyes roved over the undulating wavelets of the breeze-teased water.

Abby arrived beside her, blinking at the scene laid out before them, too.

Then Rebecca came to stand in the middle, and linked arms with them both.

All three of them were silent for a second, but Lori's thoughts were as loud and clear as though they were painted in the cloud-canvased sky.

'It's not it . . .' she whispered, her shoulders sinking.

Abby bit her lip, at a loss for words.

'Sorry . . .' Rebecca murmured, though it wasn't in any way her fault.

'Don't panic!' called Clarissa from further up the track, without even turning round. 'You're looking from the wrong end of the telescope!' she shouted back to them.

The three of them hurried after her to catch up.

'Sometimes you're in the right place, just looking at things from the wrong perspective,' she said.

The sentence seemed to roll around Abby's head on repeat.

'I was on the point of giving up there for a second . . .' Lori said. 'Not that I doubted you, C!' she added, the smile back on her face.

'I know the precise location you're looking for,' said Clarissa, leading them onwards. 'It's this way!'

They followed her, single file, along the stony path, past semi-submerged rocks that looked like lurking crocodiles, and then down to the lakeshore.

'Here,' declared Clarissa, turning to take in the view behind them, back in the direction from which they'd come.

The others did the same.

'Well, that sure is it!' cried Lori, flinging her arms in the air. 'Isn't it something!'

Clarissa pointed at the three hills that flanked the gleaming surface of Crummockwater; the same ones that made up the painting Lori's grandfather had treasured. 'Rannerdale Knott, High Stile and Red Pike,' she said, sweeping her hand from left to right.

Abby stared at the smooth slopes in the foreground, and then her gaze was drawn to the craggy rocks higher up, hidden in the shadows. *Hills are just like people*, she thought to herself. *They have gentle sides and darker, more difficult, edges.*

'You can go home happy now you've seen that!' Rebecca said, looking at Lori.

Abby noticed Lori's face fall as though she'd stepped into a patch of shade.

'Yup!' Lori replied with a flicker of a smile that didn't quite reach her eyes. She looked back towards the mountains.

'Do you want me to take your picture?' Abby asked. She'd watched Lori capture their other adventures on her camera, and was surprised she wasn't snapping away already.

'Great idea!' said Lori, a grin back on her face. She beckoned Abby to get in the shot with her. 'Hey, get over here, you guys!' she shouted to Rebecca, despite her being only a couple of metres away, and Clarissa, who'd already set off walking again. 'Come join us, C!' Lori called after their instructor.

Clarissa looked startled, as though she wasn't used to being the focus of a photo; maybe she was so at one with nature she saw herself as part of the landscape itself, thought Abby.

Lori held up her phone and the others huddled round her, the mountains making a movie-style backdrop behind them. '*Wildwater Women!*' she cried and they chorused back like an echo in a cave.

But when they sprang apart again, Abby couldn't help but notice the dampness in Lori's eyes, and the way she kept looking towards the fells as though they'd seen so much of life they were sure to understand whatever was whirling around in her head.

'Shall we carry on to the swimming spot, now you've got your souvenir?' said Clarissa, not waiting for an answer before she set off at a stride.

They headed towards a small promontory that stretched out into the lake.

Abby walked along the slim strip of land and looked back at the view once again – it was even more mesmerising from that standpoint, a little way out in the water. She almost felt as though she were *floating* above the lake.

Rebecca, however, seemed to stiffen once their attention was back on the swim rather than their spectacular surroundings. Her forehead currently resembled the wrinkles of Red Pike, realised Abby as she came to stand beside her. 'Are you okay?' she asked.

Rebecca met her gaze. 'Seem to have lost my confidence since the swim on Wednesday for some reason . . .'

'Probably didn't help having your, er, friend there distracting you,' replied Abby.

'*Ugh.* Guy. He's not my friend.' Rebecca sighed. 'Everything's so *easy* for him.' She rammed her hands in her pockets as though in protest. 'He doesn't get that not everyone is in the same boat.'

'Yeah, he might've been more understanding if he'd been in the freezing water with us, rather than that canoe,' replied Abby wryly.

'Exactly!' Rebeca laughed.

They both looked up as they heard a splashing sound: Clarissa was already lolling in the water like it was the world's largest bath.

Lori was lingering in the shallows, limbs rigid with cold.

'Go ahead,' Rebecca said to Abby with a jerk of her head. 'Join the others.'

'Are you coming in?' Abby replied.

Rebecca nodded with all the enthusiasm of someone agreeing to endure their worst nightmare.

'You don't have to do anything you don't want to do.' Abby shook her head sympathetically.

'I *do* want to . . .' Rebecca scraped her hair into a topknot, as though she were preparing for battle.

Abby thought she heard her mutter a 'but', though when nothing more followed, she didn't know whether the word had been whisked away by the wind or if Rebecca had decided to bury the rest of the sentence deep down inside her like a secret sent to the lakebed.

She wriggled into her wetsuit, while Rebecca slowly took off her coat and clung to it like a house guest who didn't want to stay.

Both their heads snapped up again when they heard Lori shriek as the icy water embraced her.

A flash of adrenaline-fuelled anticipation surged through Abby's body as she moved towards the shoreline. She looked at the scenery surrounding her and could hardly believe it was real; she felt as though she'd stepped inside Lori's painting. The landscape was a living 3D masterpiece that she could see *whenever* she liked. There were no gallery ropes or visiting restrictions. The world was right *here* for her to experience.

She waded out further and Crummockwater enveloped her in a womb of cold, fresh water. When she was submerged up to her shoulders, she lay back for a moment to steady her breathing, to appreciate being still and entirely suspended in nature. The clouds above her were an artist's palette of blended greys and smudged streaks of white, as if the sky had been painted by an old master with careful brush-strokes.

Abby turned onto her stomach and began to swim, feeling a faint ache in her arms from exercising earlier in the week. It was as though her muscles were reminding her what she was capable of, her body telling her how powerful it could be. *I'm a wild swimmer!* she thought to herself. This was only the third time she'd been out with Clarissa and the others and, already, the act of immersing herself in the water was becoming second nature. The ritual felt not so much like a new habit, but a reawakening of something that had just been waiting. Three swims in and it was a part of her life – and of the person she now was – that she didn't want to relinquish. All the elements: walking to the lakeshore; the gradual process of getting into the water; taking control of her breathing; and being more mindful than ever of her environment – each aspect was restoring her, even re-forming her, into the Abby she so wanted to be.

The countryside was healing her, but it was like medicine: one dose wasn't enough on its own, you had to stay the course.

She pushed forward, feeling the friction, forcing her way through the water even though it resisted her movement, like it was testing her, asking whether she had the strength to be an open-water swimmer.

I know I do, thought Abby. She looked over at the dappled hills where the light kept trying to break through the blurred skies above. She glanced at the water all around her; it appeared almost black each time the clouds covered the sun, but turned clear again when bright rays managed to burst through once more.

The lake's cool touch pushed all other thoughts of the world beyond this remarkable place out of her brain. As the water supported her, making her feel weightless, she felt the strain of her responsibilities lift too. Her everyday stresses seemed to be washed away, and she knew that when she stepped out of the water, cleansed and invigorated, she'd feel stronger than ever.

Abby looked over her shoulder to shout encouragement to Rebecca – but she was still on the bank.

Abby squinted.

Rebecca was wearing a strange expression; her cheeks puffing in and out like she was practising Clarissa's breathing techniques all wrong. Was she in distress or just plucking up the courage to join the rest of them? Abby parted her lips to call over to her, but the wind swept a wavelet of water inside her mouth instead. She coughed and spluttered, trying to keep her attention on Rebecca.

Then she saw Rebecca clutch her chest; her face had turned berry-red and her breathing appeared ragged.

Abby tried to stand up, but she was out of her depth. She splashed her arms and legs but it was like moving in a dream – the breeze seemed to be dragging her backwards.

She saw Clarissa shoot out of the water, one step ahead of the rest of them at all times – *thank goodness.*

Abby stumbled through the shallows, concern squeezing her insides, but she stayed well back, giving Rebecca space, letting Clarissa calm her with soothing instructions.

Lori sloshed her way out of the lake too and came to stand beside Abby. 'She looks like she's gonna upchuck,' she murmured, her eyes lake-dark with worry.

Abby bit her lip.

'Breathe in slowly, through your nose, then out gently, through your mouth,' she heard Clarissa say.

'I should have stayed with her, on the shore,' Abby muttered. 'I knew she was nervous.'

'Hey, hey, you couldn't have known this would happen,' said Lori. 'None of us did. Not even Rebecca.'

Abby started to shiver as the wind whispered against her exposed skin.

'Let's get changed,' said Lori, steering her towards where they'd left their things.

Abby focused on getting dressed; she wanted to let Rebecca recover in her own time. Then, when she was fully clothed again, she scrunched over the pebbles to see how she was doing.

Her head was bowed, and her hands were wrapped round her knees as she huddled on the ground, body curled like a hibernating hedgehog.

Clarissa was dispensing steaming soup from her enormous flask. 'Here you are,' she said to Rebecca, who lifted her head and took the cup she was being offered.

'Thank you,' she mumbled.

'Are you all right?' Abby asked, crouching down beside her.

Rebecca gave a small nod like she didn't possess the energy to move any more than that.

'Lunch. Lentil and vegetable soup,' announced Clarissa, passing a metal mug to Abby too.

Abby took the cup, brim-full of vibrant autumn vegetables and wholesome pulses, and she could virtually *taste* the goodness it contained before she'd put it to her lips.

'Lori, some for you as well,' Clarissa said, before serving herself last of all.

They sat in a protective semi-circle round Rebecca; a curve of care, like a human harbour.

'I thought I'd managed to stop having them . . .' murmured Rebecca, almost as though she was talking to herself. 'The panic attacks.' She gave a dismayed sigh. 'It's been a little while since my last one . . .' She looked up at the others.

'They can come out of nowhere, can't they?' said Abby, no stranger to an anxiety attack in the silent small hours when all was still except her racing mind and pounding heart.

'Gee, we've all been there, honey,' said Lori, nudging Rebecca's arm affectionately. 'Everyone who's anyone has 'em in New York,' she added with a smile.

Rebecca stared into her soup. 'Thank you, all,' she said, 'for looking after me.'

'It's what friends are for, isn't it?' replied Abby with a smile.

'Sure is!' said Lori. 'Hey, you guys have helped me *heaps* while I've been here, so don't mention it! I'dda been lost without you. *Literally.*'

The others laughed.

'You've all been there for me too,' said Abby. 'I honestly think joining the Wildwater Women has saved me in some ways,' she added, shocking herself when the sentence tumbled out from her mouth. But she realised it was true. She took a sip of her soup, and its nourishing warmth was like a hug for her soul.

'Why d'ya do it, C?' asked Lori, direct as usual.

Clarissa glanced up, the question seeming to take her by surprise. She stopped rifling in her rucksack to contemplate her answer. 'Because everyone needs a little assistance at some point,' she said.

'Even you?' said Lori.

'*Especially* me,' replied Clarissa. 'I could easily have had a not-so-charmed existence, if things had been different . . .'

Lori tilted her head like she was trying to figure out a crossword clue.

'But I was shown kindness I couldn't possibly repay,' Clarissa carried on. 'So, I decided to help others instead, give them a hand when they needed it most, in the small way I could,' Clarissa concluded.

'What you do is amazing,' said Abby with a nod.

'It's only taking people swimming,' said Clarissa. 'Introducing them to the outdoors, the benefits of being in nature. Simple stuff.'

'Oh, not at all,' said Lori. 'You've changed our lives!'

Clarissa twisted round to tend to the camping stove Abby noticed she'd set up behind her, as though ducking away from the praise. She clearly didn't do what she did for that purpose; it was something deeper. A desire to give back.

Lori must've realised Clarissa wasn't going to be pressed any more on the subject, as she turned her attention back to her soup, slurping the last of it appreciatively.

'How are you feeling now, Rebecca?' asked Abby, putting her empty cup down amongst the stones.

'Much better, thanks,' she replied, licking her lips. 'I think it's that soup. It was *yum*.'

Laughter rippled through the group.

'Glad you enjoyed it,' said Clarissa, turning back round with a ring-shaped pan in her gloved hand.

The homely smell of baked dough reached Abby on the breeze. *Surely not . . . is that even possible?*

Abby watched with sheer delight as Clarissa lifted the lid off the tin, and then removed a freshly made loaf from inside.

How on earth has she made that here on the shore of Crummockwater?

'Holy smoke!' said Lori. 'You're superwoman, C!'

Rebecca's cheeks had a rosy bloom again, and a big grin spread across her face at the sight of the golden-domed top of the crusty white bread.

'It's just a basic recipe, but it should keep you all toasty warm for a little longer,' said Clarissa as she turned it out of the tin to cool a bit.

Abby couldn't believe her eyes. What could be better than sharing food with friends in fabulous surroundings? Her insides were finally starting to thaw out after her dip, and a post-swim buzz of energy was fizzing through her body.

She bit into her hunk of bread, squidgy and hot, before slathering the rest of it in Clarissa's homemade damson jam, which was both sweet and tart on her tongue.

'Jeez, this is sooo good,' said Lori, closing her eyes.

Clarissa busied herself with tidying away the cooking equipment; the loaf had been devoured in far less time than it had taken to bake. 'Oh, it was only a quick something to take the chill off . . .' she said.

'Fancy coming back to New York with me?' quipped Lori.

Clarissa chortled heartily.

Abby couldn't imagine her in a manmade metropolis, surrounded by urban office blocks in place of mountains and a grid system of straight lines instead of nature's curves.

'Oh, it's a marvellous city but I'm quite content here, thank you.'

So, she's been! realised Abby, chastising herself for making assumptions. Just because Clarissa had decided to make Cumbria her forever home, it didn't mean she'd never left the county! Abby wondered what had caused her to cross the Atlantic, whether she'd been on a city break or a work trip . . . *One day I'll see the skyscrapers and the yellow taxis and all those screens in Times Square for myself,* she decided. *Show Rowan the world.*

'What am I gonna do without you, C?' Lori pouted, before popping the last piece of her chunk of bread in her mouth. 'I wanna take you all with me!' she said, glancing round the group.

I'm going to miss Lori when she goes back home, thought Abby. Her infectious zest for life and constant positivity had pulled Abby from her fug that first day they'd met on the front step of her house and refused to let her slip back into it; she'd shown her the Wildwater Women leaflet, and been so full of enthusiasm it had been impossible to forget about it. She had a boundless friendliness that was rare to find.

'How much longer do we have you for?' asked Rebecca, looking at Lori.

Lori took her time chewing. 'Um, I haven't actually booked my flight yet but, er, I gotta be back for October sixth . . .' She swallowed. 'My daughter's birthday.'

To Abby's surprise, she didn't say it with a grin; she'd seen how close Lori and Ashanti were, knew how often they spoke on FaceTime. She was starting to feel Lori was getting closer to sharing what was keeping her here, the real reason why she was reluctant to return, beyond the lakes and cakes, of course. 'Are you staying till then?' Abby asked.

Lori brushed crumbs from her lap. 'Might as well!' she said, looking up from the ground like she'd just found her smile amongst the stones. 'Gotta make the most of it, right? And there's plenty of planes, they're really regular from Manchester . . .'

Abby nodded, though she didn't know.

Clarissa stood up. 'Shall we make a move?' she said, scanning the shore to check they'd left no trace of their presence behind.

Abby took a last, lengthy look at the rolling fells and the shimmering lake. The shifting colours of the sky were reflected in Crummockwater's surface, turning it a kaleidoscope of shades.

Lori scrunched her way to the edge of the bank, picked up a smooth, flat pebble and crouched low to toss it across the top of the water – but it just sank from sight, consumed by concentric circles of blackness.

'*Hmph!*' Her shoulders drooped.

'It's a bit choppy,' said Abby, wrinkling her nose. 'Not ideal conditions.'

But Lori bent down and tried again, a lull in the breeze meaning the second pebble bounced beautifully three times before disappearing into the darkness. 'Woohoo!' she shrieked, leaping into the air herself.

Abby clapped and Rebecca cheered. Clarissa clipped her rucksack straps in place.

'You guys skip stones, too, right?' Lori asked, a little out of breath.

Rebecca shook her head. 'Nope,' she said feigning ignorance and catching Abby's eye.

Abby shook her head, cottoning on. She looked mock clueless for a moment as well. 'We *skim* stones,' she said, before breaking into a grin.

'Oh, *whatever!*' shrieked Lori, swatting the air and then bursting into laughter.

Then the three of them sped after Clarissa, who was already a fleecy speck in the distance.

171

13

'*Ohmigod!*' Lori put her hand to her forehead, miming a swoon. 'We can't walk past this,' she said, wafting her arm at the sandwich board standing outside the farm in the centre of Buttermere village.

Abby looked at the sign: Luxury Lake District ice cream. *Gosh, it does sound good.*

'It's on me, guys!' said Lori, already strolling into the yard. 'What're y'all having?'

Abby followed her. 'I'll get this . . .'

'Nope! I want at least three flavours,' said Lori, looking at the mouth-watering mounds on show in the display cabinet.

Abby gazed at the selection: one tub had shards of honeycomb sticking out from the top, others were drizzled with glistening sauces.

'Cherry ripple . . . lemon curd,' Rebecca read out, reaching the others beside the shop front.

'Good job you warmed up first,' said Clarissa, hands grasping the straps of her backpack like an astronaut braced for take-off.

'Come on, C. Whatcha want?' asked Lori, with a jerk of her head.

'Er, okay, I'll have a thunder and lightning then, please,' replied Clarissa, looking around as though she'd lost her rocket.

'What?' said Lori peering at the options.

'Cinder toffee and chocolate,' explained Abby.

'Oo, good choice,' said Rebecca, plumping for the same.

'I'll have the lemon, please,' said Abby. *When life gives you lemons . . . eat luxury lemon ice cream*, she thought to herself.

'I'll have 'em both, and a scoop of mint chocolate, too,' said Lori.

Abby had always wondered who ordered that, now she had her answer: *someone like Lori*, she thought with a smile.

Abby felt like she was Rowan's age once again as she reached for her ice cream-crammed cornet.

'What the hell, I'm on vacation!' Lori said as she licked her towering triple-cone.

Even Clarissa looked like a child with a treat as she bit into a splinter of cinder toffee.

Then a male voice shouted, '*Boo!*' from behind them.

Everyone jumped – but Rebecca gave an almighty screech and dropped her ice cream.

Abby turned round to see Guy standing there, his mischievous smile melting into a shamefaced expression as he saw the upside-down cone on the ground. 'Oops,' he said with a grimace, staring at the messy splodge beside Rebecca's feet. 'I'll get you another . . .' he murmured, taking a step towards the counter.

Rebecca shook her head. 'I don't want one.' She panted like her pulse was thumping.

'What would you like, then?' Guy asked, getting his wallet out of his pocket and clutching it like an olive branch.

'You to leave us alone, it's my day off,' said Rebecca, pulling her gloves on like she was piecing back together a protective suit of armour.

'I'm sorry . . .' Guy bowed his head. 'I didn't think—'

'No – you never do, Guy. That's the problem,' said Rebecca.

The other Wildwater Women hung back, but Rebecca's voice was loud enough for them to hear, raised with a mixture of rage and resentment.

Abby tried to strike up a conversation with Lori and Clarissa, but her brain couldn't seem to come up with a topic to talk about whilst the argument was unfolding in front of them all. Clarissa was tactfully readjusting the buckles on her rucksack, whereas Lori was watching the action take place out of the corner of her eye.

Abby glanced over at Rebecca and Guy when she realised they'd both fallen silent, unable to help herself.

Guy put his money away.

Rebecca fixed him with a glare colder than the softening splatter of ice cream that lay between them. 'What are you even doing here, Guy?' she demanded, crossing her arms.

Guy swallowed, seeming to sense her anger was growing rather than dissipating. 'What do you mean?' he mumbled. 'In Buttermere, or specifically this—?'

'Why can't I spend my spare time in peace?' Rebecca cut in before he could answer. 'I *have* to be around you at work, but I don't at the weekend.'

Guy flinched. He looked as though he'd been whacked in the stomach with his kayak paddle, thought Abby. 'Ouch,' he whispered, as though Rebecca's words had inflicted more hurt.

But Rebecca carried on, like she was being swept along by a roiling undercurrent too powerful to control.

'You were there at Coniston on Wednesday, and now I can't even get an ice cream without you popping up to ruin it.' She was breathless with fury. 'What are you playing at?'

Guy put his palms up. 'I honestly didn't mean to upset you,' he said, his voice meek. 'I was just trying to lighten the tone after last time . . . but it's obviously backfired massively.'

Rebecca glowered at him.

Guy began fumbling around in his dry bag for something, with the urgency of a criminal scrabbling about for an alibi. 'I was just here kayaking, that's all,' – he held out a licence as evidence, as though he knew her opinion of him was so low, she wouldn't believe anything he said – 'I really didn't intend to spoil your Sunday,' he said, his shoulders sinking. He shoved the permit back in his bag. 'I'm sorry, again,' he said, before turning and starting to walk away.

Abby heard a shout from the road: a man calling from the wound-down window of a vehicle with two kayaks fastened on its roof-rack. 'Where are the coffees?' he yelled to Guy, who didn't answer him, just went straight round to the passenger side.

There was the sound of a car door being slammed closed, followed by the rev of an engine, and then Guy and his friend disappeared up the hill out of sight.

Rebecca spun round to face the others, gasping like she'd been jogging.

'Got it all out?' asked Clarissa.

'No!' said Rebecca, tears starting to spill down her face. 'He has no idea what I've been through! Everything's just a big joke to him!' She gulped; her cheeks puce. 'Who does he

175

think he is, acting like he even *owns* the *outdoors*, flashing his kayaking pass . . .'

'I expect he was trying to prove he wasn't here *purely* to annoy you,' said Clarissa.

Rebecca let out an enormous sigh, the wind leaving her sails.

'He wasn't aware of the context, remember,' added Clarissa in a level voice. 'That you were already shaken up. I don't think he would have scared you if he'd known.'

Rebecca's mouth stayed clamped shut as she contemplated what Clarissa was saying.

'He's not a cruel person, I can assure you.'

Rebecca unfolded her arms, as though she was lowering her shield now that Guy had gone.

Clarissa began to lead them back to the car.

The others followed behind, Abby and Lori walking either side of Rebecca, sandwiching her in support.

'You wanna talk about it, hon?' asked Lori when Rebecca remained silent, her lips set in a straight line.

'I just wish I could get over it and move on,' Rebecca mumbled in reply.

'Oh, gee, did you guys date?' asked Lori, her forehead crumpled.

Rebecca raised her eyebrows in horror. '*What?* Me and *Guy?* God, no! What gave you that impression?'

'You just said—' started Lori.

'I was talking about my accident!' said Rebecca.

'Huh?' Lori stopped still in the lane. 'What accident?' She looked at Abby. 'Did we know about this?' She frowned.

Abby shook her head. 'No, I don't think so . . .' she said. She thought she heard Lori mutter 'Thank god' under her breath, though she had no idea why. 'We're here for you if you want to tell us,' she said, glancing at Rebecca. 'But don't feel you have to.'

They started walking again, conscious that Clarissa was already standing by the car.

'I . . .' began Rebecca, but then she seemed to become lost in her thoughts, and Abby suspected she might be reliving the past in her mind.

'You have some kinda trauma?' asked Lori. 'Is that why you're scared of the water?'

Abby's stomach squeezed in compassion. She herself had found it daunting enough joining the wild swimming group in the beginning, without having to try and overcome a fear of the lake as well.

'Yes,' said Rebecca, looking up at them both, eyes shining.

Neither Abby nor Lori spoke for a second, giving her the chance to continue if she wanted to.

Rebecca marched on down the narrow road, as though to remind herself she was pushing forward in life.

They'd almost caught up with Clarissa, who'd already loaded her rucksack into the back of the Defender and was leaning against it, waiting for them.

'When I was a child . . .' started Rebecca, 'we went to Swan Bridge.'

Abby nodded; she knew it well. A small village right next to the River Leven, just below the southernmost tip of Windermere. Boats could moor up at one of the little jetties that lined the riverbank, for a bite to eat or a pint at the pub which overlooked the water. It was a popular destination for holidaymakers and locals alike. A memory of Ben, sitting on a white wrought-iron seat, his face tilted towards the sun, beer in hand, swam into her head, then evaporated as she opened her mouth to speak. 'There's a marina, isn't there?' she said.

'Yes, there is. That's where it happened.' Rebecca looked at Clarissa as they came to stand in front of her. 'You know this tale already,' she said, in a low tone that signalled what she was talking about.

'Some of it.' Clarissa gave a nod. 'I'm glad you're sharing with the others; I think it always helps.'

Lori plonked her bag down next to the Defender without taking her gaze off Rebecca.

Rebecca sat down on the rear door ledge, as though she couldn't rely on her legs to work while she recounted the incident. 'We were on a day out – me, my brother, and my mum and dad – with some family friends.' She squinted up at the others, who were listening intently. 'They had a boat – not a big one, but it had sails and a bit to sleep in downstairs – and one summer, they invited us on it with them.' She swallowed. 'I was six years old at the time. It was a really hot day, and I remember being so excited.' She gave a wistful smile. 'I was wearing my favourite camouflage T-shirt and these khaki shorts . . .' She laughed. 'I was a proper tomboy back then.'

I had Rebecca all wrong, Abby thought to herself.

Rebecca paused for a moment; her arms braced against the floor of the four-by-four as though she was steeling herself to say any more.

'Oh, gee, I can't take this,' said Lori, pressing her palms to her cheeks.

Abby put a hand to her lips in anticipation of the next part of the story.

'My mum was putting sun cream on my brother, and my dad had gone downstairs to have a tour of the inside. So while my parents weren't looking, I took my life jacket off.'

'Oh my god,' whispered Abby.

'*Why?*' squealed Lori.

Rebecca shrugged. 'I was a kid.' She sighed. 'I didn't like having it on in the heat, it was strapped so tightly round me. I probably thought it was restricting my adventures as well. I remember my parents explaining I had to wear it, but I thought I was invincible, like an action figure or a cartoon character.' She shook her head. 'Anyway, I tried to jump the space between our boat and the one alongside it when no one was looking,' – she sucked in a deep breath – 'but I fell down into the gap and slipped under the water . . . It was so cold and dark and *silent* . . .' She wiped her sleeve across her eyes, as though trying to rid her brain of a vivid flashback.

Clarissa put a steadying hand on her shoulder. 'You're all right,' she said softly.

'Thank god you're okay,' said Abby, her insides churning as, for a horrifying split-second, she imagined how she'd feel if it were Rowan who'd gone overboard.

'How did you get out?' murmured Lori.

'My brother saw the life jacket I'd been wearing . . . a bright-orange one . . . on the deck of the boat.' Rebecca's voice had become a rasp.

Clarissa passed her a bottle of water.

She took a sip before she continued to speak. 'I don't remember the details. Just the feeling of nothingness – nothing to grab, nothing to stand on. Just the black of the water or the white walls of the boat rising out – even when I got my head above water I thought I was going to get crushed. And I couldn't shout. I couldn't make a sound.

I think I'd given up but my mum and dad managed to drag me out somehow . . .'

'Jesus, you couldda *died*!' exclaimed Lori.

Abby flinched, but it was clearly a fact.

'Yes.' Rebecca nodded. 'I very nearly drowned.'

'God, your parents musta been real scared . . .' Lori had her fingers cupped over her mouth. 'And *you* – Jeez, I can't imagine . . .'

'I don't know how long I was under for, but the panic – and the powerlessness – I felt . . . I'll never forget it.'

'But you *will* get over it,' said Clarissa. 'The memories will have less of an effect on you over time.'

Rebecca lifted her head. She gave a small smile, of relief at having unburdened herself to her Wildwater Women friends, suspected Abby. 'So, that's why I'm afraid of the water . . . and why I'm being so *pathetic* when it comes to swimming in the lake.'

'Hey!' reprimanded Lori. 'That's not true at all! You've done *so* good! You should be real proud, doll.'

Abby nodded. 'I totally agree.'

Rebecca gave a little laugh. 'You're all very kind.'

'We mean it!' said Abby, eyes wide. 'I think you're an inspiration,' she added. 'You're tackling a phobia, head on. That takes *guts*.'

'Sure does,' said Lori.

'Thank you,' replied Rebecca. 'Maybe I should have said sooner . . . but I didn't really know how. You guys seemed so confident. Walking straight in.' She pursed her lips. 'I was just trying to get on with it, I suppose.'

'Of course,' said Abby. 'I understand.'

'You've done enormously well so far,' said Clarissa. 'Look how much progress you've already made.'

'Still a long way to go,' replied Rebecca. 'I haven't even properly swum yet.'

'The lakes have been here for thousands of years,' said Clarissa. 'They aren't going anywhere.'

Lori gave a sigh, as though lamenting the fact that *she* was. In a few short weeks she'd be gone, realised Abby.

'We, on the other hand, need to get a move on!' announced Clarissa. 'There's still a lot to see on the way home!'

They clambered back into the Land Rover and started to climb the hill out of Buttermere, in a different direction to the one from which they'd come.

'This is the Newlands Pass,' declared Clarissa as they crawled up the steep incline.

'It's *beautiful!*' said Abby.

'And just a little terrifying,' said Lori, clasping the door frame as she marvelled at the twisting track they were taking along the side of the bracken-swathed mountain. 'I feel like I'm on a roller coaster,' she said with a laugh. Then she jerked her head towards Abby's window on the opposite side of the car. 'That's the log-flume ride, right?' she joked as they passed a white-foamed waterfall, cascading down the fellside like a natural fountain.

'That's Moss Force,' explained Clarissa, keeping her eyes on the road as she spoke.

It was so narrow that navigating it must require a serious amount of concentration, thought Abby. Clarissa was constantly checking the traffic flow ahead, and occasionally nipping into one of the pull-in places to let another car squeeze past.

They started to drop downwards again, the Newlands Valley stretching out below them, as they made their way back towards Keswick.

'We're going to go through your namesake town shortly,' said Clarissa, turning to Rebecca, beside her in the passenger seat.

'There's a village called *Rebecca*?' she replied.

'No, *Braithwaite*, of course,' said Clarissa, in her Jeremy Paxman tone of disbelief.

The others all giggled.

'You've got Cat Bells coming up now . . .' said Clarissa.

'Pardon me?' said Lori, peering beyond the glass to try and spot anything remotely resembling a feline.

'On the right,' clarified Clarissa.

'The mountain,' whispered Abby.

'But this isn't like that other one we saw on the way here—'

'The Lion and the Lamb,' said Rebecca.

'Uh-huh, that's it – this doesn't look like a cat at all!' said Lori, shaking her head.

Everyone laughed.

'You can see Skiddaw straight ahead of you, too,' said Clarissa with a nod.

'What's this, now, huh?' asked Lori, craning to see over the head rest in front of her.

'That peak there,' said Abby, pointing out of the windscreen. Skiddaw's summit was shrouded in a halo of cloud, making it look especially atmospheric and impressive. She strained forward to gaze at it too; even though she knew what many of the fells were called, she was still fairly unfamiliar with their features. Their curves and contours were as distinctive as the shape of a face. It was interesting matching them up, like finally pairing a name she'd heard with a person.

'You been up there, C?' asked Lori, sitting back in her seat.

'I have indeed,' replied Clarissa.

Lori raised her eyebrows. 'You know everywhere, right?'

'I've lived here a long time,' replied Clarissa.

'Have you travelled?' asked Lori.

'A little.'

'Did you say you've been to New York?' asked Abby, remembering Clarissa mentioning it earlier. 'I'd *love* to go, one day!'

'Yes.' Clarissa smiled like she'd seen a fond memory in her mind's eye. 'That's a while ago now.'

'On vacation?' said Lori.

'Well, I did all the main sights when I was there, but it was a bit of a whistle-stop trip.'

'Oh, yeah?' said Lori. 'Part of a bigger overseas tour, huh?'

'No,' said Clarissa.

Lori and Abby shared a look as though daring each other to press for details. Clarissa was a conundrum they just couldn't crack.

'Came back to Cumbria straight afterwards. I'm hefted, like a Herdwick.'

'You're *what?*' said Lori.

'I know where I belong. Just like they do. Free to roam, but well aware of where's home. I've never felt the need to stray from the Lake District for very long.'

'It's a pretty awesome place, huh?' said Lori.

And as Abby glimpsed the top of Skiddaw, as the fog shifted high above them, and she saw the smooth outline of its spine, sloping like a slumbering goddess, she couldn't help but agree.

It was mid-afternoon when they arrived back in Ambleside, and Abby felt a sinking sensation inside her chest, like her heart was a skimming stone descending into the depths of the lake. After all the excitement of the day, she was loath to return to normality. She bit her lip as they drew up outside the row of cottages.

Rebecca twisted round in the front seat. 'Thanks for looking after me today, everyone.'

'I hope you're feeling better,' replied Abby, unclipping her safety belt.

Rebecca nodded. 'Much.'

Abby glanced at her watch as she reached for the door handle. She wasn't due to pick up Rowan for over an hour. 'You're all welcome to come in for a drink . . . if you want to . . . no worries if not . . . but the offer's there.'

'Sure!' said Lori, slinging her bag onto her shoulder.

Rebecca glanced at Clarissa. 'I had a lift here with you, so . . .'

'I've got another class soon,' said Clarissa. 'But I've time for a quick cup of tea.' There was that Herdwick-style smile again, small but unmistakeable.

Abby felt a rush of happiness. Maybe real life could include the Wildwater Women; they were becoming part of her world now, after all. She smiled as the others began to scramble out of the Land Rover after her, and as she unlocked the door to Little Garth, her sense of dread began to be replaced with a calm contentment.

'How is it Sunday night already?' asked Rebecca, sliding her empty cup onto the coffee table with a sigh. She flopped back against the sofa cushions. 'I don't want to go.'

'I bet your *friend* isn't looking forward to seeing *you* at work tomorrow,' Lori said, clenching her teeth.

'Oh, Guy'll be oblivious to anyone apart from himself,' said Rebecca.

Abby heard Clarissa cough, though it could have been a coincidence.

'I still can't believe you thought we'd been a couple!' Rebecca rolled her eyes at Lori.

'Aw, it's just you get real –' Lori flapped the fingers of both hands, '– what's the word . . .'

But Rebecca didn't give her chance to finish. '*No one* irritates me more than that man!'

Clarissa slapped her thighs, then stood up. 'Righto, I really must be going.'

Rebecca got to her feet, too. 'Sorry you've got to drop me off . . .' she said, glancing at Clarissa.

'No problem,' she replied. 'I've factored it in.' She smiled. 'I always make sure I take everything into account,' she added. Her voice was gentle, but the way she looked straight at Rebecca as she spoke, seemed to leave no doubt that her words had a double meaning. She didn't want Rebecca to make any hasty decisions when it came to Guy, realised Abby. Perhaps there was more to him than met the eye.

'Yes, I need to make a move as well,' said Abby, 'I've got to collect Rowan soon.'

Lori drank the last of her tea, then pushed herself out of her chair with a puff. 'Before we go, have we gotta plan for our next swim?' she asked, glancing round the group.

'Have you been to Blea Tarn yet?' asked Clarissa, starting to make her way towards the door.

'Nah-ah,' said Lori with a shake of her head.

'I haven't either, actually,' said Abby, feeling a bubble of excitement at the idea of venturing somewhere entirely new.

'Nor me,' said Rebecca. She chewed her lip, and Abby got the impression she was still mulling over Clarissa's advice about Guy.

Clarissa nodded. 'I can do Thursday evening or next Sunday,' she said, without the need to consult a diary.

'The weekend?' suggested Abby, keen to have something to look forward to after a stretch of shifts in the bakery.

'Sure!' said Lori.

'Maybe I'll work up to an actual swim this time,' said Rebecca.

'Plenty more opportunities to give it another go,' said Clarissa. 'It takes a lot of courage to overcome your fears.'

'Oh, yeah!' agreed Lori.

'You'll get there,' added Abby. 'There are bound to be stumbling blocks.'

Rebecca smiled at them all.

'We'll be with you every step – or splash – of the way,' said Abby, feeling a burst of joy when the others laughed.

14

It started to tip down as Abby was halfway through the park on Monday morning – not a gossamer mizzle, more like walking beneath a hotel shower on the rainfall setting. But not even the prospect of getting soaked on the way to work could seem to dampen her mood. *I'm a swimmer now; I'm used to getting wet.* After spending a wonderful Sunday with her Wildwater Women friends, she had then been reunited with Rowan who'd been fizzing like a shaken soft drink, she was so full of chatter about her weekend with Maria. Abby could see now that time apart could be good for her and Rowan. She'd got so used to trying to be both mum and dad to her daughter, that she hadn't acknowledged she needed to let other people in too. *I haven't felt this revitalised in a long time,* Abby thought as she shook her umbrella at the entrance to the Plum Pie Bakery, and took a last glimpse at the glittering droplets that decorated the ledges and gutters of Ambleside like strings of fairy lights before she stepped inside.

A glance at the clock on the wall told her she was ten minutes early, and she bounded into the kitchen at the back to wish Tom a good morning and tell him how much everyone had loved the lemon meringue pie on Friday night, and how she'd been all the way up to Buttermere yesterday and felt like she herself was on holiday . . . *I'm acting like Rowan*, she thought to herself, trying to temper her excitement.

But her smile disappeared as she realised there was no welcoming whirr of the ovens, no scent of dough baking or the familiar warmth of Tom's cheerful welcome.

What's going on?

She walked round the stainless-steel units the same way she looked for a lost object in the most improbable places; she knew he wasn't there, but she was still searching for him as though she could make him appear if she willed it enough.

Maybe he has today off? she wondered. But he hadn't said so. She felt itchy at the thought of a whole day at work without him, and the fact she did, made her more agitated. *What's wrong with me?* She turned to go back to the shop floor, forcing herself to get on with her tasks – and came face to face with Joy in the doorway.

'He's not coming in.' She fixed Abby with the kind of stare that made her feel as though Joy could see every thought swirling round her skull. 'Ever again,' she added, seeming to relish the way Abby's jaw gaped open in horror.

'What?' Abby clutched the doorjamb either side of her. '*Why?*'

'He doesn't work here anymore.'

Abby tried to speak but her brain was a scramble of questions all jostling to be asked at the same time.

'But *you* do work here.' Joy raised her eyebrows. 'So do you want to get on with your job?'

'Right,' muttered Abby, fumbling with her coat zip and then hanging it on the hook beside where Tom's used to be too. 'Has he . . . is he . . .?'

'He's left. That's all you need to know.'

Abby bowed her head as she tied on her apron, feeling helplessly constricted, like she was being fastened into a straitjacket for the next eight hours.

As she walked past Joy, her boss gave her a glare that dared her to step out of line and see if she didn't get the same treatment as Tom.

Abby scurried behind the counter to continue her everyday opening-up routine.

But the bakery felt like an unfamiliar place without Tom's presence, like a home in a power cut.

She looked at the display cabinet, at the racks that should be loaded with freshly made scones by now. The shop looked bereft, like a body without life.

She jumped as she looked up and saw Joy standing in front of the counter.

'We'll be selling sandwiches and a small selection of cakes and bakes for today,' she announced.

You mean I will be, thought Abby; Joy's role was to ensure every last bit of energy was wrung from her employees. 'Okay,' she replied, her voice coming out as a squeak, as though Joy had squeezed every last breath from her lungs too. 'And what'll happen then—?' she began.

'You concentrate on what I *pay* you to do, and leave the rest to me.'

Abby nodded.

Joy rubbed her hands together like a fly, before going to hover over by the leaflet stand to watch Abby work out of the corner of her eye.

Abby flipped the 'open' sign as soon as it was 9 a.m., and it was then that she saw it. The notice in the window, typed in bold, black ink.

'Baker Wanted', it read, more like a police poster than a job advert.

How was it that Joy could make the Plum Pie seem like a prison? thought Abby. She pitied the next person to take up Tom's position, as though they were a spider about to step into a Venus Flytrap. She sighed as she unwrapped chocolatey squares of tiffin and stacked them in the glass cabinet, picturing Tom stirring the syrupy mixture only a couple of days ago, and smiling back at her as he slipped her a spare digestive biscuit. He'd poured his heart into each and every confection he'd made, tweaking recipes to make them his own and gathering a cult following of customers who came from all over to purchase his scrumptious creations. The remains of what he'd baked last week now looked like sad remnants from another time, like the rubble ruins of a once-magnificent place.

The morning seemed to pass at an almost painful pace without the light relief of Tom's humour and the sense of camaraderie that came with sharing the working day with him.

By the time the bell rang at four o'clock and Rebecca walked in, Abby was desperate to see a friend. 'Hi!' she said, waving over the countertop.

Rebecca looked up, as though she'd been snapped out of a daydream. 'Hey!'

'How's your day?' asked Abby as Rebecca reached the till. She knew Joy was in her lair – the office above – but she kept an eye on the foot of the stairs that led up there, just in case she reappeared.

'Fine, thanks,' said Rebecca. 'Just needed a pick-me-up!' she said, scanning the shelves of the display cabinet. 'No Borrowdale tea bread today?'

Abby shook her head. 'I'm afraid not, sorry.'

Rebecca put a flame-red fingernail to her lips as she surveyed the other options.

'Rocky road?' Abby said.

'Sounds like my journey to being a wild swimmer!' joked Rebecca.

Abby laughed, then tried to stifle the sound; she stole a sideways glance at the bottom of the stairs, but there was no sign of her boss.

'I'll take a piece of that, go on then,' said Rebecca with a nod.

Abby chose the biggest chunk of cake with the tongs.

Rebecca blew out a breath.

'You sure you're all right?' asked Abby, handing over the paper bag.

Rebecca's shoulders drooped as she tapped the card reader to pay. 'Yeah, fine.'

Abby raised her eyebrows.

'It's just . . . there's a spa manager position at work . . .' said Rebecca, the words bursting out of her like a bubbling spring. 'It'd be a promotion, but I did beauty therapy at college so I've got the right background . . .' She gripped her bakery bag with both hands like it was a life buoy. 'It would be a step up, but I reckon I could do it . . .' She sighed. 'If only I could get over this *stupid* phobia . . .'

'Hey, hey,' said Abby in a soft voice.

'It sounds idiotic, but I can't even look at the pool without flinching, let alone claim I could tick their health-and-safety boxes. I'm such a fraud.'

'Clarissa wouldn't let you use these negative words so neither will I.' Abby shook her head. 'It's completely understandable that you're scared after what you've been through.'

She put her hands on her hips. 'But you've come such a long way already.'

Rebecca gave a small smile. 'Thank you,' she whispered.

'Just take it slowly. These things take time,' Abby said.

'I might ask if Clarissa can still do a session on Thursday,' Rebecca murmured, almost to herself. She looked up. 'If I could get my confidence up a bit before the weekend, I might actually be able to join in and *swim*!'

'Good idea,' said Abby, a yearning to be back in the water stirring inside her at the thought of being by the lake, with the fresh air in her hair and the cold kissing her skin. Waiting six more days till Sunday seemed like an age. She wanted to go too, but decided that perhaps Rebecca needed some one-on-one tuition with their instructor, in order to make some real headway. 'Have you seen Guy?' she asked, half out of curiosity, and half wanting to make sure Rebecca had recovered after their two recent run-ins.

'God!' replied Rebecca.

'Is that what you call him now?' Abby grinned.

Rebecca shuddered. 'Absolutely not.'

Abby giggled. 'So you've talked to him since—'

Rebecca shook her head. 'No. He left a note on my desk, though.'

Abby raised her eyebrows. 'Really?'

'Yep.' Rebecca pursed her lips.

'What did it say, then?' Abby tipped her head on one side.

Rebecca rolled her eyes. 'That he was sorry.' She gave a shrug. 'It did seem pretty genuine,' she admitted. She started to search around in her handbag, then pulled out a card which she thrust over the counter at Abby. 'Here.'

'Gosh.' She took it, noticing its corners were crumpled – she suspected from the number of times it had been read and then shoved back in Rebecca's bag. Abby glanced up at her friend; a crimson blush had crept into her cheeks. She turned her attention back to the card. On the front was an arresting picture of Crummockwater, with Rannerdale Knott reflected in its glassy surface. The sky was luminescent and the water so still it made Abby feel calm just looking at the image; maybe Guy had chosen it for Rebecca because it had that effect . . .

'It's very thoughtful of him,' said Abby, testing the water to gauge Rebecca's reaction. Rebecca must have been a little touched; she'd kept the notelet after all . . . 'I think it's a kind gesture,' Abby added as she handed the card back to Rebecca.

'You can read it,' whispered Rebecca, as though she wanted Abby's opinion on what was written inside.

Abby flipped the card open. Small, scrawled letters filled the page. She blinked in surprise; Guy had certainly had a lot to say.

But then she heard the creak of a wooden floorboard, and before she could take in any of the looping little words, she flung the notelet back at Rebecca, just as Joy appeared at the foot of the stairs. 'Better get back to work,' Abby muttered. 'See you on Sunday, if not before!' she said with a wave as Rebecca turned to leave the shop, tucking the letter back in her bag as she went.

Joy came right up to the counter. 'We've a *new* baker starting tomorrow,' she declared, looking Abby dead in the eye, as if to say, 'that's how quick and easy it is to replace people.'

Abby nodded.

'I'll need you in half an hour early, so you can help get them up to speed.'

Abby opened her mouth, but a vision of another notice in the window, with her job on it, prevented her.

That evening, her thumbs hung above her phone keypad as she deliberated whether to text Tom. Were they good enough friends for her to do that? she wondered. She'd never spoken to him outside of work, but she really wanted to know whether he was okay. She tapped out a message: You weren't in today before immediately backspacing. *That was obvious!* Why couldn't she think of anything sensible to say? She typed out: Are you all right? But then deleted it. *I'm sure he's just fine without me checking in,* she told herself. She was trying to construct a third and final text, when her phone began to buzz in her hand.

She glanced at the screen.

Tom.

'Hello?' she said, fiddling with the belt of her cardigan. They hadn't talked on the phone before. *But we chat every day at work! It isn't a big deal!*

'Hey, Abs,' said Tom, in a flat tone of voice she'd never heard him use before. He sighed, making a hissing sound like a hot air balloon inflating.

'What's happened?' she whispered back down the receiver, huddling into the sofa cushions as though hoping they might envelop her in a hug if she wished hard enough.

There was silence on the other end of the line, and for a moment she wondered if the call had been cut off. She frowned as she saw she had full signal. But then Tom cleared his throat.

'I'm sorry if today was awful,' he mumbled down the phone.

'What, because it's normally such a treat working for Joy?' joked Abby.

Tom chuckled.

Abby felt a warmth in her chest as his voice vibrated in her ear.

'I didn't want to make things extra hard for you, though.' Tom paused. 'So I apologise.'

'What have you got to be sorry for?' asked Abby.

'I feel like I've abandoned you to the dragon.'

Abby giggled. 'That's probably the only way to make working at the Plum Pie sound like a fairy tale.'

Tom laughed loudly.

'So, you left, then?' asked Abby. 'I thought Joy must have sacked you.'

'Charming.'

'No, not because of anything you'd done, but because she's the Most Horrible Boss of All Time.'

'Shall we call Guinness World Records?'

Abby's stomach ached from laughing.

Then she sensed Tom's tone turn serious. 'Joy did get rid of me.'

Abby bit her lip as she listened.

'But I gave her a reason.'

Abby sucked in a breath. *What's Tom done?*

'I didn't turn up for work . . .'

The number of times I've wanted to do the same. 'Why?'

'I just couldn't go in.'

'Are you okay?'

That hot air balloon hiss again.

'You don't have to tell me anything, Tom, but I'm here if you need anything,' said Abby. 'All you have to do is say.'

'Freddie's mum . . . Sophie . . .' Tom started.

Abby felt a twist of tension in her stomach. All trace of humour was gone from his tone. 'Is she all—'

'She's been having an affair.'

Abby slapped her hand over her mouth. 'No!'

'Yes.' Tom paused as though it was hard to push the words from his lips. 'With the PE teacher at school.'

'Oh my god, I'm so sorry.'

'So in answer to your question – she's fine.' He gave a grim laugh.

'What can I do to help?' asked Abby. 'I can look after Freddie if you need some time to yourselves to work it through.'

'She's left me, Abs.'

'Oh, Tom.' Her voice cracked, as though in sympathy with his heart.

'It's not been right for a while, if I'm honest.' He gave such a huge sigh the phone crackled in her ear. 'This weekend away was meant to be make-or-break.'

Abby was speechless. *What on earth can I say to take any of the pain away?*

'I can see why you couldn't deal with the Joy of work, as well.'

Tom picked up on her pun and laughed. 'Thanks for listening, Abs.'

'Hey, how many times have you been there for me over the last few years?'

She heard a short exhalation; she knew Tom was smiling down the phone.

'And I'm sorry for leaving you in the lurch today. It wasn't my intention . . .'

'I've survived.'

'Stronger than I am.'

'Don't be silly. So, what will you do now?'

196

'Look for a new job. It might be tricky without a reference, but I'll think of something. I needed to do it sooner rather than later, anyway. I wasn't happy there.'

Abby swallowed. It was a bleak prospect working in the bakery now Tom had gone.

'I don't want to leave you there with Joy,' said Tom, as though her thoughts had trickled down the telephone line. 'You should get out too, Abs.'

'I need the job, Tom. It's close to home and school. And I've Rowan to think about.'

'I know – but remember to think about you, too, okay?'

'Yes,' she said, her voice hoarse. And when she put down the phone at the end of their call, and went upstairs to bed, Tom's words just wouldn't stop whirring round her head.

15

Abby sat on the park bench watching Rowan scramble about in the playground, grateful for the opportunity to pause for a moment. The week had passed in a blur, with the new baker starting – who'd turned out to be her boss's niece, and just as easy to bond with as Joy – and Abby felt as though she hadn't stopped. She leaned against the wooden backrest of the seat, as though subconsciously needing a little support, and sighed appreciatively as she took the weight off her feet and soaked in the simple beauty of her surroundings. She looked up at the cloud-smattered sky, like a canvas daubed with different shades of monochrome, and watched the trees cheerlead her with their wind-waving branches. *Hopefully it'll stay fine for our trip to Blea Tarn tomorrow.* She was so looking forward to swimming again. She'd missed the thrill of the chill water surrounding her limbs, the buzz of endorphins afterwards that made her feel as though she could do *anything,* and the companionship of the other women.

As Abby walked home with Rowan skipping beside her, she realised she hadn't bumped into Lori at all over the last

198

week to ask if she wanted a lift tomorrow. *I should have offered sooner.* But it had completely slipped her mind. She was about to send a text, but she and Rowan had already rounded the corner into Church Street, and Silver Ghyll's front gate was visible, so she decided to call in on her neighbour instead.

Rowan reached up on tiptoes to ring the bell, whilst Abby ran through the route to Blea Tarn in her mind. *It's past Little Langdale, that's right. I remember.*

There was no answer; Lori was out, no doubt blazing through her list of must-do sights before she jetted off back home.

Abby glanced in through the dim glass of the living-room window: no light on.

'Lori's not there,' she said to Rowan, before taking her hand and leading her down the path towards home.

Abby was just closing the gate behind them, when the door opened. She looked up to see Lori standing there, wearing a scruffy pullover and a pair of glasses that framed her raisin-sized red eyes. If she'd been anywhere other than on the front step of Silver Ghyll, Abby wasn't certain she'd have recognised her.

Rowan half-hid behind her thigh, with all the tact of a four-year-old, clearly not sure the woman next door was the same one she'd met before.

'Is everything okay?' asked Abby, putting a reassuring hand on top of Rowan's hair.

'Yeah . . . sorry – I look a real mess,' replied Lori. 'You doing good?'

Abby nodded. 'Just wondered if you wanted taking tomorrow?'

Lori blinked, and her eyes became almost invisible. 'Er . . .'

'No probs if something's come up and you can't make it . . . just thought I'd offer as I'll be going anyway . . .'

'Um . . .'

'You can think about it. Give me a text in a bit . . .' Abby smiled, wondering whether to ask again if Lori was all right.

'Sure thing.'

Abby noticed her neighbour's shoulders slump.

'What is it that's meant to be happening tomorrow?' Lori said, resting her head against the hallway wall.

'Our trip to Blea Tarn,' said Abby. 'We arranged it for Sunday.'

Lori scrunched up her face like she'd been punched.

'I forget things all the time,' said Abby, batting the late-afternoon air with her fingers.

'I should have written it down,' said Lori. She gave a sigh.

'Oh, I'm the same,' said Abby with a smile. 'Forever scribbling things on the back of my hand.'

'What for?' murmured Lori.

'To remind myself about stuff. Maybe it's a British thing . . .' said Abby, trailing off as she took in the frown on her friend's forehead.

'No, I mean why are we going to this tarn place?'

Abby bit her lip. 'To go wild swimming,' she said. 'Are you sure everything's okay?'

When Abby opened the door to Lori on Sunday morning, her spectacles were gone and her hair was swept up into a swim-ready bun. Anyone who hadn't seen her in the state she was in the previous day wouldn't suspect a thing: she looked just as she always did. *Let's keep it that way for now*, said the bright smile Lori had spread on like lipstick. She was sporting a brave face in the same way people wore

200

makeup. But yesterday afternoon she'd let Abby in, and revealed the truth she'd kept buried inside so far . . .

Abby smiled back, then saw Rebecca's little red car pull up behind Lori's shoulder, right on time, too.

'Morning!' said Rebecca, slamming the driver's side door as she got out. 'Thanks for taking us today, Abby!' she added, coming to stand on the pavement in front of Little Garth.

'Oh, no problem at all,' called Abby, locking up and leading the way to where she was parked, a little further along the street.

Lori and Rebecca followed her; Clarissa, of course, was making her own way there. She probably couldn't cope with being cooped up in the confined space of her micro car and carted about like a rustled Herdwick, thought Abby.

As she wove her way out of Ambleside, she couldn't help thinking back to what Lori had confided to her last night, but she tried to make her brain concentrate on the conversation currently taking place between the others instead.

'Have you been to Fell Foot yet, Lori?' asked Rebecca.

Abby saw her neighbour's mouth twist in the rear-view mirror.

'I don't think so.' Lori shook her head.

'Just at the bottom of Windermere,' explained Rebecca. 'Great for getting into the water as it's really gradual.' She mimed a slope with a slanted hand.

'So, you got to go out with Clarissa this week, did you?' asked Abby, glancing across at Rebecca in the seat beside her.

Rebecca nodded. 'And I have some news, girls!' She clenched both fists into two balls of excitement, then splayed out her fingers as she spoke the next sentence, like she was releasing a secret into the wild. 'I SWAM!' She smiled at Abby, then turned round to beam at Lori behind her too.

201

'Oh my god, congratulations!' Abby squeezed the steering-wheel, as though that could somehow translate into a hug.

'You've done *so* good!' said Lori.

'I've still a long way to go,' said Rebecca, settling back into her seat again. 'I wasn't in for very long.'

'But that's not the point!' said Abby with a supportive shrug. 'You did it!'

'Yep. Taken the plunge – *literally.*' Rebecca giggled.

The others laughed too.

There was a new lightness in Rebecca's tone of voice, as though her dip at Fell Foot had washed away some of the fear that had weighed on her for so long.

'We gotta celebrate!' said Lori. 'Is there some place near the tarn?'

'Hmm.' Abby bit her lip. 'Not really. There's Sticklebarn?'

'Now is that a town or what?' asked Lori, raising her eyebrows.

Abby and Rebecca shared a glance.

'It's a pub, in Great Langdale,' said Abby.

'Perfect!' said Lori. 'I still need to try some Cumbrian ale!'

Abby glimpsed her glowing reflection in the mirror and felt full of admiration for her friend: she was showing such grit – she was an inspiration.

But soon after that, Lori's head began to loll as she was lulled by the undulating lanes, and it wasn't long before her cheek was resting on a scrunched-up cardigan pressed against the window. Abby suspected she'd got very little sleep the previous night, despite the fact she was being so positive today, as always. Although she was missing the resplendent scenery surrounding them on all sides as they descended Hardknott Pass, she decided not to wake her, thinking she must need the rest.

They passed the remains of the Roman fort on their right-hand side, ravaged by time but still resembling the impressive place it had once been. It seemed to have a particular resonance for Abby now, like a reminder that nothing lasted forever, that making the most of the present was paramount. Especially in light of her talk with Lori last night . . . She found herself blinking back a burst of emotion, so she brought herself back to the moment with a deep breath.

'Did you hear any more from Guy, by the way?' she asked Rebecca. 'Sorry, my boss came and I couldn't read his card the other day.'

'Ah, it didn't say much.'

It looked like he'd written a lot to me.

'Just waffled on about wanting to make up for what happened.' Rebecca's forehead was creased in a frown.

'That's nice, isn't it?' chipped in Abby.

'That's what Clarissa would say, sticking up for him!' Rebecca then stole a glance at Lori, worried she'd disturbed her – but she didn't stir. 'It's just always Guy's way – thinks he can buy himself out of anything,' she angry-whispered.

'How d'you mean?' asked Abby.

'Oh, so he said he'd get me any treatment – a massage, or whatever I want – at the hotel spa, as a sorry.'

'That seems thoughtful—'

'He thinks because he's the heir to the Loveland empire he can act how he likes and everyone'll just fall at his feet.'

'It's still a kind gesture. Sounds like he genuinely—'

'He just wants everyone to love him.'

'I wouldn't say no to a massage,' said Abby, rolling her shoulders.

'You would if you knew what Guy was like.'

203

'He's not the one doing it, you know!' Abby laughed. 'Clarissa seems to think he's all right, though,' she added, when Rebecca just gave a huff.

'I've no idea why.' Rebecca crossed her arms.

'I can't imagine she suffers fools gladly, can you?' Abby shot Rebecca a sideways glance.

Rebecca sighed. 'She probably knew him as a kid, when he hadn't grown into the arrogant—'

'Shall we do some of Clarissa's breathing techniques?' suggested Abby and, to her relief, Rebecca laughed.

Lori jolted upright as they bumped into the rocky car park opposite Blea Tarn; a tantalising silver sliver of shimmering water. 'I fell asleep,' she mumbled, rubbing her eyes as though she'd woken to find herself in a fantasy land filled with mountains in place of skyscrapers.

They drew up next to Clarissa, who was standing, rucksack already on, next to her Defender.

The four of them crossed the road together, then followed the path on the other side; with every step they took, a little more of the tarn became visible. Abby could feel her pace begin to quicken as though the pool before her had a magnetic pull.

'This place is *unreal*!' said Lori.

It's spectacular. Abby wondered whether this was their best wild swimming location yet, but then it felt wrong to compare. Each of the places had a charm of its own, a unique character that defied competition.

They walked along till they were directly in front of the tarn, stopped in their tracks by the mesmerising view. Blea Tarn had a magic unlike anywhere else, and being here gave Abby the feeling of stumbling on some undiscovered treasure.

Its small size and sheltered situation made it feel like a private pool, more exquisite than any manmade version could possibly be.

'Probably the most famous mountain profile there is in the Lake District,' said Clarissa, looking up at the hills, hands on her hips. 'The Langdale Pikes,' she declared, like she was announcing an aristocratic family as they arrived at a ball.

The other Wildwater Women were standing in a straight line a few steps behind her, and they gazed at the three craggy rockfaces staring back at them.

Abby felt a deep sense of awe as she looked at the ancient peaks watching over them, like respected elders wrinkled with wisdom.

'From left to right,' – Clarissa waved a hand briskly through the air – 'Pike of Stickle, Loft Crag and Harrison Stickle.'

Lori snapped a photo, turning her phone sideways to capture the whole panorama. The water was so still, the mountains were perfectly mirrored in its surface.

She'll be able to turn that picture upside down, and it'll look exactly the same, thought Abby, *even though it's just an illusion*. Appearances could be so deceiving. She glanced at Lori, her smile in place, an image of relaxed calm, but in reality her whole world had been upended.

Clarissa was carrying on down the slight grass-covered slope that led towards the edge of the tarn.

The others followed the path she cut.

Abby saw that a selection of large, smooth stones scattered the shore, like a set of low seats, carved by nature and left just for them.

They each sat on one, and started to change into their swimming gear.

'We thought we might go to Sticklebarn on the way home,' said Abby, glancing up at Clarissa, who seemed to get into her swimsuit in a new personal-best time each time they went out.

'Nice. Great view. Good beer,' she replied like she'd been asked for a five-word review for Tripadvisor.

'Would you like to come?' asked Abby, wiggling to get into her wetsuit.

'Oh!' Clarissa raised her eyebrows. 'Right.'

'Just for a quick one; I'm driving so . . .'

'That's . . . grand,' she said with a nod.

'Yay!' said Rebecca.

Lori clapped.

Abby smiled and sat back down on her rock chair to put on her newly bought neoprene swim shoes. It'd seemed lavish – even *selfish* – purchasing something for her, rather than Rowan, at first, even though they weren't an item of frippery, more of a passport to improved health, like a gym membership or a therapy session. Even going into the Swim Wild shop had felt liberating. She'd assumed the staff would immediately think she was an imposter, laugh at her for thinking she belonged in a store like this. But it had been fine, more than fine. The man behind the counter was helpful and friendly and Abby realised she had as much right as anyone to be there. Her hope was that by looking after her own mental and physical wellbeing as well as her daughter's, that would enable her to be the best parent she could possibly be. *That was Tom's advice to me*, she realised. *I must give him a ring to see how he's doing.*

Clarissa coughed.

Abby glanced up; their instructor looked like she didn't know what to do with her arms, and for once she was just standing there, when she'd normally have marched off towards the water by this stage, never one to waste a second dithering around . . .

'I'm having a little get-together at my house,' said Clarissa, 'next Saturday.'

'Is that an invite?' asked Lori. 'Count me in!'

'Indeed it is,' said Clarissa with a smile.

'I'm free if it's in the evening,' said Rebecca. 'I'm on an early shift.'

'Seven-thirty,' said Clarissa. 'I'll text you the postcode, but you can't miss it: the white house on the right opposite Rydal, on the way from Ambleside to Grasmere.'

Abby had often looked at that place and wondered who lived there. It had an understated grandeur and a modest elegance, but wasn't showy at all with its simple white walls and perfectly proportioned windows. 'I'd love to come,' said Abby. 'Thank you.'

Clarissa nodded. 'Now, let's swim!' she said, striding off towards the water's edge.

'You reckon it's some kinda special occasion or what?' asked Lori, when Clarissa was already splashing her way into the shallows.

'I don't know. Wouldn't she have said if it was?' replied Abby, standing up from her stone seat.

'Maybe it's like a wild swimmers' event,' suggested Rebecca. 'Something she does every year or something?' she added, looking at Lori and Abby.

'I guess,' said Lori with a shrug. 'She is super passionate about it.'

'And very generous,' said Abby. 'Well, we'll soon find out what it's all about,' she said.

'Shall we fix a cab?' said Lori. 'You can always stay at my place, Rebecca,' she added. 'I gotta spare room at the cottage so you're super welcome to crash there.'

'That would be great!' Rebecca grinned.

'I'm excited!' said Abby, not meaning to speak the words out loud, but realising she meant it. *Saturday night plans!*

'Me too,' said Rebecca. 'I'm properly part of the group now!' she said, flexing her biceps and making the other two laugh.

'Yeah, you are!' cried Lori. 'Let's see these swimming moves, then, girl!' she shrieked as they sloshed into the shallows.

Rebecca gradually waded in up to her waist, taking big deep breaths as she did so.

Lori and Abby focused on their own acclimatisation, splashing their arms and then dipping down up to their necks; conscious not to put any pressure on her.

But when Rebecca submerged her body, stretched out her limbs, and then did breaststroke before their very eyes, they all burst into boisterous cheers.

Abby felt pride blaze across her chest. It was always easier to give advice than to take it, she knew that. But sometimes when your friends did amazing things – showed positivity and perseverance – some of that reflected back at you. Friendship was about knowing who was there for you when you got out of your depth – and she knew these women were. And as she swam in the water, melding with the land-scape, she felt truly at peace with life in that moment.

16

Abby's eyes widened as the taxi swung off the main road and drove through the wrought-iron gates that lead to the elegant white house before them. As they passed between the two enormous candle lanterns that stood on top of the pair of stone posts, illuminating the way to the party, she glimpsed a slate sign that said Herdwick Hall. She smiled to herself: there couldn't be a more apt name for the place Clarissa called home. Abby was spellbound by the sight of the house up ahead, cast in an ethereal glow by the mother-of-pearl moon that hung low above them.

But as the cab crunched its way up the gravel drive, and more of her surroundings came into view, Abby felt her stomach swirl with nerves. She blinked down at her outfit and bit her lip as the light from the floodlamps in the trees filtered through the window; the black dress that had seemed so over the top for their girls' night at Silver Ghyll, suddenly seemed so drab and dowdy.

'Jeez!' exclaimed Lori beside her, breaking her out of her train of thought. 'This place is *unreal*!'

Why am I worrying about what I look like, when I should be enjoying the moment instead? Abby scolded herself. She glanced back at Lori with a grin, then gazed once again at the vision that greeted her beyond the glass, eager to soak in every second of the occasion. *It's only down the road but I've never been anywhere like this before . . .*

'I feel like I'm in *Downton Abbey*!' Lori declared.

The others giggled; Abby felt her self-consciousness subside slightly as she laughed – she was in the company of friends, what did the clothes she had on matter? Surely their fellow wild swimmers inside wouldn't care either – after all, they usually wore wetsuits or waterproof jackets and walking boots . . .

Rebecca turned round in the front seat. 'God, this is incredible!' Her eyes were huge in the half-light. 'I can't believe Clarissa lives here!'

Abby smiled, and a shiver of excitement shot across her skin as the cab came to a stop outside. Lollipop-shaped box trees festooned with fairy lights flanked the door, which was already open, such was the stream of people arriving at the hall.

Another car drew up behind, its headlights flashing onto the group of guests being disgorged onto the grey-granite ground by the people carrier in front.

Goodness me, Abby thought, as she took in the sea of silk dresses and dark suits that flooded the steps. *Everyone's certainly made an effort!* What exactly *was* this do they'd been invited to? She would never have guessed their instructor was given to hosting events like this. Were these *really* all people she'd taught to wild swim?

The three of them clambered out of the taxi and joined the queue for the entrance. A band was playing, the music drifting out into the night as though the notes themselves were drawn towards the magnificent moon. Abby tilted her head upwards to look at the stars, which sparkled against the blackness like the sky was sequin-sprinkled velvet.

'There are *actual* waiters,' whispered Rebecca, eyebrows raised. 'Look!'

Abby craned her neck to see over the crowd. *So there are.* Serving champagne flutes filled with some sort of cocktail, and exquisite-looking canapés.

'Welcome!' boomed a familiar voice, but it took Abby a moment to realise it was Clarissa standing in front of them. Her flattering flint-shade dress nipped in at her waist and fell into a long, full skirt with flowing folds of soft grey wool, as though her outfit had been designed specifically with her in mind. *Perhaps it had,* wondered Abby. A diamond stud glittered in each of her ears and a matching solitaire pendant winked at the base of her neck.

'You look *beautiful*,' breathed Abby, before worrying she'd offended her by sounding so surprised.

But Clarissa just bowed her head, as though the compliment must have been intended for the person behind her. 'Good to see you all,' she said, her mouth curved into her characteristic half-smile. 'Have you got a drink?'

'Not yet, but we will,' replied Abby.

'Lori's invention,' said Clarissa with a good-natured glint in her dark eyes.

'Pardon me?' said Lori, her forehead crinkled.

'Sloe fizz,' declared Clarissa with a brief nod, before disappearing off into the depths of the house, no doubt to attend to the rest of her guests.

The three of them turned to gaze at a nearby tray of drinks – sure enough, the glasses were a distinctive ruby red.

211

'What we had at yours a couple of weeks ago,' said Abby, nudging Lori fondly.

'Oh, yeah! Right!' she replied, reaching for a flute.

Rebecca raised her glass. 'Let's get *wild*, Wildwater Women!'

Lori and Abby chinked their drinks against hers, their laughter tinkling in tune with the sound.

Abby took a sip of the sloe fizz and the warmth she'd felt a fortnight ago at the dinner party at Silver Ghyll returned, but it wasn't the taste of the alcohol that was making her feel content, it was the fact that for once, she felt as free on solid ground as she did in the water.

'There should be a little note next to the cocktails to say you're the genius behind the creation,' Rebecca said to Lori as she lifted her drink to her lips; her perfectly applied blusher was the same shade as the bubbles in her glass.

But Lori was busy searching out the nibbles.

Abby glanced at Rebecca. 'Speaking of little notes, have you heard any more from Guy since he sent you that card?' she asked.

Rebecca shook her head. 'He seems to be giving me a wide berth.' She smiled, to signal she thought that was a good thing, but even in the low atmospheric light of the party, Abby could tell her pleased expression didn't quite reach her eyes. She wondered whether Rebecca had a grain of regret that she'd buried deep inside her; an inkling that only grew as she watched her take a large gulp of her sloe fizz, as though that could wash the feeling away.

'I'm going to go for that job, though,' Rebecca added, draining the rest of her drink as though to swallow any further conversation about Guy. 'The spa manager one,' she clarified. 'If I can swim in a tarn, I think I can manage a heated pool.'

'That's great!' Abby clinked her glass again, as though ringing in a new topic of chat. 'Exciting!'

'*Scary*,' countered Rebecca, giving her a sideways glance. 'But it'll be better hours, and more money.'

'Sounds great. You should be proud of yourself.' Abby smiled.

'Haven't got it yet,' Rebecca replied.

'Even applying for it is a good step. You said you couldn't even set eyes on the pool when we first met. Look at you now!'

Rebecca grinned. 'Thanks, Abs.'

The unexpected nickname made Abby's spine straighten. *It's usually only Tom who calls me that. I must ring him.*

Rebecca was straining to see over the throng of guests.

'Do you think we should find Lori?' asked Abby, as her not-yet-empty glass was refilled. *I can't see her anywhere*, she thought with a frown of concern.

'Good idea.' Rebecca gave a nod. 'But I was looking for a beer,' she half-whispered before hiccuping.

Abby giggled. 'Come on, then. Let's mingle.'

They made their way through the mass of people, the music making Abby's shoulders loosen; she almost wanted to dance. When had she last felt like that?

Rebecca led the way across the drawing room, on the lookout for liquid refreshment, while Abby kept an eye out for Lori. She couldn't believe the sheer volume of guests.

Rebecca stopped walking so suddenly Abby bumped into the back of her. *Oof.*

'What are *you* doing here?' Abby heard her say. She took a step back – and saw Guy standing in front of them. *Oh gosh.* The room was so densely packed, there wasn't much space for her to move away to give them privacy; she was wedged in between the marble-topped fireplace and a

213

seemingly close-knit circle of chattering companions, who seemed to have formed an impenetrable ring, like a human fortress.

'Rebecca, hi,' she heard Guy reply as she checked her makeup in the mirror above the mantelpiece. 'Don't worry, I'm not going to ruin your night.' Abby couldn't help but glance at his reflection, saw he was holding his palms up in surrender. 'I'll leave you to it; have a great time.'

Abby watched Guy bow his head and back away as best he could, but his passage was blocked by a canapé-tray-clutching waiter.

'*You're* not a wild swimmer,' said Rebecca, tilting her chin upwards. 'Why were you invited tonight?' She crossed her arms.

'With respect, you don't know anything about me.' Guy dropped his hands and gave a sigh.

Rebecca opened her mouth, and closed it again.

'But I wouldn't have missed Clarissa's seventieth for the world.'

'*What?*' Rebecca's brow crinkled.

Abby looked up. *The party is for Clarissa's birthday?*

'What did you think all this was?' said Guy with a shake of his head.

Rebecca remained speechless.

'Anyway, I'll leave you to it, Braithwaite,' said Guy, spotting an opportunity to make his escape as a gap in the crowd opened up. 'Have a good one.'

Abby stayed where she was, studying a statue on the mantelpiece.

But as she gazed at the object, she realised it wasn't a sculpture at all—

'Did you hear that?' said Rebecca, who'd spun round and was now by her side.

'Er . . .' began Abby, unsure as to the correct response.

'We're at Clarissa's big seven-oh! How did we not know?'

'Well, she didn't tell us,' said Abby matter-of-factly, her eyes skimming over to the figurine above the fireplace, modestly displayed amongst a pair of brass candlesticks and an ornamental plate. 'She doesn't strike me as someone who likes a fuss.'

'Then why invite all these people to her house?'

Abby glanced around the room, at the heads thrown back in laughter, the buzz of multiple conversations vibrating in her ears. 'Because everyone's having the best time,' she murmured. Clarissa wasn't holding a party for herself; she was doing it for others. *Hospitality at its most generous.*

'We need to tell Lori,' declared Rebecca, grabbing her fingers and carving a path across the woven-wool carpet.

They found her ensconced on the sofa in the sitting room, next to a middle-aged man with an impressive beard and a can of craft beer in his hand.

Rebecca plonked down on the arm.

Lori didn't look up, so Abby decided to wait for a natural lull in the chat to make contact.

But Rebecca butted straight in, bolstered by the alcohol. 'This is a birthday party!' she blurted out, leaning towards Lori.

Lori blinked back up at her, tipsily trying to focus on Rebecca's face.

Abby felt a sharp pang of empathy for her; she understood now where Lori went in those moments where she looked far into the distance.

215

'Pardon me?' said Lori.

'It's Clarissa's seventieth!' cried Rebecca.

'Who?' said Lori.

Abby's throat squeezed.

'I take it you're either a trio of gate-crashers, or my sister's been up to her usual tricks,' said the grey-haired gentleman beside Lori. 'She's very humble, considering all her achievements. She shies away from attention at all costs. Which is why I myself can't wait for the next part of the evening' – he glanced at his watch – 'which should be any second now.' His wrinkled eyes twinkled in the lamplight. 'Just a bit of sibling fun.'

The long-case clock in the hallway struck nine times, then a hush descended, before a shout of 'Speech!' rang out throughout the house.

They scrambled to their feet and shuffled towards the door to listen.

But it was a man's voice who spoke next.

And it sounded unmistakably like Guy.

'Good evening, ladies and gentlemen!' he cried.

Abby caught Rebecca rolling her eyes.

'Bet he *loved* being asked to do this,' she said under her breath. 'Chance to listen to the sound of his own—'

But her comment was cut short as Guy carried on speaking.

'As we all know, Clarissa does her very best to stay out of the spotlight . . .'

A knowing murmur of agreement resounded round the room.

'Despite the fact she deserves a *mountain* of praise for all the ways she's improved so many people's lives,' Guy continued. 'I, for one, don't know what I would have done without her guidance and support over the years, even when I was a bit of a tearaway in my younger days.'

'I knew he'd make this about himself,' muttered Rebecca with a tut.

'I think he's just speaking from the heart,' whispered Abby, feeling the need to stick up for him. She couldn't see Guy, but she could sense the emotion in his voice, as though her hearing was heightened by her lack of sight; gratitude was making his words waver. She identified with that feeling, was similarly indebted to Clarissa – and the others, too – for their kindness. She'd been a different person back when they'd first met. She suspected that beneath his bravado, Guy was just a vulnerable boy, begging for approval, and that perhaps he was on a journey of self-acceptance too.

'What's *he* got to be worried about?' said Rebecca, and Abby remembered thinking the same about her when she'd breezed into the bakery, her hair bouncing and her outfit flawless. No one really knew what someone else was going through. Not until that person wanted to let it show, decided to open up and let you in . . .

'Clarissa is a *very* special person,' continued Guy. 'So, although she's tried to ignore the fact that this is *her* day – and a milestone one at that – I'd like to raise a toast to her.'

There was a pause, in which he must have sought out Clarissa in the crowd.

Abby clasped her glass, feeling a surge of affection for their instructor.

'I know you thought you could get away without being in the spotlight tonight,' Guy said loudly, and Abby could picture Clarissa's bashful expression in her mind.

'But I'm afraid that's not how it goes on your birthday,' he declared.

A ripple of laughter rumbled through the house.

'Thank you for everything you've done for all of us,' called Guy. 'For being an inspiration, for throwing a *fabulous* party, and for being the best godmother a lost boy could have.'

'*What?*' said Rebecca, her head snapping sideways to meet Abby's gaze.

'Would explain why he's at her party – and doing the speech,' replied Abby.

Then Clarissa's brother cupped his hands round his mouth beside her. 'Three cheers for my sister!' he boomed. 'Hip hip!'

'*Hooray!*' every guest in Herdwick Hall bellowed back.

But Rebecca's shout was sheepish, and her head was tipped to one side as though she was still listening intently.

The hum of happy chatter returned as the band took up a jaunty rendition of Stevie Wonder's 'Happy Birthday'.

'Grand speech, that!' Clarissa's brother grinned, then crushed his empty IPA can.

'Where did you get that?' asked Rebecca, licking her lips as though her throat was suddenly dry.

'Oh, I bring a supply with me. Can't bear my sister's home-made gin. Far too sweet,' said Clarissa's silver-bearded brother. 'I've got a crate of this chilling in the pantry. I'll bring you one back – I'm heading there myself.' He raised his eyebrows. 'Anyone else?'

'Sure!' said Lori with a smile, from where she stood on the other side of him.

'I'm fine with my sloe fizz,' said Abby. 'But thanks . . .'

'George,' said the beer-drinking, brown-eyed man. 'Pleased to meet you all,' he added, before bustling off through the horde.

'D'you guys know C's some sorta record holder?' said Lori as soon as he'd gone.

Abby remembered the trophy she'd seen nestled on the mantlepiece, half-obscured by the brass candlesticks and the decorative plate, as though it were as shy as its recipient.

'He's bin tellin' me all kindsa stuff!' Lori added, jerking her head in the direction in which George had disappeared.

'Like?' said Rebecca, leaning in.

'Oh, you'll have to get whatsisname to explain. I don't recall it all, but she's done *heaps* of extreme swims. All for charity.'

'I saw a prize above the fireplace—' said Abby.

'Wait till you go to the bathroom,' chipped in a woman beside them.

'Huh?' said Lori.

'*Tons* of them,' said the pashmina-swathed lady. She produced a hand from beneath the luxurious layers of fabric, and splayed her fingers. 'You have to see it to believe it.'

I already do, thought Abby.

'She's travelled all over the world,' the woman added with a wave of her hand. 'America—'

'Yes!' whooped Lori. 'She was in the US . . .' But her face fell as though the rest of the sentence had been on the tip of her tongue but she'd accidentally swallowed it.

But the shimmering-shawl lady was nodding enthusiastically. 'Indeed. She did the forty bridges in New York.'

'The what?' said Rebecca.

'A double circumnavigation of Manhattan island,' said the woman.

'In English, please?' said Lori, her speech a little slurred.

'She swam over ninety kilometres in the fastest-ever time.'

'Jeez!' Lori plonked down on the sofa as though the *idea* of such an undertaking had tired her out.

The woman was nodding, her lips puckered as though to stop a torrent of factoids from flowing out; it was clear she was spilling over with admiration for Clarissa. She gave a little wave before her hand vanished beneath the voluminous wrap and she turned back to talk to someone next to her.

George emerged from the crowd, arms full of beer. 'Excuse me! Coming through!' He sat down beside Lori with a satisfied sigh. 'Mission accomplished.' His eyes crinkled as he distributed the drinks.

'Thanks!' said Rebecca, coming to sit down on his other side and cracking hers open.

Abby perched on the sofa arm next to her.

'Not bad, this!' announced Rebecca as she inspected the brightly coloured can she'd just taken a glug from.

'Glad to hear it,' said George, stowing the remaining stash of beer underneath the sofa to spare battling through the packed room any more than necessary. 'Bit more professional than the sister's efforts,' he added with a mischievous chuckle.

Abby opened her mouth to stick up for Clarissa's sloe gin, but closed it again as George carried on speaking. She felt an unexpected sting in her heart as she realised with a pulse of sadness that sibling banter was something Rowan would never experience.

The sound of George tapping the side of his tin snapped her out of her spiral. 'It's my company,' he explained with a grin. 'Part of the Dimplethorpe Drinks empire.'

Abby's eyes widened; George had his own business, and Clarissa was a world-champion swimmer. They were certainly a gifted pair.

'You made this?' Lori spluttered on her drink.

'Well, not me personally,' said George, taking a slurp of his beer. 'I employ a whole team of people to do that for me.'

'Modesty runs in the family, then,' quipped Rebecca tipsily.

Abby and Lori smiled; the talent displayed by both brother and sister was impressive, but Clarissa was definitely the more self-effacing of the two.

George gave a little laugh in response; it was high-pitched, as though with surprise, thought Abby.

George turned to look at Rebecca, his head cocked on one side as though still computing the punchline of her joke. 'How well do you know Clarissa?' he asked, curiosity crumpling his forehead.

Rebecca looked embarrassed. 'I shouldn't have said that – I'm sorry . . .' She fiddled with the ring-pull on top of her drink.

'Don't be silly!' said George, nudging her amiably. 'We're all friends here, don't worry.' He reached beneath the sofa to replace her empty can. 'I just wondered what she'd said to you, out of interest.'

'Are you upset she hasn't mentioned her extremely successful brother to us?' asked Rebecca with a smile, having recovered herself.

George grinned. 'Well, *quite*.'

'She's been taking us wild swimming,' explained Abby, noticing her champagne flute had been topped up again, without her even realising. She glanced around for someone to thank, but there was no sign of a server. She turned back to the others. 'We've all just started.'

George was nodding. 'Ahhh, I see. That makes sense . . .'

They waited for him to elaborate.

'What do you mean?' asked Rebecca, when he didn't.

'I understand it now,' replied George. 'Your remark earlier.'

Rebecca's cheeks bloomed. 'I'm confused.'

221

'I get why you didn't know.' George gave a good-humoured shrug of his shoulders.

Rebecca shook her head. 'Know what?'

'Our history. It's not something I expect she discusses when she's leading classes.' George put his drink down and looked at the three of them in turn. 'However close we are, there's no biological link between Clarissa and me.'

Rebecca looked puzzled, like she was the one wrestling with a word game now. '*What?*'

'We're not blood related. We don't share any DNA,' replied George.

Abby sucked in a breath.

Lori looked a little lost.

'We were both adopted.' George settled back on the sofa.

'I had no idea . . . I can't believe I made that comment before,' mumbled Rebecca, rubbing her brow.

'Honestly, it didn't bother me in the slightest!' said George. 'I was just intrigued; I thought most people here would know. It's not something we keep on the down-low.'

Abby's gaze roamed the room. 'So, who else is here, apart from the people in her wild swimming groups?'

George scanned the swarm of guests. 'Some are fellow athletes from her competitions.' He glanced at Abby, now visibly bubbling over with brotherly pride. 'You know she's the fastest person to swim the English Channel? That man over there held the title before she smashed his time.'

Abby gasped. '*Really?*'

'Told ya C's a record-holder!' said Lori, sitting more upright in her seat.

George nodded. 'She's incredible.' He smiled. 'All of it's for charity. She's always wanted to give back, pass the good deed on.'

Abby recalled Clarissa's response when she'd asked about the fee for her wild swimming lessons. *'Pay it forward, instead.'*

'She was so grateful for what our parents did for us – I am too – they gave us everything we could have hoped for. A home filled with love, all the opportunities we could have dreamed of. We were lucky to have a privileged upbringing, a truly blessed life, but not everyone is as fortunate – so she's devoted her time to making a difference to those who need a helping hand.'

Abby brushed a tear from her temple. *Clarissa turned my world around.*

'It's thanks to her I've overcome my phobia of the water,' said Rebecca. 'I've been crippled by fear for years.'

George's eyes shone. 'I couldn't have asked for a better sister,' he murmured. Then his tone changed and he raised his beer. 'Speak of the Devil!' he boomed, back to his previous boisterous self.

Clarissa appeared in front of them all of a sudden, like a glinting piece of treasure that had been brought to them on the sea of people surrounding them.

'Are you going to circulate, George, or just sit there on the sofa drinking your own beer?' she asked, hands on hips.

'I've been getting to know these fine friends of yours!' he said, slapping his thigh in protest before getting to his feet, summoned into action by his sister.

'It's lovely to meet your brother,' said Abby, smiling at Clarissa.

'Is it?' said Clarissa, arching an eyebrow. 'I suppose he's not so bad,' she added, her mouth breaking into a gin-encouraged grin. She jabbed George's arm with her forefinger. 'But have you actually been conversing?' she said. 'Or just boring everyone to death about your beer?'

George tucked in his chin, mock affronted.

'Come on,' said Clarissa with a nod. 'What do you know about them?' she asked, jerking her head towards the sofa where Abby, Lori and Rebecca were sitting.

George pursed his lips. 'By god, you must be a fearsome teacher,' he replied, and everyone laughed.

'We were talking about you, mostly,' said Abby, standing up and smoothing the jersey fabric of her dress.

'Whatever for?' said Clarissa, whisking a hand through the air as though she were dispelling all discussion of herself.

'Because you really are remarkable,' said Abby, at the same time as George said, 'Just to annoy you, dear sister.'

They all dissolved into giggles as Clarissa swatted the sleeve of her brother's shirt this time.

'Right, well, I must obey my orders to mix,' said George with an exaggerated sigh. 'See you later . . .' He lifted a hand, Abby didn't know whether in a wave of goodbye, or in salute to his sister.

'You don't even know their names, do you?' said Clarissa, looking quizzically at her brother before crossing her arms.

'We're the Wildwater Women,' replied Rebecca, and Lori and Abby beamed back at her.

Clarissa's downstairs loo was twice the size of the bathroom in Abby's house – which was a good job, really, considering how many awards were crammed inside its four walls. Abby gazed at the prize-lined shelves, her lips parted in awe, before she began to worry that a queue would be forming outside the door. But she couldn't take her eyes off the rows of accolades in front of her. She'd never seen anything like it – medals, trophies and certificates for feats of endurance she couldn't believe were physically possible, yet Clarissa, their incredible wild swimming instructor, had completed them all, triumphing in each and every one of the challenges she'd set herself.

'*Waikiki Roughwater Swim*,' Abby read aloud in wonder. '*Farallon Islands to Golden Gate Bridge.*' Clarissa really had traversed the entire globe. There was an *actual* Guinness World Record with her name on it – *wait till I tell Tom!* – for the most southerly swim in Antarctica, without a wetsuit: an ice swim of one kilometre in water measuring one degree Celsius. *Gosh!*

Abby saw a newspaper article, mounted in a brushed-gold picture frame; she guessed that maybe one of Clarissa's friends had got it done for her as a gift. 'Goodness me,' Abby whispered under her breath as she read the first sentence: 'British swimmer Clarissa Dimplethorpe completes historic Havana to Key West swim on her third try, twenty years after her first attempt.' Abby scanned the rest of the piece. 'The sixty-five-year-old reached the shores of Florida fifty-one hours after she set off from her starting point in Cuba, a hundred miles away, becoming the first person ever to complete the swim without a shark cage.' *Oh my god!* Abby couldn't help but carry on . . . 'Dimplethorpe wore a full body suit and custom-made face mask to protect her from the poisonous stings of box jellyfish, which blighted her previous efforts . . .' Abby slapped a hand over her mouth. 'Exhausted and sunburned, Dimplethorpe still managed to say a few words from her stretcher as she was taken to hospital for a medical check-up. "Never give up on your dreams," she said to her cheering spectators. "Anything is possible, no matter what age you are, especially with the right support around you." Dimplethorpe has, to date, raised over a million pounds sterling for charities worldwide. She said: "I hope to inspire others to chase their goals and make the most of out of life – live every 'moment.'"

Abby blinked at Clarissa's words, felt them imprint on her mind.

Then a knock on the door startled her. 'Sorry, one second!' she called.

She glanced at the rest of the honours, all commemorating accomplishments at the very limits of human capability. She smiled at the way Clarissa had decorated her down-stairs bathroom with them, as casually as if she'd used wall-paper, and then with a last look around, she unlocked the door.

'There you are!' said Rebecca. 'We thought you'd got lost!'

Abby shook her head from side to side. *This house is pretty maze-like, though, it'd definitely be possible.*

'I left Lori in the sitting room and came to look for you,' said Rebecca. 'I've been standing outside here for ages.' She shuffled forwards towards her and Abby moved aside to let her past.

'You'll understand when you see in there for yourself,' she said, gesturing over her shoulder.

'Why? Is there a speakeasy bar or something?' Rebecca replied with a roll of her eyes.

Abby laughed. 'I'll wait for you, if you like.'

'Okay,' said Rebecca with a smile. 'Please will you hold my drink, then?' she added, handing Abby her can of beer.

Abby leaned against the wall and felt an unexpected wave of tiredness crash over her. She walked a little way down the hallway to sit at the foot of the stairs, where she could see that the long-case clock said it was almost midnight, its pale, round face mimicking the moon: the taxi would be coming soon. *I can't believe it's already so late!* She yawned as she pulled out her phone from her handbag; she hadn't checked if she had any messages from Maria for the last few hours, she realised. The screen lit up like she'd woken her mobile from slumber.

One new voicemail.

From an unknown number.

Someone had tried to ring her at eight o'clock. *After Rowan should have been in bed.*

Abby felt her heart start to slam in her chest.

The music must have been so loud earlier, she'd missed the call.

Now there was a lull in noise as the band had ceased to play; the party was drawing to a close. The tick of the clock seemed ominous as opposed to soothing.

What if Rowan isn't okay? Guilt ripped through her as she stabbed at the keypad on her mobile to listen to her answer-phone. *What am I doing here?*

She pressed the phone to her ear, but she didn't recognise the eleven digits the automated voice reeled off down the line.

Why would Maria call from a different number?

But it was a man's voice.

Tom.

She realised she'd been holding her breath. She blew air from her lungs as he started to speak. 'Hey, Abs . . . er, sorry to ring you on a Saturday night . . .'

Oh god, is he okay? Her insides clenched. Had he needed someone to talk to, and she hadn't answered?

'. . . I guess you're busy, and I know I'm ringing off another number . . .' – the line crackled as he gave a sigh – 'I never answer those calls either . . . er, I'm calling from my sister's phone, I'll explain why when I see you . . .' Her stomach did a strange spasm, she wasn't sure why. Perhaps at the idea he

227

assumed they were still going to keep in touch, despite the fact they didn't work together any longer.

'. . . I don't want to interrupt your night if you're out doing something nice . . . but give me a ring when you can. Oh, and don't you worry about me – I know what you're like,' there was another sputtering sound and she could tell he was smiling down the phone. 'I'm fine, I promise. Enjoy the rest of your evening and speak soon. Okay. Bye.'

Abby would've listened to the message again if Rebecca hadn't burst out of the bathroom at that moment.

'Bloody hell – can you believe we've been having swimming lessons from a *legend*!' she said, bowling down the hall.

Abby scrambled to her feet, picking up the can of beer she'd set down beside the stairs before Rebecca kicked it over in her excitement. 'We're very lucky, right?' she replied, realising she'd adopted Lori's American inflection as she handed Rebecca her drink.

'You okay?' Rebecca's beer paused halfway to her mouth. 'You look a bit funny.'

'Oh, no, I'm good.' *Another Lori-ism.*

'Just slightly tipsy – like me?' Rebecca took a slurp from her can.

Abby nodded. 'Yeah. Shall we go and get Lori; the taxi'll be here any minute.'

'Yep,' agreed Rebecca, heading towards the sitting room with a slight sway.

The three of them were seeking out Clarissa, to thank her for her hugely generous hospitality and to say goodbye, Rebecca leading the way, when they encountered Guy head on in the corridor that went to the kitchen.

'Braithwaite.' He nodded in acknowledgement; his head bowed as though physically avoiding any form of confrontation.

'Guy . . .' Rebecca stopped to speak to him, leaning forward to prevent him just edging past.

Abby held out a hand to brush Lori's arm, and they hung back to give them both some space to talk. Clarissa's house provided plenty of nooks for private conversations to take place, thought Abby. It was the sort of house where a historical saga would be set, a Sunday-night TV series . . .

'Which way was the bathroom again?' asked Lori, peering back the way they'd come, towards the foot of the staircase.

'Just over there,' said Abby. *Don't leave me here like a gooseberry!* she thought as Lori wandered down the hall.

'It was a great speech you did,' Abby heard Rebecca say to Guy. 'Clarissa's an incredible woman, isn't she?' Rebecca had at least found the one thing her and Guy could agree on.

'I know. And it's probably down to her that I'm not as terrible a person as you think I am,' he replied.

Abby glanced behind her to see the entrance hall was now awash with departing guests; George was busy bidding people goodnight on his sister's behalf. So she decided to slip away towards the kitchen, and leave Rebecca and Guy to talk. There had been no sign of Clarissa elsewhere when they'd looked. *But surely she wouldn't be in there?* thought Abby, reminded of her fruitless search for Tom amongst the stainless-steel cabinets in the Plum Pie Bakery.

Yet there she was indeed. *Classic Clarissa: hiding away from the limelight, helping others wherever she can.* She was standing at the long oak table, assisting the catering staff with their packing up. If she'd really been a Herdwick sheep, her ears might have twitched at the sound of Abby's footsteps on the flagstones, but she lifted her head instead. 'Abigail. Is everything all right?' she asked, pausing partway through wrapping a clean canapé platter.

'Absolutely,' said Abby. 'Just wanted to say thank you, that's all.'

'You're most welcome,' said Clarissa, continuing to tidy away the crockery that only hours earlier had contained such an abundant array of food.

'See you soon then, for a swim,' added Abby.

Clarissa gave a nod in reply.

Abby smiled back at her, then spun on her heel to gather up her friends.

It was only when she was in the pitch-black back of the taxi, in the silence of the countryside lanes, with Rebecca asleep in the front seat and Lori's head lolling beside her, that her thoughts returned to Tom's answerphone message. His voice had sounded strained, and there had been an under-current of urgency in his tone, yet the reason for his call eluded her. But she had no way of getting an answer tonight. She'd ring him first thing in the morning. She turned to look out of the window as they sped past Rydal's slick dark surface, then watched with delight as the moon broke through the clouds in the sky above, its silvery light bringing the lake back to life before her eyes. She smiled, then let her gaze follow the beam of the car headlights instead; they illuminated the road ahead, a few metres of treelined-tarmac at a time. *Just focus on your next steps, rather than worrying about things so far in the future*, the rustling leaves seemed to whisper, and Abby sank back into the soft leather seat and tried to settle her whirring mind.

17

Abby stretched her hand out towards her bedside table, feeling hopefully for a tumbler of water, but there wasn't one. She must have left her glass downstairs when she came in last night. Her fingers closed round her phone, and she squinted at the time on the screen. Almost ten o'clock! She shot upright. When had she last had a lie-in for this long? Her head throbbed like it was still counting the beat of the music in time with the band. Her mouth felt like it was filled with sand from the play pit in the park. What time had she said she'd collect Rowan? Eleven? She shoved off the duvet with leaden limbs, then wrapped her dressing gown round her like it was the closest she was going to get to a hug. She shoved her phone in one of the pink-fluff pockets then made her way downstairs to get a drink. She downed a pint of water, then poured herself a cup of tea that she'd been planning to take back to bed, but the stairs seemed as steep and insurmountable as Skiddaw, so she plodded over to the sofa instead.

She put her mug on the coffee table and snuggled into a horizontal position, resting her head on a scatter cushion and reliving the party the previous night. She'd never been to such a lavish do, but at the same time it had been so unpretentious. Her mind wandered through the events of the evening: she recalled Guy's speech – and wondered what Rebecca and he had said to each other in the passageway before they left at the end of the night. Abby had noticed that, thankfully, her friend had seemed relaxed as she'd clambered into the taxi, her shoulders loose and her forehead smooth, as though this time, the conversation between her and Guy hadn't been confrontational. She knew what it was like to have a toxic workplace, so she hoped Rebecca had seen another side of Guy.

Abby remembered the rows of awards Clarissa kept secreted in the bathroom, too, except for the one tucked away on the mantelpiece – the trophy engraved with the words 'Youngest Successful Swimmer', which she guessed was the first award she'd ever won. *Does that one get to stay on display as a reminder of where it all started? Perhaps the cup was there to prove to herself how far she'd come, or to inspire other young people to be ambitious, to aim high?* Abby mused.

Then she shot upright as she remembered the answerphone message from Tom.

How could I have forgotten?

She reached for her mobile and fumbled with the lock screen, her fingers slow and her hungover brain thumping.

'Morning, Abs,' he answered on the second ring.

'Hey, Tom,' she croaked, feeling a prickle of embarrassment at the hoarseness of her voice. She cleared her throat. 'Did you call me last night?' she asked, a little less raspingly.

'Yes . . . sorry if I interrupted . . .' he trailed off.

'You didn't. I didn't look at my phone,' she explained, before worrying about what that might imply. 'I was just at a friend's house,' she added, feeling her cheeks flame. 'That's all.'

'Right.'

'What was it you were calling for? Are you okay?'

'Yeah . . .'

He doesn't sound very sure . . .

'I don't really know how to say this . . .'

Abby's insides squirmed. *What?*

Tom sighed.

'Are you sure you're all right? Do you need somewhere to stay, is that it? Just tell me what's wrong, Tom!' She was babbling, her heart beating double time. *Something must have happened for him to resort to ringing me . . .*

'No, no, I'm at my sister's in Bowness . . . sorry about the random number, by the way – I had to get a new SIM. Freddie's hidden my phone somewhere,' – he blew out a sharp breath – 'possibly an attention-seeking thing, some sort of plan to make me stay . . .'

Abby chewed her lip. *Poor Freddie, caught up in the split.*

'My sister had an old brick of a mobile she's letting me borrow for the time being. Anyway, I'm getting off track here. I'm just going to have to come out and say it . . .'

'Yes, spit it out, please!' Abby pleaded, taking a sip of her tea for comfort.

'The Plum Pie is up for sale.' Tom blew out a breath.

Abby tasted blood on her tongue, she'd bitten down so hard in shock. '*What?*

'I was flicking through the *Westmoreland Gazette* and I saw it in the property pages.'

Abby swallowed. *What about my job? What if I get let go by the new owners?*

'I didn't trust Joy to give you a heads up.'

'She hasn't said anything to me,' said Abby. The huskiness had returned, but she didn't care. Tom had seen and heard far worse from her.

'I didn't really want to be the bearer of bad news,' he said, 'but I thought it was best you knew.'

'Thank you,' she said. 'I appreciate it.'

'What are you going to do?' Concern made his tone falter.

'Er . . . what are my options?'

'Well, you could confront Joyless about it?'

Abby's tummy tensed, as though her body was physically recoiling at the idea.

'Make sure you fight for your rights, Abs,' said Tom. 'Or else maybe start looking at other options.'

The thought of job-hunting felt like being dropped in a pool of water where she was well out of her depth – overwhelming and terrifying.

But you're a wild swimmer now, said a tiny voice inside her head. *You'll be all right.*

'You can do anything you want,' said Tom, as though he could hear it too.

'I like being in the bakery.'

'Apart from the horrible boss.'

'Well, yes.'

'I just don't trust the dragon to have your best interests at heart. She's already being underhand, not giving you the facts.' Tom paused. 'The premises could even get turned into something else, Abs,' he said, in an almost whisper.

I hadn't thought of that. I might get made redundant. 'I'm going to speak to Joy about it,' Abby said aloud, her conviction surprising her.

'Atta girl!' said Tom. She could tell he was smiling from the way his tone had softened, and the sound of his voice in her ear made her feel like sunshine was warming the side of her face.

Despite Abby's resolve, the news seemed to weigh down on her like she was carrying about a backpack of boulders. She couldn't break out of a constant cycle of firstly going over what Tom had told her, and then rehearsing what she intended to say to Joy the following day. All the way to Maria's, this thought-vortex circled round her head, and the idea of returning home – and being confined in Little Garth with a full-of-energy four-year-old and a mind bursting with worries about the future – made her feel as though the invisible rock-rucksack was dragging along the ground.

She craved real fresh air – not even the kind she'd breathed on the walk through town to collect her daughter; she needed cool, pure oxygen in her lungs, to stand close to the lake, and imbibe the countryside like a tonic. She knew feeling rooted was the only answer.

She filled water bottles and packed snacks for Rowan, then settled on a route from the door, so they didn't even need to go in the car. *We'll go to Rydal the way I described to Lori.* Perhaps they could call in on her on the way back.

They followed the Rothay, stopping to marvel at the famous stepping stones about a mile north of Ambleside. With Rowan straining against her grasp to get closer, Abby gazed at the row of rounded rocks, watched the way the river gushed over the top and in between them, finding a way through. Although the stepping stones appeared magical to look at now, they were in fact *obstacles*, blocking the normal flow of things, causing friction, realised Abby. It was only possible to contemplate the benefit of each little barrier when you stood back and looked them all in sequence, with a bit of distance.

They continued on till they reached the picturesque Pelter Bridge, with its slate parapet and three low arches. Abby had never properly appreciated its simple beauty before. The trio of stone arcs had been there, supporting each other as well as those passing through, for possibly hundreds of years.

'I'm hungry, Mummy,' said Rowan, tugging on her hand as they crossed through the car park just beyond the bridge. Abby took off her backpack and rooted around for a banana and a bottle of water, pre-empting the shout of 'I'm thirsty' which was sure to follow soon enough. For once she felt as prepared and organised as Clarissa, as she furnished her daughter with both food and drink, then buckled the rucksack on her back again. She was feeling better the nearer they got to the lakeside, she realised. Rydal only was a short walk away.

They carried on a few paces, before Rowan thrust the sticky banana skin towards her, and she stopped again, glancing round the car park to check there wasn't a nearby bin before she tucked it into the outer mesh compartment of her bag.

Is that Rebecca?

Abby stared at the berry-coat-clad figure standing next to the red car with her back to her on the other side of the car park.

It looks like her.

She took a few steps closer.

Yes, that was Rebecca's brunette hair, her Hunter wellies. *What's she doing here? She isn't going for a swim on her own, is she?*

Abby knew her friend was feeling much more confident around the water now, but surely she wasn't going to go out into the lake on her own. That definitely wasn't a sensible idea; it could be risky even for an experienced swimmer. She took a gulp from Rowan's water bottle.

'Rebecca?' said Abby.

She turned round with a jolt of surprise. 'Abby! Hi!' Her ruby mouth formed a broad grin a split-second later, but Abby almost got the impression she wasn't pleased to see her. Were she and Lori meeting up without her? Was that it? She told herself off for being unreasonable; Rebecca and Lori were allowed to see each other as a twosome! Her hungover heart was predisposed to feeling vulnerable, prone to assuming the worst; she was aware of that. *Stop being silly!*

'How are you feeling after last night?' asked Rebecca, her gaze darting over Abby's shoulder which only worsened her suspicions.

Don't be ridiculous; Rebecca is allowed to see whoever she likes! 'Oh, much better now I'm outside!' replied Abby. 'How about you?'

'Yeah, good. Just needed to blow the cobwebs away by getting out of the house.'

'Absolutely.' Abby smiled. 'Are you going or you've just arrived?'

'Oh, er, about to set off. Going for a stroll with a friend.'

She'd have said Lori if it was Lori! Stop being nosy! 'Well, enjoy!' said Abby, just as a sports car mounted the bridge, the rev of its engine drowning out her words. The vehicle pulled into the car park with a low rumble, and came to a stop in the space beside them.

Abby's eyes were as wide as Rowan's as she watched the driver's side door open.

Out stepped a sunglasses-wearing man that her hazy brain struggled to place immediately. But when he pushed his shades on top of his head and raised a hand to greet Rebecca, she realised exactly who he was.

Guy Loveland.

Abby turned to meet Rebecca's gaze, her mouth open. *What's going on here?*

Rebecca glanced back at her, shooting her a smile that promised to explain later.

Her scarlet lipstick had looked ridiculously flawless for someone merely off for a walk, thought Abby. How on earth had that turnaround come about, then? she wondered, watching as Guy bent to retrieve a pair of shoes from his car boot. This was the man Rebecca claimed to dislike more than anyone. Now she was meeting him for a Sunday wander.

Guy crouched down to do up his laces and Rebecca mouthed, 'I'll ring you afterwards,' to Abby.

'Okay, have fun!' Abby enunciated back. But as she started to lead Rowan towards the path on the other side of the car park, she began to panic that she would be impinging on Rebecca's date – she and Guy were surely heading the same way, down to the lake, too. Abby didn't want them to feel hampered by her and Rowan, as though they had to check over their shoulders to make sure two pairs of prying eyes weren't following them. She spun Rowan round in a one-hundred-and-eighty-degree turn, and hurried back towards Pelter Bridge with a cheerful wave.

Right. Time for a rethink.

'Where are we going, Mummy?' asked Rowan.

Good question.

'We're exploring, sweetheart.'

Think. Her hungover brain scrabbled for a backup plan.

They reached the road on the other side of the river, and walked a little way along the narrow pavement, but the traffic was roaring as though each passing car was a raging tiger. Rowan gripped her hand tightly, tucked as far away from the kerb as possible.

This was no good; it wasn't the replenishing day Abby had intended to spend surrounded by nature at all.

They crossed the road when they saw a lane forking off to the right. Abby glimpsed a signpost that said 'Rydal Hall'. *Gosh.* A memory almost winded her. An image of Ben sitting opposite her at a picnic bench. The hiss as they'd cracked open bottles of sparkling elderflower, the fizz and clink as they poured the drinks over ice cubes in the bottom of chilled glasses, the liquid bubbling like a river running over rocks. It had been scorching that day. The last summer before he'd got sick. Abby remembered the smell of sun cream as Ben squirted too much of the stuff into the palm of his hand, the way he'd rubbed it over her neck and beneath the straps on her back. They'd stumbled across the tea shop not long after setting off on their hike, had stopped to just bask in the warm rays, revelling in the weather. Spontaneity had run through their relationship like a mineral layer through rock. The nights had been light, and time had seemed limitless, then. They'd delighted in taking an impromptu detour to wander round Rydal Hall's beautiful gardens, too, in disbelief that such a place was open for the public to roam through. They'd gone down to the grotto on the river, a picturesque viewing station with a square-shaped window that looked up to the waterfall above, framing the landscape like a dynamic piece of art.

Now, as she once again set foot on the estate, for the first time she felt *grateful* for the past she and Ben had shared, instead of sad. Her husband was here with her, in Rowan, she realised, as they wended their way towards the symphony-like sound of Rydal Beck tumbling down the hillside.

There it was: the café by the stream. The rushing, gushing sound of the river grew louder as they got closer.

'Look, a waterfall!' Abby said, lifting her daughter up so she could see the water cascading over glistening stones a little further up the brook.

She felt a tug in her stomach with every step she took, as though she couldn't help but retrace her and Ben's steps from all those years ago; perhaps, somehow, that would mean he could be part of their day too.

It was only a mile to the exact place where they'd ventured to on that glorious summer's day.

She knew the way; it was a straightforward route, alongside the river.

Only about a mile.

She felt as though a climbing rope had been looped round her middle and she was being pulled towards the spot.

They walked northwards, taking their time, until it came into sight.

Buckstones Jump.

A private-seeming paradise.

A fellside oasis.

Abby sucked in a breath as she gazed at the large, freshwater pool, and the waterfall that flowed into it from above.

They wandered to the beach-like bank, and stood on the pebbles to stare at the smooth-rock sides of the basin.

Abby couldn't believe she was back here.

She glanced at her daughter, who was entranced by the white-froth waterfall in front of her. She and Rowan had the place all to themselves; there was no one else there.

Abby looked back in the direction they'd walked from; she could see Windermere below, a gleaming slice of grey on the horizon.

They sat down on the little shore.

She and Ben had paddled up to their ankles, the water cooling their sun-baked skin.

Today she wasn't dipping so much as a toe in the water. Not without her Wildwater Women friends.

She'd heard of daredevils hurling themselves off in the height of summer, from the rockface at the top of the waterfall, but the thought made Abby shudder. From this vantage point the pool was stunning, its wind-crinkled surface reflecting the spectrum of colours in the sky. But it was hard to determine its depth, or whether there were hidden dangers concealed beneath – jagged stones, slippery edges, icy temperatures.

Abby and Rowan had their picnic on the shore, like she and Ben had done, then stretched out on the grassy bank, the musical sound of falling water ringing in their ears.

Rowan rested her head on her mother's tummy, and Abby felt the rise and fall of her breathing synch with her own. Soon her daughter was snoring, soft snuffles that made Abby smile as she watched the clouds pass overhead; nothing was constant, everything changed, and, in many ways, that was what made the world so magnificent.

She heard two voices in the distance, but she didn't want to disturb Rowan by sitting up. They were semi-concealed amongst the long grass that made the beach area feel like a secret. There was a certain delight in feeling as though you were the first people to discover this hillside haven, and she didn't want that joy to be taken away from the approaching couple, so she stayed where she was.

But the rustle of footsteps seemed really quite close now. *Wait, was that Rebecca giggling?*

Oh god. She and Rowan had come up here specifically to be out of their way! But Rebecca and Guy had been heading here – not Rydal – all along.

Abby kept still, hoping to remain out of sight so as not to spoil the mood. Rebecca and Guy seemed to be having a good time from the sound of it, chattering away to each other. She couldn't tell what they were talking about, but the tone seemed light and happy. *Well, that's a change for the better!* But Abby was unsure what to do. She didn't want to ruin any potential romance by revealing herself, but surely they were going to spot her and Rowan any moment now?

To Abby's relief, their voices started to become more indistinct; they must be moving off in the opposite direction now, walking up towards the top of the pool, perhaps, to look back down to Windermere.

Yes, it sounded like they were far enough away now. She shuffled upright, and stroked Rowan's cheek till she woke up. 'Shall we get going, poppet, before we get cold?'

Rowan rubbed her eyes and yawned. 'I'm tired, Mummy.'

'I know, but you don't want to stay here all night, do you, sweetheart?' said Abby, stuffing the picnic things back in the bag.

Rowan shook her head.

'Let's go home then, my love.' Abby got to her feet and held out a hand to Rowan.

Just as a raised voice made her glance round. It was coming from above the waterfall.

A woman's high-pitched pleading, her exact words blurred by the sound of babbling water.

Pinpricks of fear pinched Abby's spine as she saw Rebecca standing with her arms outstretched towards Guy, who was standing on the top of the steep stone face that formed the sheer side of the pool far below – in just his boxers.

Jesus.

He can't be going to—

'Is he going to jump in, Mummy?' asked Rowan.

Abby's pulse thumped. Her feet were like tree roots planted in the ground. Her gaze was locked on Guy. 'I don't know, darling.' She squeezed her daughter's hand. 'You mustn't ever do anything like that, okay?' she said, terror distorting her voice. 'It's very dangerous.'

She watched Guy inch forward, skin winter-white, limbs rigid with cold.

He must be experienced, or he wouldn't be attempting it, Abby reasoned. *Maybe he's an extreme sports aficionado?* Abby's gut twisted as Rebecca, her features muddied by distance, gave a piercing shout.

Abby watched as Guy propelled himself off the top of the rock and plunged down towards the dark water below.

'Oh my god,' she breathed, instinctively trying to shield her daughter's face from the sight of someone plummeting off a precipice, but Rowan squirmed out from behind her fingers.

'Where is he, Mummy?' Her daughter's eyes were round and huge.

Abby didn't know what to say; Guy had disappeared from sight. *Is he okay? Please, God, let him be okay.* Her jaw clenched as she stared at the surface of the pool, willing Guy to appear. She glanced up at Rebecca, who was peering over the edge of the ledge above, hands over her mouth in horror.

Abby's heart pumped a frenzied beat as she remembered the panic attack her friend had had. *This could trigger a relapse . . .*

She watched as Rebecca raced round the edge of the water, down to where Guy ought to be wading out of the shallows.

Seconds passed.

Then Guy popped up.

Abby felt a brief rush of relief.

But his pale face was a bleary oval, and there was no shriek of victory or fist punch of success. He looked depleted and limp.

Christ almighty, is he all right?

Abby scrambled closer, pulling Rowan with her.

Guy was attempting to do breaststroke towards the beach, but he was hardly moving, as though all his strength had been sapped away. *Is he hurt? Did he hit something on the way down?*

Rebecca was on the shore now, her back to Abby. She splashed into the water up to her knees, to take some of Guy's weight as he stumbled out, his bare flesh covered in goosebumps that had turned his muscled body into pimpled chicken skin.

His mouth was moving, and he was making gasping sounds. *He's hyperventilating,* realised Abby, trying to recall what Clarissa had taught them in her safety talk.

But Rebecca looked to be in control. She sat Guy down on the ground, ripped off her quilted jacket and laid it over him whilst she tried to calm his breathing. She pulled her phone out from the coat pocket.

Christ, his clothes must be back up at the top of the water-fall, thought Abby. She rushed round the edge of the pool to look for them, with Rowan running alongside her. She spotted the pile just beside the point where she'd seen him launch himself into the water.

She grabbed the clothes and jogged back to the beach. 'Rebecca!' she called, the sound vibrating off the rocks which surrounded them.

'Abby?' Rebecca cried, her mobile clamped to the side of her face. 'Guy's collapsed!'

Abby flung herself down beside the two of them.

'I'm calling 999,' said Rebecca. 'Can you keep talking to him? Make sure he stays awake?' She blew out a steady breath. 'What else did Clarissa say to do? We need to keep him warm, right?'

Abby took off her coat and spread it over Guy too. He was shivering violently, his lips a purply blue. *Is this hypothermia?* She felt a jolt of dread. 'Keep looking at me, please,' she whispered, as his lids began to close.

Rebecca put her phone down. 'The police are sending Mountain Rescue.' Her eyes met Abby's; they were shining with fright.

'What was he *doing*?' Abby asked.

'Showing off. Trying to impress me, I suppose.'

Abby put her hand on her back. She couldn't say, 'He'll be okay.' She knew what it was like to hear those words and to want to shout back, *But how do you know?*

Then the hum and whir of a helicopter pounded overhead and they tilted their faces skywards to search for it.

Few things sounded more serious than the spinning rotor blades and thundering engine of an air ambulance.

The noise was deafening as it came into land, drowning out all thoughts from Abby's head. She clutched Rowan's body to her tightly as she stood back to let the professionals get to Guy, watching with awe as the medical team moved

245

in. Rebecca stayed close to answer questions: his full name; next of kin.

Oh god.

Guy was stretchered into the helicopter's bowels, and then it took off, blasting an icy breeze in its wake.

'They're taking him to Royal Preston Hospital,' said Rebecca, brushing her hair from her face. She blinked at Abby, her cheeks damp with silent tears.

'I'll drive you there,' said Abby, without hesitation.

'No, don't be silly.' Rebecca swallowed.

'I'm not,' replied Abby. 'I'm being your friend.'

They hurried down the hillside back to Pelter Bridge, where the sight of Guy's Porsche parked up next to Rebecca's car, quiet and motionless, seemed like an unpleasant omen.

'He's in the best hands,' murmured Abby, noticing the anxious twist of Rebecca's lips.

'Look, I'll be fine getting there on my own . . .' she replied, mouth quivering.

'I know you're capable,' said Abby. 'But if you want some company, then I'm coming with you.'

Rebecca's face crumpled and she flung her arms round Abby's neck, mumbling a thank you into the collar of her coat, before they leaped into the car and set off south. They dropped Rowan off at Maria's on the way through Ambleside, then made for the M6, driving the first half of the hour-long journey in almost silence. The songs on the radio seemed too trivial a soundtrack in the circumstances, and neither did Abby want to utter platitudes that would provide no real comfort for Rebecca. She remembered what that felt like herself. She waited for Rebecca to talk if she wanted to, and in the meantime concentrated on getting them to the hospital, so they could deal with the facts face on, together. But as they passed a sign for Preston, Rebecca started to speak.

'D'you think he'll be all right?' she asked, turning her head towards Abby in the passenger seat.

'I don't know,' whispered Abby. 'At least he's getting treated . . .'

'The paramedics said someone had been paralysed doing the same thing . . . it's called tombstoning, apparently.'

'Oh god,' said Abby.

'I can't believe he jumped in . . .' muttered Rebecca. 'I tried to stop him.'

'I know, I saw.' Abby glanced at her. 'Rowan and I went up there to leave you to it . . . I just assumed you were off to Rydal.'

'I'm so glad you *were* there,' murmured Rebecca.

'Me too, but you were already doing everything you could,' said Abby with a reassuring smile. 'You stayed calm and put into practice everything Clarissa told us to do.'

Rebecca pressed the back of her head against the seat, as though she was braced for bad news.

Distract her from thinking the worst. 'How come you decided to see Guy today, anyway?' asked Abby. 'He must have done some sweet-talking at the party last night,' she added, attempting to turn the conversation to happier times.

To her relief, Rebecca smiled. 'He didn't do any, to be honest. Everything he said seemed to be genuine.' She gave a sigh. 'I'd started to wonder whether I *had* been too hard on him. And I saw him in a different light at Clarissa's . . .' She trailed off, as though slipping back into sadness.

'Go on,' said Abby, encouraging her to continue, and keep her mind off the ever-diminishing miles on the road signs;

with every minute that passed, the tension seemed to be mounting. 'What changed your mind?'

'Well . . . when we were chatting in the hallway, just before we were about to leave, he told me . . .'

Her voice broke and Abby saw her wipe her face with her sleeve out of the corner of her eye.

'I got the job – the spa manager one I went for,' Rebecca finished.

'Oh my goodness – congratulations!' The words seemed to stick in Abby's throat and then came out as a squeak, as though they knew any hint of celebration was inappropriate.

'Thanks,' mumbled Rebecca.

They were coming into the outskirts of Preston now. *Keep her chatting, make sure her brain's occupied.* 'So what else did he say?'

'Er . . .' Rebecca bit her thumbnail as though so much had happened in the last few hours it was a struggle to recall the night before. 'Oh, he said he knew I really wanted it, and he was pleased for me.'

'That's nice.'

'He seemed to mean it. I saw a different side to him, I suppose . . .'

'And so how did you get from a chat about work to going on a—'

'Walk?' said Rebecca. 'I thought I might as well learn to get along with him if I have to see him even more around the hotel.'

Abby nodded, but the way Rebecca squirmed in the seat beside her as she stumbled over her explanation, seemed to indicate that she'd been keen to go on the date. *I knew Herdwick Hall was the perfect setting for romance,* Abby thought to herself.

248

'And the fact that he and Clarissa are close had to count for something; he admitted he'd been a bit of a tearaway, that it was Clarissa who kept him on the right path,' added Rebecca. 'She always sticks up for him; I realised there must be a reason.' She sniffed, and Abby got the impression that perhaps she'd just been starting to discover a little of what Guy was really like before the incident at Buckstones Jump. Then Rebecca blurted out, 'I feel terrible about how I was towards him. You and Lori were right – I can see now he does struggle with living up to what his parents want him to be.' Abby turned to look at her: her face was crumpled in anguish. 'I misjudged him . . .'

'Hey, hey. You mended your differences, though,' Abby said.

'Oh god, I hope he's all right.' Rebecca closed her eyes as though she were praying.

Abby felt her chest squeeze in sympathy with her friend. 'I do too,' she murmured.

18

The clinical smell hit Abby like a punch as they walked through the sliding doors of the hospital; so many milestone moments in her life had been accompanied by that clean, medical scent. Ben's death. Rowan's birth. She bit her lip as she contemplated the outcome of today, and linked Rebecca's arm as they went over to the information desk.

They followed the instructions they were given to Guy's ward, hurrying down shiny-floored corridors past muralled walls.

Abby took a seat in the waiting area, while Rebecca spoke to a nurse. Then she was led away, only glancing back at Abby fleetingly over her shoulder before she disappeared round the corner, her mascara-smudged eyes seeking a last dose of support.

Abby studied the ceiling tiles for what seemed like an age but must have only been a few minutes – until Rebecca reappeared, face red and cheeks streaked with tears. Abby leaped up from her chair and wrapped her in a hug. *Oh, Jesus, no. Is he—*

Rebecca dissolved into sobs.

Abby smoothed her hair. *I can't believe it—*

'He doesn't want to see me!' Rebecca wept.

Abby pulled back from her. 'He's alive?'

Rebecca nodded.

Thank Christ. Abby let out a deep breath.

'He told me to leave him alone!'

Abby's spine stiffened. 'What?' She tried to steer Rebecca towards the rows of plastic chairs. 'Come on, sit down for a moment.'

'I don't want to stay.' Rebecca shook her head. 'I want to go.'

Abby gave a nod. 'Okay.'

'He . . . he . . . *recoiled* away from me,' Rebecca stammered. 'He hates me!' she cried.

Abby's chest ached at her friend's pain. She rubbed Rebecca's arm.

Rebecca was pushing air out of her lungs the way Clarissa had taught them to acclimatise to an uncomfortable situation.

'Let's get you home then,' soothed Abby as they walked towards the way out. She noticed a well-dressed, middle-aged couple approaching the automatic doors from the other side. As they got nearer, she realised they weren't just hunched against the cold; they were huddled into each other for mutual support. *Parents of someone*, realised Abby, feeling a tightness in her tummy. She couldn't even imagine coming here for news about Rowan. She scrunched up her eyes as though to dispel the thought, but when she opened them, the man and woman were close enough for her to see their expressions more clearly. Recognition niggled at the edges of her mind. She'd seen the scarf-swathed face of the woman somewhere before, and the navy-wool-coat-wearing man looked familiar too.

'Mr and Mrs Loveland,' said Rebecca, as they met on the threshold of the sliding doors.

'*Rebecca Braithwaite?*' said Mrs Loveland, springing upright as though showing any emotion was an affliction.

'I . . . I was . . . with Guy . . .' Rebecca started to explain.

'What, when the accident happened?' asked Mrs Loveland. Rebecca nodded.

Mrs Loveland winced as though Rebecca's words had further wounded her. 'Why?' she murmured.

'We went on a walk . . .' said Rebecca.

Mrs Loveland tipped her head to one side like a beady-eyed bird.

Mr Loveland lay a hand on his wife's arm. 'It's okay, Amelia. They said he's doing all right.'

'Yes, I just want to see him, Martin,' she replied, taking a step forward towards the doors.

'I'm sorry . . .' mumbled Rebecca.

What are you apologising for! thought Abby. *You saved his life!*

Mrs Loveland's gaze burned into Rebecca, blazing with unspoken blame. She took a breath, but bowed her head as a blustery gust of wind buffeted them all. Instead, she lay a gloved hand on the scarf knotted at her neck as though restraining herself from saying any more.

'Rebecca was the one who called 999!' said Abby, consumed by a need to defend her friend.

'Well, thank you,' said Mr Loveland, with a nod at Rebecca. 'In that case we're hugely indebted to you.'

'But Guy wouldn't have even *been* in that situation if it wasn't for *her*.' Mrs Loveland jabbed a black leather-clad forefinger in the air at Rebecca.

'What do you mean?' muttered Rebecca with a frown.

'If he hadn't been *showing off* to you, he wouldn't be in hospital now,' replied Mrs Loveland, with a tilt of her chin.

'It isn't her fault—' said Abby, standing up straighter.

'Then why is she apologising?' retorted Mrs Loveland. 'Hm?'

'I just meant I'm sorry that he's . . .' Rebecca glanced beyond the glass doors.

Mr Loveland held up a hand. 'He's going to be fine,' he said, directing the statement at his wife. 'Come on, let's go and see him.'

Abby opened her mouth but Rebecca spoke first: 'I tried to stop him jumping in the water! I begged him not to do it!'

'I find it hard to believe that, when you're the one who's been babbling on to him about the benefits of wild swimming.' The look Mrs Loveland gave her was as icy as a lake at midnight.

Rebecca was speechless, no doubt astounded Guy had mentioned her to his mum at all.

'Hang on a second . . .' started Abby, but the wind stole the sentence from her lips, carrying it away across the car park.

Mr Loveland was already guiding his wife towards the sliding doors.

But the breeze whipped up the words that they spoke and whispered them in Rebecca and Abby's ears.

'Who *was* that?' asked Mr Loveland. 'Is she Guy's new girlfriend?'

Mrs Loveland gave a brittle laugh. 'Oh, goodness me, no. She just works on *Reception*.'

Abby looped an arm round Rebecca's shoulders. 'Ignore them. She's lashing out because she's had a shock. Guy's their everything.'

'Yeah, and I'm *nothing*.'

253

'Hey, that's not true. They're just being snobby and horrible.' Abby was reminded of the story Lori had told her, about her grandfather and his sweetheart. 'Who cares what they think?'

'I'm going to hand in my notice tomorrow,' said Rebecca suddenly. 'I've decided. It's for the best. None of them want me around.'

'What? Why? You've only just got your promotion!' Abby dropped her arm.

'I don't want it anymore,' croaked Rebecca.

'But you were so excited about it!'

'I was. But not now. Guy can't stand me – you should have seen the expression on his face – and you heard his parents.'

'They're just being protective. Why didn't you tell them what happened?'

'What's the point?' Rebecca gave a rasping gasp. 'Guy doesn't even want to *look* at me.'

'You can't just walk away from that manager role when you've worked so hard to get it. You've come so far – been through so much for it! Don't throw your dreams away.'

Rebecca sighed.

'I should have stood up for you more,' said Abby. 'If it wasn't for you, Guy could have been . . . in a *far* worse state.'

'If it wasn't for me, he wouldn't have been at Buckstones Jump at all – his mum was right. He obviously thinks that too.'

Abby shook her head.

'He was like a different person when I saw him just now.'

'Just don't do anything hasty, okay? Promise me.'

Rebecca pursed her lips. 'Okay.'

'Give them all time to calm down,' said Abby.

Rebecca linked her elbow again. A squally gale battered their backs as they crossed to the car park. Darkness made everything look different to when they'd arrived. Abby felt disorientated. 'I don't know where the car is, do you?' she said to Rebecca, glancing round the tarmacked bays.

Rebecca peered at the rows of vehicles. 'No, I don't either.'

They'd been in such a rush when they arrived that she hadn't paid enough attention to where they'd left it, realised Abby.

'Where's Clarissa when we need her?' said Rebecca with a small smile, craning to look down the next line of cars. 'She always knows the way.'

But it was the face of the fourth member of the Wildwater Women that swam to the forefront of Abby's mind. *This is how Lori must feel.*

19

Abby was trying to collect up enough courage to confront Joy about the Plum Pie Bakery being up for sale, when Rebecca walked into the shop on Monday afternoon.

'Hey! How are you doing?' she asked, making a quick check of the shop floor to make sure Joy wasn't lurking anywhere nearby. 'Have you heard anything more about Guy?'

'I'm fine, but I haven't made contact with him. I decided not to ring the hospital, or bother him at all. I'm just going to leave him be. He made his feelings clear yesterday . . .' Rebecca slipped a square pink envelope onto the counter, face-down. 'I'll leave that there.'

Was it a leaving card for Lori? Or belated birthday wishes for Clarissa?

But Rebecca carried on speaking. 'I took your advice, though, and I'm not going to jack in the job.'

'Good!' Abby gave a nod.

'Guy and I can just go back to not really speaking, like before . . .' She trailed off, as though the sadness inside her had swallowed up the rest of the sentence.

'Did you want something to eat?' asked Abby, trying to drag Rebecca's attention back to the present.

'Oh, er, yes please.' Rebecca glanced down to look at the contents of the display cabinet and her eye shadow shimmered.

'You sure you're all right?' asked Abby when Rebecca added a slice of Borrowdale tea bread onto her order. *She only does that in emergencies . . .*

'Yeah . . . I think what I really need is a swim,' Rebecca replied. 'I'm sure that would sort me out.' She took the paper bag with her lunch in, and tapped her card to pay. 'I'll message Lori and Clarissa, too, see what they say. Maybe Wednesday?'

Abby noticed a glint of light had returned to her eyes. 'Great idea.' *I could do with one too.* All the adrenaline of the past twenty-four hours had left her feeling drained and in need of an energy boost: a blast in the outdoors would be the best way to fix that.

'Okay, I'll be in touch.' Rebecca turned to leave.

Abby waved goodbye, feeling full of admiration for her; Rebecca hadn't been put off being around the water after the events of the previous day. Abby was proud of her; she seemed to have well and truly broken down her phobia, come to understand that if the rivers and lakes were treated with respect, and you took great care, you could enjoy them safely. The reason the incident at Buckstones Jump had come about was because Guy had been *reckless*.

Joy appeared at the foot of the stairs in front of her.

Abby swept the fondant-pink card off the worktop. She held it behind her back like a talisman, taking strength from it, as though it were a physical connection to her friends. She'd promised herself she'd tackle Joy, ask her outright about what was happening with the bakery. She had a right to know.

'Everything okay, Abigail? You're standing about when there's work to be done . . .'

'I . . .' Abby cleared her throat. 'I heard the bakery was up for sale.'

Joy raised her eyebrows, as though to say '*And?*'

Abby clasped the envelope tighter, like a good luck charm.

'It's in the estate agent's window, in plain sight,' replied Joy, with a jerk of her head towards the door.

Abby nodded.

'I'm retiring,' said Joy.

Abby had always wondered whether it was just her boss's miserable attitude that made her look older; now she had her answer.

'So d'you have a buyer, or . . .?'

Joy frowned, as though to ask, 'Do I have to run all my business decisions past *you?*'

'I'll tell you when there's anything you need to know, don't you worry,' she said.

'Thank you,' murmured Abby. *At least I've said something.*

'*Well done,*' she heard Tom cheer her on in her head.

Once Joy had disappeared again, and when there was a pause in between people coming into the Plum Pie, Abby opened the envelope Rebecca had given her.

There was a card inside, with a photograph of a lake on the front.

Looks like Crummockwater, thought Abby, flipping it over to look at the credit on the back. *It is!*

An image of the four of them, the Wildwater Women, there on the shore, smiling for the picture Lori had taken of them, flashed into her head – sowing the seed of an idea in her subconscious . . .

Inside the card there was another slip of thick cream paper, placed face down, obscuring Rebecca's message.

Abby slid the oblong sheet down to read Rebecca's words:

To Abby,
Thank you so much for yesterday, not only for driving to the hospital, but for being there for me when I needed it. You're a great friend.
Love,
R x

On the back of the rectangle of embossed card the colour of vanilla custard, she'd written: *A treat to say thank you. Don't argue. You deserve it. x.*

Abby turned it over. *Very high-quality stationery.*

She gave a gasp as she saw the logo for the Loveland Hotel was printed at the top, above the words 'gift voucher' and 'spa treatment'.

'*Reviver massage*' was written in looping gold lettering on a black line below.

Abby stared at it, remembering the conversation she'd had with Rebecca on the way to Blea Tarn; '*I wouldn't say no to a massage,*' she'd said. *And Rebecca had remembered.*

Abby bit her lip; she couldn't believe it.

She typed out a text, thanking Rebecca for the thank-you, and almost forgetting to say yes to the swim. Then she put her phone back in the pocket of her apron, and bent to check the stocks of cakes in the display cabinet. *How thoughtful of Rebecca. She didn't need to do that.* But already the present had had a profound impact on her, going some way to reframing the Loveland in her mind. The place she'd avoided for so long was now somewhere she'd be greeted by a friend.

She'd never been to the spa there; it would be a new experience. Entirely unrelated to the past. Besides, the thought of having a massage seemed beyond luxurious—

'Service!' bellowed Joy's niece from the back, like she was a celebrity chef in a restaurant kitchen.

Abby put the gift certificate back in the card, and tucked it out of sight beneath the counter, taking a last look at Crummockwater, reflective and calm, as though it would restore her for the rest of the afternoon. As she walked towards the kitchen, the picture seemed to linger in her mind, sparking a plan that started to take shape throughout the remainder of the day. In the gaps between serving customers, the idea began to burgeon in her brain, until by closing time, she was bursting to tell Rebecca about it too.

20

When Rebecca came to pick her up at 5.30 p.m. on Wednesday, Abby was already in Little Garth's hallway with her swimming bag on her shoulder. Her body was fizzing with excitement at the thought of being at High Pool Tarn again. It was a haven away from the rest of the world, a secluded sanctuary that seemed to only be visited by a handful of hardy, all-weather swimmers and well-wrapped-up walkers. She yearned to feel the satisfying ache in her arms as she pushed through the dapple-patterned water, every centimetre of her skin, each cell in her body, tingling with life . . .

'Hey!' Abby said when she opened the door, a smile on her lips. A thrill of anticipation zipped down her spine. She'd been tired when she got home after her shift, but now she was looking forward to the post-swim sensation of pure exhilaration.

'Hi!' said Rebecca grinning back. 'Ready?'

Abby nodded. 'You betcha, as Lori would say.'

'Have you seen her today?' asked Rebecca.

I haven't seen her since Saturday . . . Abby shook her head. The first half of the week had flown by faster than a peregrine falcon. She'd had so much on her plate, what with work and Rowan and starting to put together the plan she'd come up with at lunchtime on Monday in any spare moments, she'd only had the briefest of text exchanges with her neighbour. 'Just chatted a bit on WhatsApp,' said Abby as they walked round to next door. 'She sent me the photos she'd taken of us swimming. I asked if I could have them for a talk I've been roped into doing at one of Maria's WI meetings.'

'Oh, nice,' said Rebecca, raising her eyebrows as she rang the doorbell. 'I've got a few I can ping over to you, too,' she added as they waited for Lori to appear.

'We'll have to get some more today, to add to our collection,' said Abby.

'Definitely,' said Rebecca. 'I'm going to set up a group chat, for when she's gone back to America, too.' Rebecca jerked her head at Silver Ghyll's front door as she pressed the bell a second time. 'So we can share stuff and keep in touch.'

'That's a good idea.' Abby bit her lip. 'Do you think I should ring her?'

'Yeah, maybe. I'm sure I said half five in my message,' said Rebecca, pulling out her phone to check. 'Yep. Maybe give her a buzz in case she's got mixed up.'

Abby gave her a sideways glance. *Has Lori said something to Rebecca too, then?* 'Er, okay.' Abby dialled Lori's number, but they both heard the sound of an electronic ringtone chime behind them, a little way down the street. They turned round, to see Lori walking along the pavement, then she stopped to search for her mobile in the depths of her handbag.

'Lori!' called Abby.

Rebecca waved. 'It's only us!'

Lori lifted her head and blinked at them.

Abby saw her shoulders droop as if to ask *what's going on?*; she let the hand holding her iPhone drop from her ear.

'Still up for wild swimming?' said Rebecca.

'Oh, yeah, sure,' replied Lori, finally finding her phone and frowning at the screen. 'Who's this calling me . . .' she muttered.

Abby swallowed as she ended the call. 'We were just checking you still wanted to come,' she said with a smile.

'I forgot . . .' Lori said with a sigh.

'Stuff slips my mind all the time,' said Rebecca with an empathetic roll of her eyes. 'You should see my notepad at work; I'm just endlessly scribbling things down.'

Maybe Rebecca doesn't know, then, thought Abby.

'This is different,' murmured Lori.

'Is everything all right?' asked Rebecca.

Lori pressed her palms to her eyes, before beaming back at them both. 'Absolutely! Just let me get my swimsuit . . .' she said, bustling in between them to unlock the cottage's door. 'You go make yourselves comfortable on the couch a minute . . .'

Rebecca looked at Abby, confusion crinkling her forehead, before stepping inside Silver Ghyll.

Lori went upstairs to gather her things.

'Does she seem herself to you?' Rebecca whispered.

Yes and no. This is nothing new, sometimes you can only see things when you're told they're there. 'I didn't know if she'd told you too . . .'

Rebecca's brow furrowed further.

'It's Lori's place to say . . .'

Their friend's footsteps began to descend the stairs.

'Alrighty, let's go wild swimming, girls!' said Lori, her eyes like two watery wishing wells filled with hope.

'Thank you for an *amazing party* last weekend,' Abby said to Clarissa as she huffed up the path that led to High Pool Tarn in her wake.

'I'm glad you enjoyed it,' replied Clarissa, not remotely out of breath despite her fast pace.

'Yes, very much.' Abby sensed Rebecca close behind her, racing to catch up with their instructor, as though there was something she wanted to ask her.

Abby hung back, to let her overtake, and turned to talk to Lori. 'How are you?' she asked, keeping the question general so Lori could be as open as she liked with her response.

'Oh, good. Thanks.' Lori glanced up from the leaf-strewn path and smiled.

'Is there anything you still want to do while you're here?' said Abby. 'It's your last week, after all.'

'A moonlit swim,' said Lori with a grin. 'I've been thinking about it, and for my last one, I want it to be really memorable.'

'Are you sure that's a good idea?' asked Rebecca, slowing down to join in the conversation. 'Sounds dangerous.' She frowned.

Abby chewed her lip; the events of Sunday were something that would surely stay with her.

'Not if we have C with us!' said Lori. 'How 'bout Friday?'

Clarissa looked over her shoulder. 'I can take you for a night-time swim, if you like. But, Rebecca, don't feel any pressure.'

Does Clarissa know about Guy? wondered Abby.

Rebecca was level with Clarissa now; the path had widened into an autumn-mottled track. 'Mr and Mrs Loveland ought to be very grateful you were there on Sunday,' Abby heard their instructor say.

Rebecca looked across at Clarissa, her skin pinched with concern. 'Is Guy okay?'

'He will be, thanks to you.' Clarissa reached out in a rare display of affection, and touched Rebecca's arm. 'Well done for remembering what to do, when you needed to.'

Abby saw Rebecca smile back at her, her cheeks flushing red with relief. 'I had a good teacher. The umbles are *engraved* in here.' She tapped her temple, and Clarissa gave a small laugh. Then, to Abby's surprise, Clarissa turned round. 'You did a sterling job too, Abigail.'

Abby felt heat flood her face. It wasn't often she received praise, and it echoed about her head like a meaningful song lyric. 'Thank you.'

'Whassgoin' on?' said Lori, noticing Clarissa had stopped still.

'These two rescued Guy from a very sticky situation at the weekend.' Clarissa nodded at both Rebecca and Abby in turn.

Lori put her hands on her hips. 'Who?'

'Master Loveland,' said Clarissa.

'Canoe man,' explained Rebecca. 'The one who gave the speech at the party.'

'Oh, *right.*' Lori said, wide-eyed, as they started walking again. 'You guys went out at the weekend, huh?' she said.

'Go on, Rebecca, tell her,' prompted Abby.

'Oh my *god!*' said Lori, slapping her hands to her cheeks, when Rebecca recounted what had happened at Buckstones Jump.

'She stayed so calm,' said Abby, feeling a burst of pride for Rebecca – ultimately she'd saved Guy's life. *His parents ought to be told that*, she thought to herself, and wished she'd said more to stand up for her friend at the hospital.

'What a story!' said Lori. 'I love a romance where the female's the hero, right?'

Rebecca's jaw tensed. 'We're not . . .'

'Oh!' Lori grimaced. 'I thought you guys were on a date?'

'We were,' began Rebecca. 'But . . .'

'It didn't go well?' asked Lori. 'I mean apart from the whole hospital part.' She flapped a hand awkwardly.

Rebecca reached for a bottle of water from the side pocket of her rucksack, as though her mouth felt like a dry riverbed all of a sudden. 'He . . .' She took a gulp of her drink. 'I did see a different side to his personality, I suppose.'

Abby noticed Clarissa glance at Rebecca, her kind eyes wrinkled at the corners, her lips clamped together despite the fact Abby was sure the words 'I told you so' would never spill out from her mouth.

'We were having a good time,' explained Rebecca, her gaze glazing over for a few seconds, as though she was reliving a snippet of the afternoon she and Guy had spent together. Then she looked up. 'He wasn't at all arrogant away from the hotel, almost the opposite. He opened up to me about how his Mum and Dad want him to expand the Loveland brand abroad, be in charge of developing new hotels as well as running everything here when they retire – when all he wants to do is teach watersports.' She rubbed her forehead. 'It was actually nice, just out in the countryside on our own.' She made a strange sound, a cross between a smile and sigh, demonstrating her surprise.

'So, what else did he say?' asked Lori.

They were standing on the edge of the tarn now, but everyone's attention was on Rebecca, rather than the puckered expanse of graphite-grey water in front of them. Even Clarissa was motionless beneath the opalescent sky.

'Just that he loves being out on the lake, in his kayak, and he wanted to inspire others to be active and enjoy the outdoors . . .'

Abby raised her eyebrows.

Rebecca looked at Clarissa. 'He said you're his role model.'

Clarissa coughed as though compliments were hard for her to digest. 'Have you spoken to him since he came out of hospital?' she asked, shifting the subject from herself.

'No.' Rebecca fidgeted with the cuff of her coat. 'So he's home? Is he all right?'

Clarissa nodded. 'Fully recovered.'

Phew, thought Abby.

'Thank god.' Rebecca put a hand to her chest. 'Have you seen him?' she said to Clarissa.

Clarissa shook her head. 'Talked on the phone. I told him off.'

Of course, thought Abby.

'I doubt he'll be so thoughtless in the future,' said Clarissa, crossing her arms. 'I think he's somewhat embarrassed about his behaviour,' she added. 'Don't hold it against him, though. We all make mistakes.'

Rebecca bowed her head. 'Oh, he . . . I don't think he wants to see me again.' She took another sip from her water bottle. 'I mean, he'll have to at work, but aside from that . . .'

Abby dipped her gaze in sympathy.

'What makes you say that, huh?' asked Lori, tucking her hair behind her ear.

'How he was with me at the hospital . . .' said Rebecca, desperately trying to blink back a disobedient tear, but it absconded down her cheek.

Rain was starting to fall, as though the clouds had taken their cue from Rebecca; droplets hit the canopy of leaves above them with a soft pattering sound, like the four of them were standing inside an enormous tent made of trees.

'Heyyyy,' soothed Lori. 'Whatcha cryin' for?'

'I'm just upset that . . . oh, I don't know.' Rebecca sighed. 'I didn't even like him to begin with, but when we chatted at the party, and then went on the walk last Sunday . . .' She sniffed. 'I feel like he showed me the real him; let me in.'

Abby and Lori came to stand either side of her, a forcefield of friendship.

Clarissa was frowning. 'Well, what's the issue then?' she said, straight to the point as ever. 'He clearly likes you back or he wouldn't have tried to impress you by throwing himself in at Buckstones Jump like a prize idiot.'

Rebecca gave a snort of laughter despite herself, but it was short-lived.

Abby remembered the state she'd been in at the hospital; almost hysterical when Guy had sent her away . . .

'You do know he was diagnosed with Transient Global Amnesia, I take it?' Clarissa said, her gaze on Rebecca.

'Pardon me?' said Lori.

'I . . . no, I didn't . . . *what?*' spluttered Rebecca.

'Short-term memory loss triggered by cold water,' explained Clarissa. 'I wouldn't take anything he said straight after the accident seriously,' she said. 'He'll have been very confused. His body suffered extreme trauma.'

Rebecca bit her thumbnail. 'But how come he hasn't said anything since . . .'

'He's had a hugely distressing experience,' Clarissa said solemnly, and Abby got the impression she'd seen the shocking effects of sudden immersion first-hand before, or perhaps even felt her own system start to shut down in similar icy conditions on one of her endurance challenges.

'You said he was fully recovered, though . . .' said Rebecca in a small voice.

'I think his pride took the biggest knock,' said Clarissa.

'Does he know Rebecca rescued him?' asked Abby.

'The medical staff gave the Lovelands your name,' conceded Clarissa.

And they haven't said a word of thanks? Abby suppressed a tut.

'I haven't seen them at work, actually,' admitted Rebecca. 'Must have hit them quite hard.'

God, I couldn't have borne being in their position if it was Rowan, thought Abby. *Guy was their only child, too . . .* She gave a shiver.

'Right, well, before we all freeze just standing here, shall we get on with the swim?' said Clarissa.

The rain had subsided to a drizzle, and the breeze had dropped to a gentle breath of fresh, earth-scented air.

Abby looked up at the pearly sky as she filled her lungs; the last of the light was fading fast, leaving a luminous glow above them.

She started to get changed, then heard Lori sigh beside her.

'You okay?' she asked. Clarissa was splashing her way into the tarn and Rebecca was rummaging in her rucksack.

Lori glanced up. 'Oh, yeah.' She shrugged as she tussled with her wetsuit.

'Sure?' pressed Abby, stretching the neoprene material up over her midriff.

Lori wiggled as she pulled her outfit on. 'It's stupid . . . I guess I kinda feel . . . *jealous* of Guy almost . . .'

Abby finished zipping up her suit and her arms flopped to her sides. 'How d'you mean?' But as soon as she'd said the sentence aloud, she realised why. *His situation was temporary. Oh, Lori.*

Her friend was holding the heels of her hands to her eyes, as though she could physically push her emotions back inside.

'You don't have to pretend around us . . .' said Abby. 'It's all right, you can let it out. Are you going to tell the others?'

'Not tonight,' replied Lori. 'I want us to have a nice time.'

Rebecca was walking over to them from the far side of the rounded mound of rock that acted like a windbreaker, shielding them from the biting breeze. She was clutching her phone. 'Photo?' she suggested.

Abby smiled back at her. 'Definitely.'

Lori cupped her fingers round her mouth. 'Hey, C! We need you in the shot!' she shouted.

Clarissa waded out of the water with dripping limbs and a bemused look on her face that seemed to say this modern obsession with selfies was something she'd never understand.

But it isn't just a picture for social media, thought Abby as her plan was coming together, *it is for a purpose.*

21

Once Rowan was in bed, and she'd washed the tarn from her hair and skin in a warm shower, as though it were a lover's perfume, Abby snuggled up beneath her duvet, stretching diagonally across the bedsheet as though breaking away from the idea she was half of a whole, not enough on her own. She was exhausted but comfortable, not just because her head was resting on double pillows and her feet were toasty on top of her hot-water bottle – life felt *better*. Her world wasn't the same as it had been before; she'd discovered a new hobby she adored, met great friends while doing it – and she was becoming herself again. She had *energy*. A healthy daughter, a home. A circle of people who cared about her. There was a lot to be grateful for. There was the problem of her job, though . . . Abby wriggled under the covers as the thought popped into her head. She stared at the ceiling as she contemplated her situation. She'd brought the topic up with Joy, so she'd have to let her know any developments. Surely that was the law. Employers had to tell their staff what was happening, didn't they? Her mind turned to Tom. She wondered how he was doing, if he'd found a new job yet.

She reached out to grab her phone from the bedside table and shuffled upright against the headboard. She started to tap out a message, but after fifteen minutes of typing then backspacing – *what should she say?* – she dialled his number instead.

'Hey, Abs.' The lightness had left his voice, like the sun slipping from the horizon at nightfall.

'Hi, Tom.'

'One second, I'll just go out of the room,' he whispered.

Oh god. He isn't alone! What am I doing ringing him this late at night! He's with someone. Maybe he and Sophie are back together—

Abby heard the sound of a door close, as though he'd shut one behind him to separate his home life from his work one.

'Sorry, I can talk now,' he said.

'Oh, I wasn't ringing with anything in particular to say . . . I didn't meant to disturb your evening.' Abby felt the cold air in her bedroom chill her bare skin as though it were chastising her.

Tom didn't speak for a second.

Abby's stomach squeezed. *What am I doing? It was a ridiculous idea to call him!*

'You're not interrupting,' Tom muttered, so softly she was sure he couldn't mean it.

'Well, I won't keep you long.' Abby pulled the duvet up to her shoulders like a comfort blanket. 'Just wanted to see how you were getting on, but it sounds like you're busy . . .'

Again, Tom was silent for a moment.

'Look, let's speak another time—'

'I was sitting next to Freddie's bed, that's all.'

272

'Oh.'

'He's struggling to settle at night, needs me to sit with him till he falls asleep. It must be stressful for him, going between two houses, getting used to having separate parents . . .'

Abby's heart hurt on Freddie's behalf. *Bless him.* It couldn't be easy for him to comprehend. 'So, are you renting a place now?' she asked.

'Yeah, couldn't stay with my sister forever, but luckily her friend has a holiday cottage they said I can stay in for a bit seeing as it's low season, just while I get myself sorted, look for somewhere more permanent.'

'That's good,' said Abby. *What am I saying? None of it sounds great.*

'Thanks.' Tom sighed. 'You speak to Joy?' he asked, as though talking about himself wasn't something he relished at present.

'Er, yes. She said she'd let me know any developments as and when.'

'She tell you it's sold, then?'

It was Abby's turn to fall silent.

'I take it that's a no.' Tom gave a grim laugh at his ex-boss's ruthlessness. 'I was going to ring, but—'

'Oh, you've got plenty to deal with, don't worry about me.'

'I don't anymore, actually,' replied Tom.

Abby disliked the way her tummy tensed when he admitted that.

'Because you seem to be much brighter nowadays,' he said.

Oh, right.

'Think I need some of whatever you're having.'

'Come and get in the lakes, then.'

Tom laughed.

'I'm serious.'

'Ah, I don't think it's for me.'

'I said the same. But I bet there are tons of groups around and about. Have a look online. Or go with our instructor, Clarissa – she doesn't only teach women.'

'Okay.'

'I can tell you're just humouring me,' said Abby with a laugh.

'Well, then, I'll promise.'

Abby smiled. 'No harm in trying it once.'

'Okay. It's definitely worked for you,' Tom conceded.

'It's completely changed my life,' said Abby, and as she uttered the words out loud she realised they were true.

'Oh, well, in that case, sign me up!' quipped Tom.

'Tom, is there anything I can do to help?'

He exhaled. 'To be honest, it's just nice talking to another adult – one who actually cares . . .'

Abby's cheeks ached as what he'd just said echoed round her head, cementing the fact their bond seemed to have segued from colleagues to genuine friends.

'. . . Not just someone from the Craft Tap,' concluded Tom.

Concern erased the smile from Abby's face. She didn't want Tom to turn to alcohol instead of the people around him. She wasn't judging, she'd done the same after Ben died. But it hadn't helped, only numbed the hurt for a short while, then ultimately made things worse. She hated to think of Tom sinking pints to ease his pain—

'Did I tell you I got a new job there?' he said, stopping her spiralling thoughts.

So he works in this beer place! Abby pressed her palm to her chest as though that could slow her thumping heart. 'No, you didn't,' she said, closing her eyes with relief.

'I haven't heard of the Craft Tap.'

'You don't like beer, though, do you Abs?' he said with a chuckle.

The way he remembered that made her grin. 'Correct,' she replied.

'It's in Windermere; a taproom attached to a brewery, and there's a shop, too. I've got some shifts there for the time being.'

'That sounds good. Not too far away – I mean for seeing Freddie.' Abby felt her skin flush.

'Yeah, they've been pretty flexible with my hours, so I'm grateful for that.'

'I'm really pleased.'

'Thanks. So, what are *you* going to do? Hang tight or look for something elsewhere?'

'Er . . .' Abby bit her lip. 'I suppose it would be stupid if I didn't even start to search for other options, because who knows what'll happen? I just don't really want a different job. I like seeing the regulars and walking to work and—'

'You can't just *will* things to stay the same, though, Abs – you and I both know that.'

He's right.

'Wishing doesn't make things happen.'

'What do you think I should do, then?'

'Ah, you really reckon I'm a good person to ask for life advice right now?' He laughed, a low rumble down the line.

'I value your opinion,' Abby replied.

Tom didn't speak for a beat, as though he was savouring her remark, letting it sink into his skin as though it might strengthen him.

'Well,' he said after a moment, '*I* think it'd be sensible to have a Plan B.'

Abby nodded, even though no one could see her, as though the physical action was like making a pact with herself. *I'll look on my laptop later.*

'I wouldn't start scrolling through job ads now, in bed, Abs.'

Her face flushed at the idea he'd guessed she was probably already tucked up at this time. She glanced down at her cupcake-print pyjamas and pulled a face.

'I'm not saying it'll happen, but I'd just be prepared for leaving the Plum Pie – be one step ahead of the dragon.'

Abby pictured Joy with flames coming out of her mouth; maybe if *she* could be persuaded to go wild swimming, the water would put out her fiery fury at the world . . .

Tom's tone turned more serious. 'You've taken enough punches in life already, Abs. If we can pre-empt this problem, you'll be in as good a position as possible.'

We. The word warmed her insides. Even though she was alone in the room, she felt Tom's protectiveness wrap round her like an invisible hug.

'Anyway, it's late, I'll let you go,' he said suddenly.

I appreciate your advice, Abby wanted to say, but Tom was already winding down the call.

'It was kind of you to ring. It's been good to chat.'

'Any time,' said Abby.

'Right back at you.'

He wished her goodnight and then, when he'd gone, she realised with a jolt of surprise what Tom must have just noticed too: it was past ten o'clock, and they'd been talking on the phone for well over an hour.

22

Abby ran a finger over the front cover of the photo album, traced the gold-leaf lettering that spelled 'Memories'. *No.* She wasn't going to open it. She put it back in the presentation box. She had to get a move on, the others would be arriving any minute. She'd had too much time for the temptation to look at it to build, what with Rowan away at Maria's, and the later meeting time tonight – the swim had been pushed back from its usual hour to mean it was definitely a moonlit one, in line with Lori's request.

Abby packed everything up that she needed, and, on the spur of the moment, popped a bottle of Prosecco in her bag for a toast. *Lori's last evening ought to be special.* They could have a small glass each by the side of the lake, after—

The doorbell summoned her to the hall.

The night was clear and Abby's breath clouded in the air as she greeted her friend. 'Hi!'

'Hey!' said Lori, her voice as bright as the star-sprinkled sky above. Her blonde hair shone in the silvery light and her eyes were twinkling – though what exactly she was feeling, Abby couldn't tell. *Is she okay?*

'All set?' asked Lori.

Abby nodded back at her. They were meeting Rebecca and Clarissa at White Crag car park, for their final swim as a foursome at Rydal – the place where it had all begun. *What an adventure it's been*, thought Abby, a curious mix of sadness and joy swirling inside her as she thought back to the first time she and Lori had driven there in the taxi, not knowing what to expect nor what to make of each other. *Now look at us.* She was going to miss Lori hugely, and the dynamic of the group the four of them had formed.

She must have sighed as she fastened her seatbelt, as Lori looked across at her and said, 'You good, doll?' snapping her back to the present.

'Yes – fine!' Abby smiled at her as she started the engine. *Just enjoy the moment*, she told herself. It was no good worrying about what was to come. Life could switch lanes or do a complete U-turn at any point, you had to find happiness in the here and now.

'Ready for home tomorrow? All packed?' asked Abby, as they headed out of Ambleside, the car headlights illuminating the weaving road ahead a few metres at a time.

'I guess . . .' said Lori, face still turned towards the passenger window. She lifted her left hand, and Abby wondered whether she was wiping away a tear.

'Sure you're okay?' she asked. No one ever wanted to return home after a holiday, but Abby knew this trip had been different . . .

'I'm scared, I guess.' Lori blew out a breath.

'Of going back home?' Abby prompted.

'Uh-huh. It's kinda crunch time . . .'

Abby chewed her lip as she gripped the steering wheel, not quite sure what to say to make the situation any better – so she decided to just listen instead. 'Tell me what's worrying you.'

'Ah, tellin' people . . . Ashanti, mainly. It's not the news anyone imagines having to break to their daughter, right?'

Abby shook her head. 'No.' *How would I feel having to say the same to Rowan, if it were me?* She couldn't even imagine.

'You know, if you ever want to talk when you're back in America, I'm only on the end of a phone line,' she said.

Lori didn't reply, and Abby felt a flash of foolishness flood her body. *Lori probably has plenty of people she can ring – friends she can see in person, not someone she met on vacation—*

'Thank you so much,' said Lori. 'That means a lot. It really does.' Her voice cracked as though with the weight of gratitude her words carried. 'It's nice of you to say that.'

'I mean it,' said Abby.

'I know you do, hon.' Lori was silent for a second before she spoke again. 'Don't think bad of me if I don't call, okay?' she said, and for a moment Abby felt her stomach clench with awkwardness. *She was just humouring me – why on earth would she want to keep in touch with a single mum who lives thousands of miles away?* Before she suddenly realised what Lori meant with all the force of a physical slap.

'Of course not. I understand.'

'Thank you for *getting* it,' said Lori. She pursed her lips momentarily, as though biting back a wave of emotion, then carried on. 'It's weird, it's not like a death – it's totally different – but it's still kinda like a loss, in a way, you know?'

Abby nodded. 'Yes. You're right.'

'It's one thing for it to concern me, but I hate the thought of it affecting Ashanti.' Lori squirmed in her seat as though she was in pain.

Perhaps she is. Emotional agony was harder to bear than any bodily hurt, Abby knew that.

'She'll have to go through some kinda grieving process, at some point, I guess, there's no getting around it.'

Abby swallowed. She felt her heart swell with compassion.

'Anyways, enough of that already,' Lori said with a flick of her wrist. 'At least I know now. I got strategies to deal with it, and I'm goin' back stronger, that's for sure.' She sat up straighter, as though determined to banish all sadness from her system. 'I wanna enjoy tonight with you guys.'

Abby was filled with admiration for her friend: ever positive and refusing to dwell on the unknown. After all, no one could predict what might happen in the future . . .

The others were waiting for them at White Crag ahead of time, clearly wanting to make the most of their evening together too. They were both standing beside Clarissa's Defender with their hands wrapped round cups of something steaming.

As soon as Abby and Rebecca joined them, Clarissa thrust mugs at them too. 'To *fortify* you,' she said with a nod.

'Gee, it's gonna be freezing, isn't it,' said Lori with an exaggerated shudder, taking a sip of the drink she'd just been handed.

Hot chocolate. Abby smiled as the sweetness settled on her tongue. *Just like we had after our very first swim.* She watched as the heat evaporated into the atmosphere like ectoplasm. *The ghosts of the people we were before*, thought Abby to herself with a smile.

The car park was deserted now it was dark. There was no way they'd be doing this without a professional like Clarissa present.

Abby looked around: winter was fast approaching. The beech trees had lost more leaves, but there was a stark beauty in their moon-bathed bareness; their bark like smooth skin, their branches like limbs. Underneath nature's spotlight of a cloudless night sky, faint fissures were visible in their trunks, like wrinkles that came with experience. But more than just the seasons had shifted. Her own outlook was entirely different. The Wildwater Women had altered her life so much for the better.

'Right, shall we get cracking?' said Clarissa, collecting up their cups. 'Marvellous night for it,' she said as she glanced at the moon, as though it were the fifth member of their group.

'I'm gonna miss this place,' murmured Lori, looking up at it too, as though she could hardly believe it was the same one that gazed down upon New York City.

'D'you think you'll come back and visit us sometime?' Rebecca asked Lori.

Lori studied the stone-scattered earth beneath her feet for a second, then gave a sigh. Anyone else would think she was just not looking forward to leaving after a long holiday, but Abby knew better. 'Oh, I hope so!' Lori replied.

'Us too,' said Rebecca with a smile.

'Lemme know if you're ever in the US, too, you guys. It'd be super nice to catch up.' Lori grinned back.

Abby nodded, but she was about as likely to be off to the Big Apple any time soon as she was to win the Euromillions. Both required buying a ticket, for a start.

But that was okay; she was content here, just like Clarissa.

As they set off along the path towards the lake, Abby noticed how the fallen leaves danced at their feet in the breeze, the way the beeches swayed like a waving crowd as they walked along.

'So, have you seen Guy yet?' she said to Rebecca, as they fell into step side by side behind their leader, with Lori in the middle.

'I have,' said Rebecca, but it was hard to read her expression under cover of the trees.

'And?' said Abby, leaning forward, trying to make out her features in the darkness.

Rebecca didn't reply for a moment, but the woodland cleared as they neared the river, and light spilled down to show that she was beaming at them both. 'Things are back on track.'

Abby smiled.

'Oh, c'mon!' said Lori. 'Tell us all the gossip!'

Rebecca laughed. 'Well, we went for a drink last night, actually.'

'Great!' said Abby.

'No, you gotta start at the beginning!' said Lori.

'Okay, okay!' Rebecca giggled. Then her face turned serious. 'He came in to work for the first time after the accident yesterday.'

The others waited for her to continue.

Even Clarissa seemed to have slowed, so she could listen to the developments too.

'I saw his parents first, though,' said Rebecca. 'When I got to Reception in the morning, they were waiting for me. Said they owed me an apology.'

Abby noticed Clarissa give a small nod of her head, the back of her grey hair bobbing up and down in the half-dark. *Was she responsible for setting them straight?* Abby suspected so. 'I'm glad they said sorry,' she said.

'Yeah, they were really nice to be honest. Thanked me and said they were so grateful – Guy was their only son and the most important thing in the world.'

Maybe they'd had a change of perspective since the accident? wondered Abby. *Seen that it was people that mattered, not money.*

'Perhaps their priorities will be a bit different, now,' said Rebecca, as though she was thinking the same thing. 'If Guy doesn't want to run the hotel, then they shouldn't force him.'

Abby shook her head.

'Absolutely not,' agreed Lori.

'So, at least that's some good to come out of it,' said Rebecca.

They came to the wooden slatted bridge where Lori had taken a selfie of them as they began their wild swimming journey. Abby shifted the canvas bag she was carrying on her shoulder with its precious cargo inside; it seemed to be getting heavier as the path became steeper.

'Anyway, Guy came in just as I was leaving for my lunch-break,' continued Rebecca, as the four of them crossed over the Rothay. 'Said when he woke up in hospital, he had no idea where he was or how he got there.' She paused on the other side of the river, struck still by the horrifying idea of having no memory at all. 'Can you *imagine*?'

Abby bit her lip.

'Awful,' mumbled Lori, looking at the ground.

'Let's carry on,' encouraged Clarissa, starting to climb the stone steps that led to the lake, guiding them all onwards as usual.

'It would be the worst thing ever, though, wouldn't it?' Rebecca said to Lori. 'Not being able to remember stuff, feeling like you'd forgotten everything – what you'd been doing, who you *were*.'

Abby reached out to touch Rebecca's arm.

'What?' she said, turning to glance at her.

'It's all right,' said Lori to Abby. 'It's my fault for not sayin' somethin' sooner.'

'Why do I get the impression everyone else knows something I don't?' asked Rebecca in a quiet voice.

'I wasn't keepin' it secret,' explained Lori. 'I was just tryna come to terms with it myself first, I guess.'

'I don't understand,' said Rebecca.

Clarissa was waiting for them up by the gate, leaning on its post.

The others hurried up the hill.

'What's happened?' asked Rebecca through ragged pants as she puffed to the top.

'Nothin' new,' said Lori.

'What's going on?' Rebecca huffed.

'I didn't just come here on vacation to have a real blast with you guys and see the place in my grandpop's picture.' Lori stood in the middle of the path with her hands on her hips, to catch her breath.

'Then why?' asked Rebecca, sweeping a strand of hair from her frowning forehead.

'A couple days before I flew here,' – Lori swallowed – 'I got diagnosed with Alzheimer's. I'm young for it, I know, but it can start early . . .'

Rebecca pressed her hand to her mouth. 'Oh my god.'

Lori sighed. 'Yeah.'

'Did you know?' Rebecca murmured to Abby.

Abby nodded.

'I blurted it all out one day,' admitted Lori.

'And Clarissa?' asked Rebecca.

'The questionnaire we filled in for that first session . . . I had to write it all down in there,' replied Lori. 'It's why I started wild swimming – I heard the cold water's meant to help dementia.' She pursed her lips.

Rebecca bowed her head. 'I wouldn't have said any of that about Guy if I'd known . . . I didn't mean to upset you—'

'Hey, don't worry,' said Lori with a smile, setting off up the stone stairway again, as though needing to push forwards. 'It's not that I didn't wanna tell ya, it's just I was enjoying having fun with you guys. It was nice not thinking about it every second, after all the appointments and tests.' She gave a shrug. 'I guess I wanted to get away for a while . . . be independent, before it gets worse . . .'

'Oh, Lori,' said Rebecca.

'I'm just scared.' Lori's voice shook on that last word.

Abby looped an arm round her shoulder.

They all looked to Clarissa, having finally caught up with her.

'Do you think it's helped, coming to the Lakes, having some time to yourself?' she asked, opening the gate for Lori to go through, like that would enable her to pass from her previous state of mind to a new one.

Lori smiled. 'Absolutely.'

Rebecca and Abby joined them on the grassy bank that overlooked the lake.

'I guess I'm a little more at peace with it now – as much as I'll ever be.' Lori's gaze was on the gleaming water below, as though the sight of nature in all its splendidness was a salve. 'I've got strategies in place, to help deal with it. I carry my notepad everywhere, and having the swimming to focus on's made me feel a whole lot more in control.'

285

Clarissa nodded at her.

'And I've finally worked up the courage to tell the folks back home. It's not just my daughter I've not told, I've kept it from Joe, too.' Lori looked up at the milky-white face of the moon. 'Well, he must know there's something up,' she muttered under her breath.

'That's why you wanted the photos—' said Rebecca to Abby, suddenly realising what they were for.

Abby raised her eyebrows to stop her saying any more, and Rebecca fell silent.

But Lori didn't seem to be listening, she was staring at the glazed surface of Rydal stretched out below them.

Clarissa began to descend the path to the shore, and the others followed one by one.

'Anyways, tell us about your date,' said Lori to Rebecca. 'Let's get back to that. We wanna hear *all* about it.' She grinned.

'Oh, never mind about that,' said Rebecca, waggling a hand.

'Whaaat? Go on!' said Lori.

'We just went to the Craft Tap in Windermere. I hadn't been there before . . .'

That's where Tom works now! thought Abby.

'Like a bar?' asked Lori.

'Yeah, locally brewed ale. But you'll never guess who owns it!' Rebecca said, a smile spreading across her face again at last. 'Well, perhaps *you* will, Clarissa,' she called ahead to their leader.

Clarissa turned round. 'I hope you didn't praise it too much.'

'I loved it in there!' said Rebecca. 'Great atmosphere and the beer's top notch.'

'He'll be even more unbearably big-headed if you tell him that,' said Clarissa, carrying on walking.

'Who?' said Lori.

'Clarissa's brother!' replied Rebecca. 'We met him at the party, remember?'

Oh my goodness! thought Abby. *So George is Tom's new boss!*

'Small world, huh?' said Lori.

'It sure is,' agreed Abby. She pushed away the niggling worry about her job – it wouldn't solve the situation, dwelling on it during their swim.

They were by the edge of the water now, and the four of them took a moment to appreciate the landscape in its night-time serenity. The lake was cast in an otherworldly light and the surrounding scenery was mesmerising, even though the colours were muted beneath the monochrome moon. Everything looked different at this hour, but still beautiful – like a face without makeup at bedtime.

'Can you remember how I was, when we came here the first time?' asked Rebecca with a roll of her eyes as they got changed.

'Yes,' said Abby. *And I couldn't even look at the Loveland, across the water*, she recalled.

'You've all come so far,' declared Clarissa. 'You should be proud of yourselves,' she added, her feet already in the water. 'I hope you all keep it up.'

As she waded out into the liquid ripples of the glittering lake, Abby made a silent promise to herself in the presence of the stars: *I'm going to carry on swimming*. It had become a self-care ritual she didn't know how she'd existed without. *But I'm not just surviving now, I'm living again.*

Rebecca and Lori came to stand either side of her, as though they were sharing in her wonder at how the last few weeks had intertwined their stories, bonded them together.

Clarissa was several steps ahead, as usual, waist deep in the water.

'Wildwater Women!' called Rebecca into the night sky all of a sudden, throwing her hands above her head. Lori and Abby echoed her, their faces tilted upwards too.

When she lowered her body into the lake, a sense of empowerment swept over Abby. In that exact moment, she felt as though she could do whatever she put her mind to. No matter what was to be thrown at her in the future, or what happened with her job at the Plum Pie, she could handle it. She realised that if she switched places with someone else, and was looking at her own journey, she'd be in awe of her ability to acclimatise and adapt – not just to freezing conditions when swimming in the lake, but in terms of the obstacles she'd had to overcome both for herself and as a mother. *See what you're capable of?* whispered the wind.

'Woohoo!' Rebecca shrieked beside her, her eyes gleaming in the moonbeams.

Lori was floating on her back, contemplating the sparkling canopy above.

Clarissa swam back towards them, slicing through the water as though propelled by urgency.

Abby's heartbeat increased. *Is something wrong?* She glanced over at Lori and Rebecca, but they were calmly doing breaststroke through the blackness.

Clarissa was heading for *her*. Suddenly she was there, splashing alongside her, parallel with the shore. 'So, the bakery's sold,' she said.

Wait a minute – how did Clarissa know? Had everyone else in the world seen it advertised apart from her? Or maybe one of the other women had mentioned that she was concerned about work . . .

'Yes,' said Abby feeling a chill creep across her skin at the thought. The water felt icier all of a sudden. She tried to put her feet on the ground, but she was out of her depth. 'I don't know if I'll be kept on by the next people, or what'll happen.' She started swimming closer to the shallows, craving some solid land to stand on.

'Well, I didn't want to make a fuss about it, as this is Lori's farewell party, but I just wanted to put your mind at rest about that,' said Clarissa.

Hang on – why would Clarissa know her job was safe? Unless . . . oh my god. Could she be? Who else would have enough money to invest in it? Abby broke into a grin. 'Oh my god, are you saying I can stay?' She felt stones beneath her soles and a surge of relief hit her system. 'This is *wonderful!*' she cried.

She saw Clarissa nod in the darkness.

'What's happenin' over there?' called Lori, reaching the shore as well.

Rebecca wasn't far behind.

'My job's safe!' shrieked Abby, shaking out her arms as though her body was suddenly bursting with energy. Would Clarissa be her boss, or just the person putting up the capital? Either way, it was brilliant news. No more Joy! And she didn't have to look for work elsewhere! 'I can't believe it – I'm so happy!'

'That's great, hon,' said Lori. 'I'm real pleased for you!'

'Me too!' said Rebecca as she grabbed her towel.

'Oh my goodness, Clarissa!' Abby shrieked. '*Thank you!*'

'What for?' said Clarissa, pulling on her dry robe.

'For getting the bakery!' said Abby, oblivious to the cold.

'Oh, it's nothing to do with me.' Clarissa shook her head.

I don't understand. 'So, who's the new owner then, if it's not you?' murmured Abby.

'My brother,' said Clarissa. 'George.'

23

Once they were dressed, Abby popped open the bottle of Prosecco, the celebratory sound reverberating out over the lake.

'Look at this!' said Lori as Abby handed her a plastic glass.

'To toast the time we've all spent together, and wish you a safe journey home,' she said, giving the others their drinks.

'Cheers!' said Rebecca.

'Indeed!' added Clarissa.

'And to your job, too!' added Lori, smiling as she clinked her glass. 'Those cakes are works of art, I tell ya!' she said.

'They are!' agreed Rebecca.

'You know Tom, I take it?' said Clarissa, turning towards Abby. 'Used to be the baker at the Plum Pie, I hear.'

'He's the cute one,' interjected Lori. '*What?*' she added, when Abby frowned at her. 'Just sayin'. . .'

'Yes,' Abby said to Clarissa, the fizz warming her throat. 'I worked with him – till our monster of a boss gave him the boot.'

'Ah, Joy's just bitter,' she replied.

'You know her?' spluttered Abby.

'C probably knows everyone round here, huh?' said Lori.

'Well, she is part of my family, I suppose . . .' explained Clarissa. 'Albeit an estranged member nowadays.'

'What d'you mean?' asked Abby. She couldn't imagine Joy being related to Clarissa! *Perhaps she was her adopted sister?*

'She's George's ex-wife.'

Gosh. 'Really?' said Abby.

'Yes,' replied Clarissa.

'But she's *horrible*,' blurted out Abby, before she could stop herself.

'George loves his business more than anything – or anyone. He wasn't the best husband.' Clarissa shook her head. 'I've tried to keep in contact, but I think it was her way of coping, to sever ties.'

'But she sold the bakery to him, so that's something,' said Abby.

'I bought it on my brother's behalf. She'd never have gone through with it if she'd seen his name on the papers. But he's the real owner – I'm just the facilitator. And Tom's coming back on board. They seem to get on really well, the two of them,' Clarissa added. 'George seems to be treating him like the son he never had.'

Abby smiled, but, if she was honest, it was because Tom would be returning . . .

'Going to be a bakery by day, and then serve pizza and beer in the evening,' explained Clarissa.

'Sounds amazing!' said Rebecca.

'Sure does!' said Lori.

'You'll have to come back and we'll go,' added Rebecca.

'Yes, about that,' said Clarissa. 'I had a little idea. Shall we do the Great North Swim next year, as a reunion?'

'Something to look forward to,' said Lori. 'Count me in.'

'When is it?' asked Abby.

'Summer. Mid-June,' replied Clarissa.

'Oo, it'll be waaaarm,' said Rebecca.

'You can do different distances, depending on what you're feeling up to,' said Clarissa.

'So, I could do, like, a half mile or somethin'?' asked Lori.

'Whatever you want.' Clarissa nodded. 'You'll have to keep up the swimming back home.'

'Sure thing. I already Googled open-water groups. It's gonna be the thing that keeps me going,' said Lori with a smile.

'And how about you two?' said Clarissa, looking from Abby to Rebecca. 'Are you going to carry on training too?'

'Definitely,' replied Abby without a moment's hesitation.

'Yes,' said Rebecca.

'That's sorted then,' concluded Clarissa.

Abby set her bubbles down on a flat-topped rock, and rummaged in her bag. *This seems like the right time.* The tissue paper she'd wrapped the present in rustled under her touch.

A hush descended on the group as she lifted the ribbon-topped parcel free of the canvas material.

'This is something to remember your trip by,' she said, holding out the neatly wrapped rectangle for Lori to take.

'Oh, you guys! You shouldn't have got me a gift!'

'Abby organised it – all her idea,' said Rebecca with a smile. 'Now I get the thinking behind it,' she murmured, meeting Abby's gaze.

Lori began to peel back the gold folds of paper, fragile like the petals of a rose, beautiful but for a fleeting moment.

The others peered over her shoulder.

'Hang on, I've a torch here somewhere,' said Clarissa, scrabbling about in her rucksack. 'Here you are,' she said, shining a bright light on the item which emerged from the wrapping like a mountaintop from mist.

Lori cupped her hands over her mouth. 'Thank you,' she said, her voice muffled by her palms.

'It's to remind you of all your adventures,' murmured Abby.

'And us,' added Rebecca with a grin.

Lori blinked down at the book on her lap. The gold letters shimmered on the front.

'Are you going to open it?' asked Clarissa.

Lori ran a finger over the letters on the cover, just like Abby had done earlier.

'Go on, have a look inside,' encouraged Abby.

Lori turned the page. 'An album with all my memories,' she whispered, her words wavering with wonder.

'That way you won't forget.' Abby reached out and squeezed her arm. 'And there's space for loads more – see.' She flipped past the photos of the four of them, to the blank sheets that were yet to be filled with images. 'So you can put in Ashanti's birthday, and all the big moments – or little ones – that you want to look back on.'

'Whenever I want to,' murmured Lori.

Abby nodded. 'Exactly.'

'They won't be lost.'

Abby shook her head.

'It means the world to me,' said Lori, hugging the album to her chest. 'It's been real great meeting you all.'

'You brought us together, Clarissa,' said Abby, raising her glass in tribute.

The others lifted theirs too.

'Well, it's been a privilege to get to know each of you,' said Clarissa with her Herdwick-style smile. 'Help you feel the power of wild swimming. And to see the relationships

293

between you blossom. Thank you for including me in your drinks, having me round for dinner, and always making me feel welcome, too.'

It hadn't struck Abby until now, that maybe Clarissa had appreciated the sense of belonging brought about by their group as well.

'Honestly, this has saved me,' said Abby, fingers splayed to indicate the friends sitting next to her, the star-speckled sky above them, and the peaceful panorama they were part of . . .

'I couldn't have got over my phobia without you,' said Rebecca. 'I feel like a completely different person now.'

'I think maybe we all are,' said Abby.

Epilogue

Abby had only ever been to Brockhole, on the banks of Windermere, to take Rowan to the adventure playground in the gardens of the big house, before now. But today, swarms of people, of all ages, lined the stunning shore of the largest lake in England. The hum of conversations taking place around her, mixed with the occasional bubble of happy laughter, created a buzz that made her skin tingle with anticipation. The water was diamond-bright in the June light, and she held a hand up to shade her eyes as she searched for the others. She'd got here in plenty of time. Been unable to sleep, she was so eager to see her friends again this morning, even though they'd had dinner together at the Pizza Pie the previous night to fight off Lori's jetlag—

'Abby!' squealed Rebecca.

She turned to see her, waving as she made her way through the crowd.

Lori was following. 'Hey, girl!'

Abby held her arms wide to envelop the two of them in a hug.

'Clarissa's here, too,' said Rebecca. 'She's just helping someone fix their tracking chip to their ankle – she'll be over in a sec.'

Abby felt a blast of adrenaline as she glanced down at her own timing device. She couldn't believe she was about to do this, that they all were – together. She beamed at the others.

'Can I leave my stuff with you?' said Lori, over Abby's shoulder. 'That all right?'

'Of course,' said Tom with a nod, a hand on Freddie and Rowan's shoulders.

Lori bent down to greet the children. 'Good to see you, darlin's.'

Rebecca looked around with a frown on her face.

'Don't worry, Braithwaite!' came a shout from behind them. 'I'm here!' said Guy, reaching the group and leaning in to give Rebecca a kiss.

'You're gonna stop calling her that when y'all are married, right?' asked Lori with chuckle.

Rebecca smiled. 'Probably not. I'm keeping my surname,' she said. 'Better give you this to look after, actually,' she said, pulling a solitaire ring from her left hand and holding it out to Guy. 'Don't want it to drop off in the water.'

'Definitely not,' said Guy, clutching it tightly in a closed fist. 'Can't be buying another one on my watersports instructor salary.'

Rebecca raised her eyebrows. 'And I don't want you jumping in after it!'

Guy grimaced.

'It's *so* pretty,' said Lori, jerking her head towards Guy's clenched fingers. 'Congratulations!' she added, before she began to look around as though she herself had lost something. Then a smile spread across her face.

Abby turned to see Ashanti, walking through the throng next to Clarissa.

'Alrighty,' said Lori, once they were all assembled in one spot. 'We better say our goodbyes, huh?' she joked.

'You'll all be fine,' said Clarissa, glancing at each of the Wildwater Women in turn. 'You've prepared for this – and, remember, you're not fighting the water, you're at one with it.'

They all nodded in response.

'Okay, well, when you're ready, we'd better make our way over to the starting point.'

Abby took a deep breath, and blew the air out of her lungs slowly. The summer sun was warm on her back, and her heart felt full – she looked about her, at the joyous faces of the friends and family gathered together, and couldn't help but grin with gratitude. Her chest swelled at the sight of Tom standing there with the children, waiting to cheer her on.

'See you afterwards,' she said to Guy and Ashanti, before she crouched to cuddle Rowan close, and ruffle Freddie's hair.

'Good luck,' said Tom, as she stood up and her gaze met his. 'I love you,' he added in a low voice, his brown eyes like two melted chocolate buttons shining back at her.

'I love you too,' Abby murmured, just before Lori and Rebecca linked her elbows and the three of them began to walk to the starting line on the edge of the sparkling lake, with Clarissa leading the way.

Clarissa's Cumberland Rum Nicky

This version has a hazelnut rum twist and is perfect for sharing with friends and family.

Preparation time: 30 mins
Cooking time: 35 mins
Serves: 6
Dietary: Vegetarian
You will need a 20cm/ 8in metal pie dish for this recipe.

Ingredients
For the filling:
225 g/ 8 oz dates, roughly chopped
100 g/ 3.5 oz dried apricots, roughly chopped
50 g/ 1.75 oz stem ginger, finely chopped
50 ml/ 2 fl oz Belgrove hazelnut rum
50 g/ 1.75 oz soft dark brown sugar
50 g/ 1.75 oz unsalted butter, cut into 1 cm/ 0.5in cubes

For the pastry:

200 g/ 7 oz plain flour

2 tbsp icing sugar

100 g/ 3.5 oz unsalted butter, chilled and cut into 1 cm/ 0.5 in cubes

1 egg, beaten

2 tbsp cold water

For the rum butter:

100 g/ 3.5 oz unsalted butter, softened

225 g/ 8 oz soft light brown sugar

75 ml/ 2.5 fl oz Belgrove hazelnut rum

Method

1. Apart from the butter, mix together all the ingredients for the filling in a bowl. Set aside to soak while you make the pastry.
2. Mix the flour and icing sugar together in another bowl. Add the cubes of butter and rub it in gently with your fingers until the mixture resembles breadcrumbs.
3. Mix the egg with the water and then make a well in the centre of the flour mixture, and pour it in. Using a cutlery knife, work the liquid into the flour. When the dough begins to stick together, use your hands to lightly knead it into a ball shape. Wrap in cling film and leave to rest in the fridge for at least 15 mins.
4. Preheat the oven to 180C/350F/gas 4.
5. When the dough has rested, cut off one-third, so you have two pieces. Roll out the larger piece onto a clean and lightly floured worktop. Line the 20cm/ 8in pie dish with the rolled out pastry, leaving any excess hanging over the rim.
6. Spread the filling in the pastry case and dot with the butter.

7. Roll out the remaining piece of pastry and cut it into eight strips, about 1cm/ 0.5 in wide. On a sheet of greaseproof paper, use the pastry strips to create a lattice with four strips going each way, passing them over and under each other.

8. Dampen the edge of the pastry lining the tin with water, then turn the lattice upside down onto it from the paper. Press the ends of the strips to the pastry base to stick them on.

9. Bake for 15 mins, then turn the oven temperature down to 160C/325F/Gas 3 and bake for a further 20 mins.

10. Meanwhile, to make the rum butter, beat together the butter and sugar, then gradually mix in the rum. Keep in the fridge until needed.

11. Serve Clarissa's Cumberland Rum Nicky either warm or cold, with a spoonful of rum butter to taste. Enjoy!

Acknowledgements

There are many people who've contributed to this book in direct or indirect ways, and have made it what it is. I am forever grateful, and this book is for all of you. Thank you to everyone I've met on my journey, not just on the road to publication but in life: you've helped shape my story, and in turn this novel.

Massive thanks to Genevieve Pegg for believing in me and my writing and giving me the opportunity to bring the Wildwater Women to life.

Thank you to Alice Murphy-Pyle, Meg Jones and everyone else at HarperNorth for your enormous enthusiasm and hard work.

Thank you to Anne Williams at KHLA for championing me right from the start.

Thank you to all my friends and family for your unwavering support, always being so full of excitement at every stage, and for never doubting that I could do it.

Seeing the book out in the world is a dream come true. I hope readers enjoy it, and if it encourages one person to reach out when they need help, get outside amongst nature, or enjoy small pleasures like the sun simply shining on a brand-new day, then I couldn't ask for more.